T0348875

The Last Culprit

"We are always the last person we find the courage to forgive. Scott Brighton awakens to that challenge as he unpacks years of guilt over his role in a youthful prank that went terribly wrong. But the truth could come at a price he's unwilling to pay. Through deft storytelling and empathetic insight, Alisa Weis takes us into the heart of her character's passage from darkness into light."

> ⋙ D.L. FOWLER, author of *Lincoln Raw*,
> *The Turn*, and *Lincoln's Angel*

"We like to think our actions are benign, and any harm we cause can easily be undone. But what if we're wrong? What if a 'harmless prank' extends into years of injury and guilt? *The Last Culprit* reflects on this question, exploring how both victim and perpetrator search for restoration and wholeness. It is a wise and beautiful story, well worth reading."

> ⋙ CONNIE HAMPTON CONNALLY, author of
> *Fire Music* and *The Songs We Hide*

The historical accuracy of *The Last Culprit* is fun to read. Gee, I wonder who Alisa—I mean the author—could've consulted to get 1973-Gig Harbor so right?

> ⋙ GREG SPADONI, writer of local history
> for *Gig Harbor NOW*

"There are few Pacific Northwest writers that can better capture both location and dramatic intent than Alisa Weis, and her new novel, *The Last Culprit*, once again delivers. In a coastal sea town, there is an old scandal better left forgotten. But that's not how secrets work. So when Scott Brighton returns to his hometown of Gig Harbor, the old ashes of high school revenge are once again stirred up. In Weis's gifted pen, we are offered a spectrum of raw emotions, where bitterness, fear and guilt hang in the balance of redemption. Like her superb second novel, *The Emblem*, Alisa Weis continues her mastery in *The Last Culprit*.

⊶ E. HANK BUCHMANN, author of *Darling Liberty,*
Until The Names Grow Blurred, and others

theLast Culprit

A Novel by

ALISA WEIS

INKBLOTS PRESS

ISBN: 978-1-945062-17-9

The Last Culprit is a work of fiction.
Names, characters, places, and incidents
either are the product of the author's
imagination or are used fictitiously.

Cover Image by Nancy Archer
Cover Typography by Elli Seifert
Interior Design by Elli Seifert
The Last Culprit is set in PS Fournier
Author Photo by *Sage West Photography*

First Edition, Printed in the U.S.A
Published by Inkblots Press
Olalla, WA

For my dad, STEVE TRILLER,
who has always had a heart
for the underdog.

The Last Culprit

1

Harbor Winter

*T*he boats were settling in on darkening waters, safe and sure
along the harbor he'd known since childhood. Returning after
all these years to stay, he finally saw this place as a visitor might,
one step removed, in sudden awe of the quiet beauty that had
existed here all along. He heard faint laughter down on one of
the docks, noted the festive lights decking a few of the boats. Did
people really live down here all year long? Scott stopped the drift
of his thoughts as he stood, waiting on the sidewalk just above
the Gig Harbor waterfront. He dug his hands in his pockets, felt
a few loose coins, and played over in his mind the lines he hoped
to remember before a captive audience in less than half an hour.

*It's an honor to be back among you. Such a friendly, giving commu-
nity. It's hard to find a place that compares.* Did it sound too forced?
For the first time since practicing his remarks, he worried that
his words wouldn't land well and that people would find them
too contrived.

"You won't find a place that compares," Scott said, testing out
slightly different wording. He studied a crack in the sidewalk and

traced his shoe over it, hardly realizing he was speaking aloud.

The murmur of female voices came up behind him—*I'm so glad it isn't raining . . . it's so clear for December.* He straightened up and checked his wristwatch for the time. Their black and caramel dress coats came into his periphery and he nodded a hello.

It was then his eyes locked with hers, unmistakable and dark as dusk. The twenty-some years they'd been apart evaporated into nothingness. It didn't matter that the sun had merged with the tree line some hours before, that he hadn't seen her in two decades, or that she no longer wore her studious frames—he'd know her deep brown eyes anywhere.

"El, you alright?" the woman beside her asked, offering him a puzzled smile. She tucked a few strands of dark hair behind her ear. He should have introduced himself, but he was lost for words.

From the way Elli's steps froze on the pavement, he knew that she'd recognized him too. But there was no offer of recognition, no hand extended to say how are you, no small talk about the sudden drop in temperature. Why would there have been? They hadn't parted on promising terms.

He watched as she drew her caramel duster closer to her frame and turned her attention to a closing car door, to the figure who now approached her quickly—a man he especially didn't want to see. Not even after all this time. Scott suddenly craved a drink of water despite the winter cold. He turned away as the man joined them and the three walked into Anthony's Boat House and Grill, just where he was headed.

Time had taken much, but not the beauty of the girl—now woman. His heart didn't fall, but it pulsated in his chest, and he wondered how he would make it through the night. How he would manage to file in after her and get up to speak.

No snow fell, but the wind's force made attendees pull their coats tighter as they walked toward the restaurant. He was still lost in his thoughts when he felt a pressure at his elbow. Charlotte had emerged from the car. She'd been finishing up her makeup, insisting that she wasn't ready without her mascara. He turned around and took in the questions beating in her blue eyes.

"What's wrong, Scott? You parked just fine. Perfect, in fact."

He shrugged and straightened his tie but didn't answer. He sought his wife's hand and clasped it tightly in his own, led her to the restaurant at such a clip that further conversation was out of the question.

Once inside, the rosy glow of candlelight shimmered from elegantly set tables. The attendees could finally remove their gloves, rub their hands together and gaze out the large windows overlooking the Harbor, at the lights that shone upon quaint shops and houses and played in the still, dark waters below.

Laughter filled the air within seconds of their arrival. It was the merriment that comes with the joyful sounds of Ella Fitzgerald, wine on the tables, the promise of seafood fettuccine and Dungeness crab within half an hour. But first, the program for which all had assembled. The chatter inevitably died down as the host tapped the microphone and called the room to order.

"Thank you one and all for clearing your busy schedules and being here for our Harbor's Best in Business Christmas party," a lady in a green velvet coat began, pressing her mouth into a pristine smile. Her red lips were prepared for this moment.

Scott Brighton's throat closed in on him; they would call him up to speak in a matter of minutes. He was one of the only, he noticed, who didn't so easily give in to the small talk and cheer of the other guests. He'd mustered up a tight smile to a few people that he recognized, but quickly found his designated table and threw his dinner napkin into his lap. Charlotte was more amiable from the start, taking the time to wave and say hello to the people she'd come to know in the last few months.

This might be Scott's hometown, but he'd left it so long ago. He didn't think he was recognized by too many people. He'd only been invited to say a few words because his parents were distinguished members of the community. How could he have said no?

As the new director for the family business, Brighton's Insurance, it was up to him to thank the ladies and gentlemen for joining him this evening. It wasn't difficult for him to present in a conference room to other professionals, but this formal occasion made his heart jolt as if he'd taken an extra shot of caffeine. He tore at his cuticles, a habit that hadn't left him since high school days, way back when he wore his Peninsula High School Seahawks jersey. He hoped he wouldn't falter.

He took a breath, straightened his silver tie again. It wasn't a lengthy speech—more of a thank you for coming tonight. A recap of the success his family's business was experiencing, then a close-out concerning their charity projects. A few nods to other community members doing the same brand of work. Nothing too strenuous.

But now, at 42 years old, he suddenly felt like he was in high school again, standing in front of his peers to deliver a persuasive speech. Hands gone sweaty. Breath staggered. Rocking back and forth in the wrong-sized shoes. He couldn't recall the order of the notecards he'd written up just last night.

A dark curl fell in front of his eyes. He smoothed it back and feigned a smile. So many years had passed, but so much remained unchanged. His ability to feel ever the impostor no matter what skills and abilities he possessed. His concern that people would take one look at him and still remember what he'd done. Hold it against him.

Stop being stupid. He chided himself for the guilt that lingered still. *It's been over twenty-five years, and you're not a kid anymore. Everyone here has moved on. Why can't you?*

The lady in the green coat finished her speech and motioned him to come forward. Scott stepped up to the microphone and breathed a prayer that it would go well. His eyes fell over the beautifully arranged place settings. The utensils gleamed, reminding him of his audience's eagerness to use them. He cleared his throat and thanked everyone for coming.

"Word has it that this year's running back beat my record from '74. That was a nice, long stretch, but it's great that a young buck is taking my place. And the year I return, no less," Scott said with a smile in his voice. "So surreal that we just enrolled our son at Peninsula." He sought out Charlotte's steady gaze. He longed to keep his focus on her and only her for the rest of the evening.

He did his best to connect with people without locking eyes with anyone in particular. Didn't want to linger on his notecards too long, stare down at his trembling hands. But in glimpsing at the crowd, his eyes found his former classmates in no time. Randy, Phil ... Jesse. There he was at a far table, sitting next to her.

The man had the faintest stubble on his face, a furrowed brow. He wore a tweed suit, one that gave off the hint of another time, but it fit well with the intellectual he was, would always be. The woman he'd once known, stared at him, but her dark eyes were grave.

He lost his words for a moment, looked down at his cards to catch his place, but this was no natural transition. How could he proceed without it seeming he'd panicked in front of all these people? He looked out to the audience and surprised himself by addressing his old classmate. "Jesse ... There are more familiar faces back in the Harbor than I realized."

An entirely different script ran through his head. *How could you come back here, Jesse? I thought you wanted nothing more than to escape this place and what it did to you. What I did to you.*

But Scott coughed into his sleeve and resumed his speech with the gracious words, "We're fortunate to have your talents here."

He felt himself color at the neck and wished he could unbutton his shirt.

Jesse gave a brief nod of acknowledgement, but Scott couldn't help noticing the tension written large across the woman's brow. Feeling flushed and wanting nothing more than to step from this stage, Scott pressed on as quickly as he could, skipped his next two notecards. "I wish you all a merry Christmas and a happy New Year! Take that first bite, if you haven't already."

When he took his seat, Charlotte leaned over and whispered, "You were so good up there, Scotty. But what was that last part about?" Her voice trailed when Scott looked at her with pleading eyes and reached for a wine glass instead of answering her. She frowned at him. He didn't even drink wine.

Sometimes the past still loved to taunt him, grab him around the neck and sink in its claws. The past still had leverage—Jesse Sander had leverage—and that time was still holding him captive all these years later. How long would it be before he could put past deeds to rest? If the past was still bothering him after twenty-five years, was it even possible to silence it?

2

Class of 1974

Fall of 1973

"*Huzzah!*" Scott cheered as he lifted his green helmet against the deepening blue sky. He'd just run the ball into the end zone and won the game for his team. The raindrops grazing his face didn't bother him. He even welcomed them.

Half a second later, the rest of the Peninsula Seahawks joined in, circling him, jumping up and down around him. They'd taken out their arch rival, the Curtis Vikings. Coach had promised them if they won this one, they could dump a cooler of water over his head. Scott found himself enjoying the thought of this reward a little too much—Coach Johnston worked them hard and didn't ease off on the burpees, the pushups, or running the tires even when it rained heavily. Why should they spare him?

They were working so well as a team; one reporter had described them as "poetry in motion." Their quarterback, Bobby Minter, had rolled his eyes at that, but on second thought said, "If that gets recruiters following me, I'll take it." Scott hadn't even minded so much when Bobby flashed that white smile that the girls fell for damn near every time.

It had taken pains to get here, and not only the relentless, physical kind. Now that they were entering their upper years, courses weren't so simple, and chemistry had its way with more than one of them, putting them on the tightrope of "will I pass this test and be able to play?" It didn't help that their science teacher wasn't at all concerned about their compromised play status. But for now, those stressors were tucked in the back of Scott's mind.

It was a lot more fun to join the revelry spreading among them— Randy Clauson doing a backflip on the field, Ty Parsons doing a jive, Sam Fields letting out a warrior's cry. Their energy was so charged they were commanding the interest of even those who didn't know the difference between a field goal and a two-point conversion.

"Sea-HAWKS! Sea-HAWKS!" spectators cheered from the bleachers. It was only the beginning of November, but it might as well be Christmas. The only time Scott could recall being this pumped was the time his dad had surprised him with a brand new bike when he was ten-years-old. It was tough to access that brand of natural high anymore, that pure elation. He wanted to capture it and never let it go.

Scott clapped a hand to Ty's back. "We did it again, man. We did it again." When the quietest guy on the team cheered that hard, they'd done something great. Something life-changing.

"I'm getting the water cooler," Ty said, a devious smile lighting his face. "Make sure Coach stays true to his word."

Scott let out a laugh and was about to join his team, when he remembered to find his girl in the stands. In his peripheral vision, he could see his parents clapping, and he normally would have narrowed in on the triumph across his dad's face alone. But he wanted to see Elli's admiration first. In the three months they'd been dating, he'd been careful not to bore her with talk of the game. She gravitated toward the theater, and he loved that she was artistic—so different from himself. He tried to find her in the stands. *Els, where are you?*

His eyes scanned for her caramel-colored coat among the more prevalent black ones, but he couldn't find her. Earlier she'd been sitting beside his mother and his annoying little sister on the other side, but that spot on the bleachers was empty. His heart lurched despite his inner call to reason: Elli Grayson had said she'd find him after the game, and she was someone who stood by her word. He shouldn't let doubt bloom just because she was busy with rehearsals and National Honor Society and tutoring students in every subject.

"Hey, come on, we're about to get Coach real good," Bobby said, the eagerness snapping in his eyes.

"Ha! Sounds fun. Be there in a minute," Scott said, mustering up his enthusiasm and aware that the enjoyment of this moment was beginning to dull already. *Stay in this moment,* he told himself, *you don't want to miss this.*

"Scotty, you comin'?" Ty asked, his eyes glinting with mischief.

"Hell yeah," Scott said, a natural smile returning to his face. He couldn't recall the last time Ty had looked so animated. Amusement replaced the impassive expression, and Scott wanted to indulge this side of his friend that hadn't shown itself since Ty's older brother had left for Vietnam.

Just as Scott was closing in on the water cooler and the coach, Elli surfaced at his shoulder. He took a step back to assess her—bundled-up coat and the hand-knitted ivory hat with the pompom on top. Her cheeks were chapped from the wind, but they gave her a rosy glow. She wasn't wearing her glasses tonight. Her eyes were dark, sparkling. She couldn't be any more beautiful. The unease at not seeing her at the end of the game dissipated. His shoulders felt lighter, and his breath settled into his chest.

"Scott! I couldn't stay in the stands. I had to come and tell you congratulations myself." She smiled, and he crushed her toward him, his cheek brushing her own.

"Thanks, Els. I'm so glad you're here. It means the world to me."

In the space of saying those words, he missed the opportunity to help soak Coach Johnston, but there were enough guys raring to do it, and Scott savored the aftermath—that glimpse out the corner of his eye at the coach laughing and shivering in the cold before someone handed him a towel.

"Deserves it," he laughed under his breath before turning to Elli. He took her hand up in his own, squeezed her mittened fingers. He felt like kissing her right here on the field in front of everyone, but just as he was drawing her close to his side, she looked up at him and said, "I gotta run. Nicole's waiting for me in the parking lot. Last-minute costume stuff, remember? But I wanted to be the first to tell you I'm proud of you."

His heart swelled. He thought once again of his dad in the stands, wondered if those were words his old man might echo if he were to head on down to the field.

"Go have fun with the guys, and call me?" Elli said, sounding hopeful. "Maybe we could go out tomorrow after my rehearsal."

He nodded. "Most definitely."

"See ya tomorrow," she said, tossing a smile over her shoulder.

"Bye Els. Elli . . . ." She paused upon hearing her name a second time. "I'll see ya," he said, his smile unwavering.

What he had really meant to say was that he loved her before she walked off the field, but something held him back. He was certain he loved Elli Grayson and had been since before he'd even asked her out. But now didn't seem the time nor the place. He didn't want her to think that he was running off the current of an emotional high when he expressed how he felt for the first time.

He turned toward the guys who were still holding their sides, laughing hysterically at the sight of their drenched-to-the-bone coach. "Did you see that? Did you see it, Brighton?" they asked him, summoning him closer. "I didn't think we'd live to see the day!"

·❦·

Monday morning dawned much too early, but the members of the Seahawks Football team wandered the halls with the afterglow of Friday night's win and all the accolades that came with it. Someone littered the hallways with green balloons. There were countless shout-outs from fellow students about their victory. Tired smiles rested on most of the team members' faces.

Scott wasn't one of them. He'd only been able to put his slipping performance in chemistry to the back of his mind for so long. The formulas scrawled across the board were incomprehensible. The smug delivery of the concepts didn't help any either.

If he was grateful for anything, it was that Elli was in a different chemistry class. He was spared the distraction and her ability to see right through him—that this course was seriously stressing him out and pushing his limits. He'd mentioned it wasn't his favorite class in passing and she'd offer to help him, making light of his hang-ups. Saying that he was just overtired when working on equations.

His ineptitude in this subject had nothing to do with being overtired.

He wasn't alone in begrudging chemistry class. Last week Bobby Minter, who struggled with the equations even more than he, had taken matters in his own hands and signed up to be a teacher's assistant.

Scott's eyes had widened at this unlikely arrangement, but their chemistry teacher was in need of the help. Mr. Sellers had been laid up after hip replacement surgery, and he put Bobby to work returning papers, passing out textbooks, and making photocopies.

Scott didn't have a light-bulb moment about Bobby's true motive until he realized that Bobby wasn't stressing about the next test.

"You're cheating, aren't you?" Scott asked when he was able to slide in the question out on the practice field.

"Don't make such a deal of it," Bobby said. He squinted at Scott. "I'm more than earning this grade with all the things Sellers asks me to do."

"I didn't say you weren't," Scott said, wishing it had occurred to *him* to sign up as teacher's aide. "I just don't want things to go south for you."

Bobby scratched the side of his head and gave Scott a puzzled expression. "I don't get you, man. You're dating Ms. Chemistry Queen herself, and you're still barely getting by. Doesn't she tutor you? Or are you too busy getting handsy—"

Scott shook his head abruptly, shutting his teammate down. For one thing, he wasn't going to kiss and tell. And for another, he hated the notion of showing her the depth of his ineptitude. She hadn't started dating him thinking he was a dumb jock. In fact, he'd written a few poems modeled off Robert Frost's poetry that had sparked her interest in him. She'd said he had depth and range and wasn't merely going through the motions of an assignment. He couldn't risk losing her belief in him by admitting how between a rock and a hard place he was when it came to this other subject.

"How are you going to pass? We need you for the next game."

Scott didn't answer.

Bobby stopped prying and let the topic of Elli's intervention rest.

"I'm pretty discrete about changing answers," Bobby said. "I only have a few minutes when I'm at the back of the room, cleaning the counters. I take a look at that kid, Jesse Sander's test, and borrow a few of his answers, is all. I can borrow a few of his answers and put them on your next test if you want. Ty's too. I know you're both having a tough time in this class. Let's be honest."

Scott sighed, his breath letting out a visible plume in the cold autumn air. He didn't like the idea of Bobby stealing answers from anyone, least of all, an earnest kid who would probably be a professor one day. Jesse was one of the chemistry tutors, along with Elli, and she'd said kind things about him and his abilities. *He has a humble heart. I really like that about him.*

The comment had stuck in his mind. So Jesse had a humble heart for a smart guy. It was probably good he had something going for him. The kid didn't have a knack for athletics. He was confined to his studies, and his social life—or the lack thereof—reflected this truth.

Couldn't they find a better avenue for bumping their grades? But the more he contemplated it, the more he felt there wasn't any ready alternative. He had barely squeaked by on the last exam, and since then, the equations had only intensified. There was no more squeaking by. He was certain of it. And failing would mean he'd be sidelined for the next game. He couldn't have that happen, and neither could Ty or Bobby. The Peninsula Seahawks couldn't afford to have their key players side-lined.

"Fine," Scott said suddenly, resigned to Bobby's assistance, even if it was a mark against his character. "Do what you need to do so we can suit up for the next game."

·⟨⇔⟩·

Do what you need to do. It was a sentence Scott wished he'd never uttered. By the following Thursday it was too late to take any of it back. As he walked down the hallway that afternoon, he saw Elli coming toward him on the way to her rehearsal. Elli exchanged glances with him in the hallway and shot him a disappointed look. Something was up. He hadn't been able to speak with her since last Saturday, when they'd walked her dog around the Harbor and grabbed hot apple ciders after her rehearsal. He had loved it, spending time with her and watching her animated about her role as the Ghost of Christmas Past in *A Christmas Carol*. She kept telling him she wished he had the time to audition for a play and that she knew he'd be really good at it—he had an appreciation for the arts, and he really should explore that side of himself more.

"Only if I got to be your leading man," Scott had said, walking beside her and threading her fingers between his own as they walked Harborview Drive.

How far away that moment seemed now. Just as he was about to break the divide and push through the students in the hallway to ask her what was wrong, Bobby brushed up to his shoulder and said, "I really messed up, man. This isn't good at all."

Scott turned to his friend and before thinking to check his facial expression, said, "What's not good? What are you talkin' about?"

Ty slid up to him next and whispered loud enough for others to hear, "Jesse had a hunch something' was up 'cause Bobby started smudging out the correct answers on Jesse's test last time. God knows why. Well, lo and behold, your girl came back to the class right when our stud here was changing answers on his test. On some of ours. Jesse was right behind her as a witness. She took a handful of tests, and Jesse went with her to the principal's office. Nice of her to tattle, wasn't it?"

Scott felt a wave of dizziness, but he couldn't so easily lose his footing with the crush of students surrounding him. "Elli?" he asked slowly. "She ratted us out to the principal?"

He'd tried calling her after dinner last night, but her mother had told him she'd gone to bed with two aspirin and a pounding headache. He'd thought she was overly stressed from last-minute play preparations, but now he saw her actions in a different light. She'd been deliberately avoiding him.

"Should have known better than to trust a girl like that. Too smart," Bobby scoffed, leaving his own role in the matter out of the conversation. "Didn't think to give her boyfriend a heads-up now, did she?"

Scott grimaced. Even now, when Elli's distance and anger toward him were making sense, he was defensive of her. He hated it when the guys asked how he could date someone so studious. So serious. So devoted to her craft. So unlike most girls in cheer who clamored around the guys' lockers, wanting to be asked out on a date.

"I bet she'd slap your hand if you tried to make it to second base," Bobby had joked soon after hearing the two of them were together.

But there were things Scott had kept to himself. There was that one afternoon when Elli's mom had been out running errands, her sister out with friends, and her lawyer father still at work. She'd said something witty (didn't she always?), and he'd kissed her and let his hands got lost in her dark tresses. Her kiss tasted of the peppermint stick she'd just bitten into. His breath quickened and his hands grazed her stomach, found their way under her clothes.

She drew him closer to her, her kisses more urgent and matching his own. That was until they heard a car edge up the drive. She snapped to attention, placing her glasses firmly on the bridge of her nose. "We're going out to the study. We're working on our theme collage for *A Tale of Two Cities*. Scott, fix your hair."

He'd straightened up and wet down his hair with his own spit before dashing to the study, where the two of them should have been all along. He'd noticed the deepening of Elli's cheeks and had wanted to apologize to her right then and there, not knowing how she felt about getting a little too lost in each other. But she had already started skimming the pages of the dense novel.

In the weeks since he'd kissed her so deeply, they hadn't revisited that territory, as charged as it'd been. There was still that spark of chemistry between them, that knowing in each other's eyes, but Scott stayed on safer ground. And Elli didn't invite him back over when no one else was home. He thought this was something they did out of respect for each other. A deliberate slowing to take their relationship deeper. To make it more meaningful. But now he didn't know about that. The distance was growing—not because they needed to slow things down, but because in the time they were spending apart, she'd started realizing what he was tied up in.

It was one thing to realize he was in trouble. It was another to learn that it was at Elli's volition, and that she hadn't had the consideration to let him know. He was tasting the edge of disappointment and hadn't the reserves to defend her now.

He also hadn't the time. Less than ten minutes into their next class, Scott, Bobby, and Ty were summoned to the vice principal's office. He'd known something was coming, but how could it happen so quickly? None of them had the forethought to come up with a defense.

I wasn't the one who took Jesse's answers and passed them off as my own, Scott thought, his jaw set as walked down the fluorescent lit hallway, about to meet his consequence. *There's only so much trouble I can be in when I didn't make any of these changes on the test myself.*

But he was wrong on that count. The three boys were seated together in hard-backed chairs, and Coach Johnston sat there facing them with the vice principal, Mrs. Cole. Frustration painted their coach's features far more than the vice principal, who dealt with disciplinary action far more often. Gone was the jovial spark in his eye, the hearty laugh, the—*how's it going guys?* In its place was distilled anger—the type that was brewing, but could boil over at any moment. How could they do this to their team?

"Scott," Mrs. Cole began, her voice somber. "Did you know that Bobby was going to cheat on your behalf? Did you know that he was going to take answers from Jesse Sander's test and put them on your own?"

Scott was already starting to sweat at the back of his neck, and he could feel his heart quicken. He wished he'd taken a longer time fool proofing his teammate's strategy for getting ahead. How could he have been so stupid?

"I ... uh ... knew there was a chance that Bobby would change some of our answers," he said, folding and unfolding his hands in his lap. "We're all struggling a lot in that class."

"And you, Ty?" she said, as her eyes cut away from him to address their quieter teammate. "Did you know that Bobby was going to cheat on your behalf?"

Ty nodded slowly. "I wish we hadn't gone for it, but we didn't stop it from happening. I'm sorry." He bent his head to the floor, stared at his shoes which had come untied.

"Walk me through this," Mrs. Cole said, crossing her arms over her chest and turning in her chair to address Bobby head-on. "Right as you were stealing answers off Jesse's test, Elli Grayson enters in the room to retrieve something she forgot, and sees what you're up to. And not only that, but sees that you're erasing answers Jesse wrote down so that *you* can deliberately lower his score. Then Jesse himself walks in and she tells him what you've been doing?" Her voice had a biting tone to it as she sought the admission from Bobby's own tongue.

"You pretty much captured it," Bobby said, sounding far more irritated than contrite. Scott swallowed with difficulty as he heard this account of Elli's discovery. Had she instantly known he was involved? And how was their quarterback so curiously detached and disinterested in answering the vice principal's questions?

He glanced at Bobby, hoping that through the pleading on his face, he could trigger some sense into him. Ty was giving Bobby a look, too. Didn't he realize they were at her mercy? Bobby had nothing more to say other than, "It's a real hard class. Have you taken chemistry, Mrs. Cole?"

Scott winced. He could only wait for their vice principal's words to hammer home an uncomfortable reality: they would pay for their blunder. Their team would be dealt the blow of their poor choices. The school couldn't *not* penalize them for their academic dishonesty, especially now that word was out and spreading.

"I'm glad to hear that at least one of you is apologetic," Mrs. Cole said, her tone still grave. "As a result of this infraction, the three of you will be benched for the next two games, and you'll be required to write an apology note to Jesse for taking his answers. While you're at it," she said, standing and dusting her hands on the front of her black trousers, "I'd take some time for some self-reflection, perhaps hire a tutor if you're needing a hand up in this class. Try a little humility, and ask for help when you need it."

Scott felt the color drain from his face. It might only be two games to her, but to them it was the difference between lining up for playoffs or not being in the running at all. How was he supposed to break this news to his dad? His father had been pulling for him for so long, and he hated to see disappointment settle over his features.

He'd fought so hard to be in this lineup. Now with the power-three on the bench, havoc would be loosed on the rest of their season.

"You are better than this, boys," Coach Johnston said, as they were ordered to stand and take their punishments with them. He had no choice but to help them regroup. "We'll come back strong, won't we?"

It was all Scott could do to nod and leave the office in one piece. As daunting as it was to be found out for cheating and made to suffer the consequences, his singular focus right now was finding Elli. She'd been angry enough to charge into the office with her findings. She'd known that he was caught up in this and hadn't bothered to let him know. He ruffled a hand through his hair. He'd prefer that she come at him with a burst of indignation rather than send him charged expressions from across the room.

The bell rang. They'd spent all that time in the office having their punishment doled out. Once released, Bobby paused them in the hall. "Apology letters to Jesse?" he scoffed. "Not happening. That's not the response he's getting from me or any one of us. You hear me?!"

Ty frowned slightly. "What do you mean? You saying you're not gonna write one?"

"Hell no," Bobby said, laughing. "None of us are. I have something else planned for that kid."

"Haven't we done enough damage, Bobby?" Scott said. "You're just going to make it worse."

"I'm just getting started with that kid. He's going to find out his rightful place." Bobby took off down the hall.

Several anxious teammates tried to stop Scott to hear what happened as he walked down the hall. But Scott shook his head, indicating he didn't have time for that now. His only focus was on finding Elli, though his stomach twisted at the inevitable disgust she'd show him. Or even worse, the disappointment. Shame was ready to catch up to him and settle over his shoulders.

As he'd expected, Elli was tilted toward her locker, reaching for her literature binder. Dread invaded his senses—he'd forgotten which class was next. He wasn't prepared for the way she'd distanced him before he'd even had the chance to explain his desperation, why he'd agreed to things he shouldn't have. It didn't excuse him, but perhaps she'd understand that he'd made a mistake and give him another chance.

Scott tried to close the distance between him and Elli's locker, but just as he was saying her name, he saw that she was engaged in conversation with another guy and that she was laughing at something he'd just said.

As he came closer, Jesse Sander reached out his arms to carry Elli's books to the next class. The bell rang. Scott felt gut-punched as he followed the two of them into the classroom.

·☙·

It had never been such agony—sitting through literature class. Elli acted indifferent to his presence. She hadn't turned from her seat in the front to look at him even once, and that was uncharacteristic of her. It was all he could do to stop tapping his pencil nervously to the desk and make it through the hour. He watched her adjust the clip in her dark hair, caught her small smile at the mention of Sydney Carton's self-sacrifice and studied her as she took careful notes on plot aspects she'd probably already committed to memory from *A Tale of Two Cities*.

He only caught up with her after class because he was willful and determined. He watched as her beautiful, dark eyes went from their glow to lifeless upon seeing him. "Els. We need to talk."

"I didn't know you were involved when I went to the office," she said, her tone flat. "Bobby flipped a lid on me when I caught him, and I had to tell what was going on. So they could deal with him."

Scott's nostrils flared at this admission. "He flipped a lid on you? What do you mean by that?!"

She glanced away, but her lower lip trembled. When she turned back to him, she didn't answer the question. "Why would *you* do this, Scott?" she asked instead, hurt flickering in her eyes. "You could have asked me to help you out if you were struggling. I'm a tutor, after all."

"So what," Scott started in, weary at the notion, "my John-Hopkins-scholar-girlfriend can see how much I'm lagging behind? Did it ever occur to you that . . . ?"

"I have to go," Elli said, clutching her books close to her chest.

"Did it ever occur to you that it wouldn't go well when I found out you cheated off Jesse Sander? He's my friend, you know. He didn't want me to say anything about it, but Bobby's started sending him threatening messages. For what, though?! As if it's Jesse's fault he's good at chemistry. He hasn't done *anything* to deserve this. He's sweet and smart and . . . ."

What kind of threatening messages? Scott was about to say something, but Elli started in about how great Jesse was again. He bit down on his tongue hard enough to taste iron.

"Scott, we'll have to talk about this later." Sparks of indignation brewed in her eyes. "But what you did was dead wrong, and that isn't something I'll change my mind about. I'm not sure you and those boys deserve to win any more games." She clutched her textbooks closer as if to shield herself and was gone before he could say another word.

·◌·

Scott set out for Elli Grayson's house shortly before the dinner hour. He didn't like the idea of a static phone line and her father possibly overhearing him apologize. Face-to-face was best. His stomach twisted at the thought of knocking on her front door, not knowing how she'd receive him, but he wouldn't rest until she was no longer glaring in his general direction.

Several minutes later, he was greeted by her elegantly dressed mother, and could tell from her welcoming spirit that she didn't know he'd done anything to make her daughter mad. "Scott, come on in. Elli is practicing lines in her bedroom. I'll have her come out and meet you in the study."

For whatever reason, Scott's face began to burn at the thought of the time he'd spent making out with Elli in her room when neither of her parents were home. Her mom was so resolute about having them go to the study, but they'd found a way around the unspoken rule that once, and he couldn't forget it.

Scott reminded himself to lower his shoulders and unclench his jaw. He was so far from experiencing a repeat afternoon like that with Elli, that there was no use burdening himself with thoughts of getting caught.

"Please wait here a moment while I get her," Mrs. Grayson said, grazing a hand over his shoulder as she left him in a room encased with books, so many of them hardbound. How many had been read, he wondered. His eyes found a beautifully framed map of the Pacific Northwest while he waited for her to materialize. He thought about what Elli told him—that Bobby had started sending Jesse threatening messages—and knew that it would be a sticking point if it came up in their conversation again. Torn pages of scratch paper in his locker. Pages strewn over Jesse's textbooks, laid conveniently over his seat. Notes warning him to watch his back. Notes that proclaimed—*we know where you live*. Notes that reminded Jesse that next time he wanted to assert his academic smarts, he might not want to bring an entire football team down upon him. It would be a sticking point because Scott knew what Bobby was up to. Their quarterback was incapable of keeping his nose to the grindstone and taking the punishment. *He wants that boy to toss and turn at night and not know what's coming to him.*

"That kid needs to know who he's dealing with," Bobby had said after school. "He thinks it's worth it to tattle about a few test answers. I'm gonna have him start second guessing the day he—"

Ty had drawn a hand to Bobby's forearm. "Wait a minute, man," he'd said. "You're blaming this all on Jesse when it's really Scott's girl who ratted us out."

"You leave Elli out of this," Scott had said. "Do you really want to mess with someone whose father has his own law firm? Seriously, you don't have to think hard about that."

Bobby let out an exasperated sigh. Scott knew he had him on that count if nothing else. "I'm well aware of who her father is. 'Member her older sister and I kinda had a thing?"

Scott tried not to betray his emotions. *Kinda had a thing?* That was one way to put it.

Bobby leveled with Scott. "I'm leaving Elli out of this. But I'm not done messing with Jesse. You aren't either," he said, eyes flickering from Ty to Scott. "Your girlfriend might have convinced him to tattle, but Jesse went with her to the office with his test in hand. He could have made things a lot easier for himself if he'd just asked me about it. But since he went over me—over us—he's gonna pay. And you two are gonna help me."

Bobby leaned toward Scott and whispered in his ear. "You should hate him more than anyone, Brighton. Have you seen the way that kid looks at *your* girl? He's into her. And she seems to like it."

3

Retaliation

There was no undoing the punishment, so Scott did his best to adjust. No use bemoaning two lost games and the opportunities to stay on top this season. But disappointment still seeped in like mud slowly filling his shoes; it was a sludge that stayed with him.

Late afternoon, after their first football practice back since it had all gone down, Scott walked into the Pogie Bait, Gig Harbor's sandwich and ice cream joint. He had taken the fastest shower he could manage, and his hair was wet against the hood of his orange windbreaker as he lowered himself into one of the open booths in the roomy establishment.

A framed photograph of a weathered ship hung above the booth and unsettled him. He had the sudden feeling of being adrift at sea, amidst choppy waves. Some of his friends took their daddy's sailboats out on the Sound, but Scott didn't envy them, much preferring the solid ground beneath his feet over the turning tide.

He ran his fingers over the clear resin surface of the weathered boat-hatch-turned-table and studied the wooden planks that held it up. Undoubtedly stories could be told about where they'd come from, but all he really cared about was whether Ty would show up or not. He had to talk to him.

Scott looked at the root beer float on the table. It no longer appealed to him. Not before he was about to do such a substantial ask. Scott had ordered one for Ty too, hoping to entice him to listen. It was minutes away from melting. *What if Ty didn't even like root beer floats?* Scott thought, second guessing himself. The weather was brisk, even for November, and it wouldn't have hurt to order him a hot chocolate. Too late now.

He picked at his cuticles as he waited for his teammate, but stopped when he drew a drop of blood. A few minutes later, Ty opened the front door, making his entrance in black sweats and a dark green Peninsula Seahawks sweatshirt. His blond hair looked dark, wet from the shower or the rain. As soon as Ty looked toward him, Scott tasted relief. He wouldn't waste words about plays out on the field—if he didn't get out what needed to be said quickly, they might be interrupted.

But Ty hadn't come alone. As he moved on through the door, Marianne Prather came into view behind him. She was a junior cheerleader, with golden hair and sun-kissed skin. Her eyes were an unexpected hazel that lent her a more distinct beauty. She smiled brightly at Scott, even as she drew one of Ty's spare sweat-shirts closer to her frame. There was a bookbag slung across her shoulder.

Scott felt his hopes collapse and was certain his frustration showed. He hadn't told Ty this meeting was only for the two of them, but Ty was smart enough to read into Scott's urgent tone and his off-campus location. With Marianne there, he wouldn't be able to mention the prank they'd dreamed up at the height of their anger, much less the fact that he didn't want to be involved anymore. Scott sipped his float, unable to dissolve his unease. He needed to get it together before the irritation of this moment started telling on him and made him stammer.

Before Scott could gather his composure, Marianne approached the table. "Hi Scotty," she said, her voice unexpectedly low.

"I . . . I didn't know you were coming," Scott choked out and then tried to recover from his fumble. "I could get you a root beer float too."

Ty's blue eyes flashed at the mention of a root beer float, and he stepped in front of his girl to claim the beverage from the table. "Don't worry about it, man. I'll order her one. Thanks, though. This is just what I needed after a grueling practice. I don't know what Coach Johnston is doing, but I think he's trying to kill us."

"He is," Marianne said, unfazed. "Not much has changed in the years I've been cheering . . . ." She cleared her throat. "You two get to talking. I'm gonna order some coffee and do some homework over by the window while you guys catch up. I want something warmer."

Scott tried to conceal his relief, though the corners of his mouth were already turning up. He tried to let his remaining agitation simmer down. Attention fixed on Ty, he said in one breath, "Take a seat for a minute, Ty . . . I—I'm having second thoughts about this plan."

"We just need to get it over with. Look, we won't leave Jesse out there for long. The point is to shake him up a bit and get him home. None of us want to get in more trouble than we already . . . ."

Scott couldn't bring himself to take another sip of his float. "We're going to get in trouble no matter how fast we get him out of there, don't you see that?"

Ty narrowed his eyes. "Not necessarily, Scotty. Bobby's gonna work it out with the kid. He's not taking him back home until he admits he messed with the wrong guys and that he'll never do it again."

"Here's a better idea. One of us—ideally Bobby—pulls him aside, sets him in the car even and threatens him. No off-site business."

But he'd already lost Ty to Fleetwood Mac's "Hypnotized" playing over the airwaves. After a few lines, Ty turned back to Scott. "What were you saying?"

Scott straightened his shoulders, afraid that he wasn't going to get Ty to change course. "Only that I think taking Jesse to the old boat is the worst idea that I've—"

Ty drank noisily through his straw. "You've got more reason to hate him than I do . . . Elli ending things with you and spending more of her time with—"

Scott's chest hurt. "They both tutor chemistry nitwits like us. You know this." He winced at the pang in his heart.

Ty leaned across the table and said in a loud whisper, "Whatever the case, Bobby's mind is made up, and this isn't as big a deal as you're making it."

Before he could give a response, Scott saw Marianne turning from the front window to study the two of them. She set her pencil down, and it rolled across her open textbook. Questions spilled from her eyes.

Ty gave Scott a look and placed his hands firmly on the table. "If you want us to get in trouble, keep talking as loud as you are now. My girl's watching us, and she's not the only one."

Sure enough, Scott scanned the interior of the Pogie Bait and saw his next-door neighbors, the Housers, looking in their direction, waving with agreeable expressions on their faces. Scott waved back and tried to offer a genuine smile before cutting his eyes back to his teammate.

Ty lowered his voice. "Bobby and us go way back . . . we need to get that kid off our back for good. He never should have messed with us in the first place. And look," Ty said in one last effort to rationalize Bobby's scheme. "We—you and I—will find a way to get back to Jesse. We won't leave him out there for longer than an hour. Just long enough to make him keep his damn mouth shut. We gotta show Bobby we're a united front. We've lost the last two home games, and we need to get back out there stronger than ever. We gotta show him that we're on his side. That we're in this together."

As soon as Ty finished his speech, Marianne edged up to their table and peered down at them, her Styrofoam coffee cup now in hand. "Sounds like you guys didn't work everything out on the field today. Anything I can help you two sort out?"

Scott mustered up a smile. "Bobby's been a little hard on us lately, so we've had to put our heads together. Come up with an improvement plan, so to speak."

Marianne chewed on the inside of her cheek. "And it works to make those plans without him?"

"I don't know if you've spent much time with Bobby, but he doesn't like ideas unless they're polished," Scott said, taking a napkin and wiping the stickiness from his face. "He's particular."

"That's one way to say controlling," Marianne smirked, raising her cup to her mouth. "No, I haven't spent much time with Bobby, but his older brother was quarterback before, you know. And I've met their father. Let's just say the apple doesn't fall far . . . . I think the Minter men are a lot alike."

Marianne arched an eyebrow at Ty. "You almost ready to go?" she asked, her voice infused with sudden sweetness. "I don't feel much like studying after all." She gave him a playful wink.

Ty gave an eager nod and clasped a hand to her waist. "Thanks for the treat," he said, motioning toward the empty glass as he rose to his feet. "Our next game will be good, Brighton. We'll get it right again."

Scott's plea had gone unheard. And what did Ty mean about finding a way back to Jesse—just the two of them? Was Scott making more of this than he needed to? It wasn't as if they were going to leave Jesse alone in the hull of the boat indefinitely. They weren't monsters—they just needed to shake the kid up a little bit so he'd think twice before ever compromising their college prospects again.

· ⟨⊷⟩ ·

The late autumnal sky was steely gray each time Scott looked up that Wednesday afternoon. He wished he was anywhere but here, standing in the lower parking lot of Peninsula High School with Bobby and his teammates. Practice had wrapped half an hour ago, and they had all showered off quickly and traded out their uniforms for street clothes to ensure their prank went off as planned. Before it got too dark.

Scott's heart beat fast, and his palms were already sweating. He thrust his hands in the pockets of his Levi's, an attempt to anchor himself and his thoughts to earth.

What was left of the late afternoon sun glinted in Bobby's eyes as he faced his two teammates. "Here's how it's gonna go," he said as though he were leading a squadron. "The kid leaves the science lab either alone or with Elli Grayson around *now* most days."

Scott bit his tongue at this cruel reality. It had only been two weeks since she'd broken up with him and sent his heart reeling. So much for their winning streak. That had ended too. But any loss of glory there dulled in comparison with how it felt to lose her.

"If Elli is with him," he continued, smoothing his hands over his letterman jacket, "it might not work today." Bobby waited for Ty and Scott to nod their agreement. "It all depends on whether Elli's sister swings by to pick her up. Within five minutes, we'll know. If Nicole doesn't come, the kid will walk her home, and we'll have to call it quits for the day."

Ty removed a box of Marlboros from his back pocket, lit one, and took a puff. "I don't see why Elli has to be a deal-breaker. She's almost as annoying as Jesse, and she had the biggest part in ratting us out."

Scott ruffled a hand through his tousled hair. He opened his mouth to defend her, but closed it when he thought better of it.

As far as he was concerned, they were all stupid for thinking they could ever cheat off Jesse on those chemistry exams. Bobby should have known that he might be seen through the window, and that Elli would be the first one on to them. Something about her acting in all those school plays made her search out villains around every corner.

"We're not doing anything if Elli is anywhere around," Bobby said staunchly. "She's a bigger risk since her daddy's a rich lawyer. Something goes wrong, we find ourselves behind bars, and that's not worth it."

Ty closed his eyes and let out a spiraled breath of smoke. Was he envisioning handcuffs and oppressive gray walls surrounding him, Scott wondered? Man, he didn't want to be involved in this anymore. Nothing had happened yet, and he felt like the lights on their nonchalant hangouts were already going out. What he'd give to be leaning back in his chair right now, a Coca-Cola in his hand, unable to stop laughing at a dry joke one of them had told. Probably Ty.

Scott drew his focus back to the present moment. He was allowing himself to drift like an unmoored boat. The quarterback was watching him. "Stop your daydreaming," he said, snapping his fingers close to Scott's face.

Bobby glanced at his wristwatch. Scott's stomach turned. If he second-guessed any of Bobby's directives, chances were that he'd become as much a target as Jesse Sander.

"We have five minutes," Bobby said in an undertone, with a

heightened awareness of his surroundings. He glanced at his 1968 red Chevelle. "Good thing I was able to park in the lower lot." The trunk and doors remained unlocked for a quick escape, the keys lingered in the ignition, and the wheels were ready to peel down the back road the moment they needed to go.

They'd already discussed the logistics a few days before. Scott had felt an unease in the pit of his stomach then too, but his low-grade anger at Jesse for befriending the girl he loved had prevented him from interrupting Bobby. He didn't like the severity of the plan, but Jesse would come out relatively unscathed—if a little shaken up.

They wouldn't leave Jesse in the trunk for long, only ten minutes at most. It couldn't be that mean, could it?

"There he is. Heading across the parking lot!" Bobby whispered.

Scott told himself to breathe. *Please let Elli come up behind him*, Scott prayed, though doubting God would listen to him now. *Please don't let her sister pick her up today. Jesse needs to walk her home. He just needs to. It's our only way out.*

Perspiration rolled between his shoulder blades. His hands were sweating too. For sure they would slip him up as they attempted to grab Jesse. If this setup would only crumble right now, he would accept the zero from the chemistry exam that he, Bobby, and Ty rightly deserved for cheating. He'd gladly face his parents and accept losing the black '65 Mustang fastback he'd been working on with his dad these past two summers, as they'd threatened.

Scott was afraid to raise his eyes to see if Elli was with their target, but he had to know what was going on. If he wasn't paying attention, Bobby would charge forward and he'd be two steps behind.

Crouching behind a huckleberry bush, brash branches poked into his skin. He couldn't stop thinking of own discomfort. He had to pee and he wouldn't be able to do anything about it for quite some time. He tried not to think of running creeks and waterfalls.

They waited, Ty only a few feet away and watched as the kid emerged from the science lab. He was pitiful, really, this Jesse Sander. Scott watched in irritation as Jesse patted his dark blue satchel at his side. Why couldn't he keep anything to himself? Why must he abide by the rules to the letter? He saw with relief that Elli was hovering close to Jesse's side. This was the only occasion where he wanted to see those two standing shoulder to shoulder.

Scott had always detected something in Elli that those other boys hadn't seen—potential. Though she carried herself well, she kept her framed eyes pressed to textbooks or scripts and didn't betray much interest in attracting the opposite sex. She was really something when she lifted her chin up. Her cheekbones were high, her eyes were beautifully almond shaped, and her figure would probably make most girls envious. She kept much of herself hidden behind oversize sweaters, like the shapeless cranberry one she wore today. Her older sister, Nicole, was pinup material, but Elli could be too, if she wanted.

He wasn't here, waiting in the bushes after school, to be distracted by the Grayson sisters, however. He was here to focus on Jesse, "the kid," as Bobby preferred calling him. The kid's frame was small, though he was an average height for his age. He held his arms close to his body—skinny arms like chicken wings, the kind you effortlessly tear once you open the greasy box at the drive-through joint. Jesse scarcely ever looked up to make conversation, so intent was he on mastering chemistry equations and scientific code. And he barely spoke to anyone, unless it was the teacher or another science geek.

No one really knew Jesse, except for maybe Elli. He'd only moved to the Peninsula last year and hadn't channeled through the same grades and teachers as the rest of the kids. He was one of those students that most of his peers left alone: mature beyond his years and independent. But several weeks ago, Bobby had started intercepting Jesse's homework assignments from the wire basket in the back of the classroom soon after class was dismissed, and everything had changed.

Ty had followed Jesse home one afternoon after school: down the hill, across the highway and through the neighborhood beside quiet, woodsy roads. The kid lived only ten minutes' walking distance from Peninsula High. His house was painted green—small, nondescript. The drapes were sealed tightly shut, and there was no garden or evidence of family life except for a friendly blue heeler traipsing around in the backyard. The house felt lonely, Ty told his teammates. The yard wasn't tended, and the paint on the shutters hadn't seen a new coat in years.

It was Scott who learned that the only family member the kid lived with was his father, who'd served as a medic in the Vietnam War. That vital piece of information was harder to come by, but he asked around a little and learned that Ed Sander was currently working as a traveling physician.

When Bobby had realized that Jesse didn't have any siblings or doting parents overseeing him, he'd clasped his hands together. "We've got him!"

The only wrench in their scheme was Elli Grayson. Scott had seen her glaring at members of the football team on several occasions now, including him. She'd undoubtedly written the lot of them off as "dumb jocks."

Bobby hoped she would leave the premises in her sister's car, but Scott found himself wishing that she could curtail their best laid schemes, that she'd put an abrupt stop to their entire prank by walking Jesse home. He didn't want to be part of this ploy. It wasn't worth it, but who would listen to him now?

"Will you put that cigarette out?" Scott whispered impatiently to Ty as they waited to see if Elli's older sister would arrive.

They weren't visible from the sidewalk where Jesse and Elli prattled on about God knows what, but Ty's need for a nicotine fix was more than Scott could bear right now. They didn't need one more reason to compromise their eligibility on the team, and Ty should know better.

Ty took another long draw and exhaled slowly so that the plume of smoke filled Scott's eyes and made them burn. He gritted his teeth, feeling his eyes start to water.

"Put it out now or I'll do it for you," Scott said tightly.

Bobby cast them both a threatening glare. If they didn't follow through, and quickly as he'd planned, Bobby would make their life miserable for the rest of the season. He'd throw them the ball to win games, but he'd be moody and terse.

Ty stomped the half-smoked cigarette out under his gray sneaker and said to Scott, "There. You happy now?"

What was with Ty lately? Though he could come across as withdrawn, he was increasingly combative. He nearly gritted his teeth when answering questions, and Scott didn't get it. Since Marianne Prather had gone steady with him, Ty Parsons was the envy of all the guys.

"Will you just shut up!" Bobby snapped, just as a late-model blue Cadillac pealed into the parking lot. Nicole was there to pick Elli up.

Scott gulped, the lump in his throat painful—their prank was still on. They were really going to do this. He was cold enough to feel his teeth chatter. His eyes darted across the parking lot desperately, and he actually prayed for Elli to refuse her older sister's offer of a ride home in favor of walking beside Jesse.

"Bobby, we can't . . . ." he started, his voice wavering.

"We will," Bobby said, squatting close to the ground, as if savoring this moment before they went in for the kill.

There was nothing quite so deliberate as retaliation, and Bobby had maintained that there was none more deserving than Jesse Sander to receive it.

4

Revenge Begins

Scott raised his eyes to the stone-colored sky and narrowed in on the merging clouds. All signs pointed to torrential rain before they were halfway through this so-called prank.

"Bobby," he said sharply, motioning above their heads to the afternoon's foreshadow of unruly weather. Why hadn't any of them been smart enough to check the news reports? What else should they expect for the Pacific Northwest?

Their ringleader glanced at the sky dismissively and threw Scott an irritated look. "We've played ball in worse weather than this," he said. "Don't tell me you'd let a few raindrops interfere with our plan."

At this point Scott was willing to let anything interfere. But Bobby's unnerving determination prevented him from saying a word even now. Twice Scott could have sworn that Elli glanced in their general direction before jumping in her sister's car, but he couldn't be certain. Perhaps she'd heard some rattling in the shrubbery and scanned for a squirrel.

Bobby's focus followed the Cadillac until it was completely out of sight. Suddenly the tension between the quarterback and Elli's older sister came back to him. The only reason it had slipped Scott's mind was because Bobby was anything but monogamous when it came to his approach with girls. It usually took him less than a week to find a replacement for the last girl he'd had swinging on his arm.

Sure enough, once Elli and Nicole left the premises, Bobby's shoulders began to relax. He stood to his full height, stretched his long, muscular arms over his head and fastened his eyes on Jesse, who began to leave the parking lot, walking with his head bent to the leaf-strewn sidewalk. The green vest he wore over his flannel gave the illusion he had an extra ten pounds on him. Jesse swung his satchel over his right shoulder. The heft of it slowed his footsteps.

Scott concentrated deeply, as if warming up for a play on the field, but this time there was no flicker of anticipation surging through his veins.

"Now," Bobby said, snapping his fingers, summoning his teammates as he would in a huddle.

Now was the time to make their move.

Ty rose to his feet. "Should have changed my shoes," he murmured, glancing down at his new Pumas. Scott could tell from a quick glance out the corner of his eye that they weren't broken in yet.

Before Bobby could scoff at him for his oversight, Ty redirected his focus. "Let's do this," he said, moving to the quarterback's shoulder.

The three headed after Jesse, Scott's limbs feeling slow and heavy. The kid turned as they ran toward him. But Scott would get him out somehow. He'd borrow his dad's truck and return to the boat. Set him free.

The boys closed the gap, encroaching closer and closer on Jesse's territory. His expression was one of confusion at first—it obviously hadn't occurred to him that their appearance had anything to do with him and not a football drill. Scott could see panic written on the kid's face.

Jesse drew his arms closer to his body, but he didn't immediately break into a run. When their breath was quick at his heels, he finally attempted to pick up the pace. He could only move so fast with his satchel on his right shoulder.

Bobby reached him first, spun him around with force. Jesse's blue bag tumbled to the ground, and notebooks, pens, and pencils spilled onto the ground.

Scott could see the terror in his cloudy gray eyes behind his lenses. The next breath the kid took was ragged and terrified. Scott winced. They should stop now. They'd already put the fear of God in him.

Bobby didn't give the kid a chance to speak. He took a step closer and gripped Jesse at the top of his collared shirt. "You chose to mess with the wrong guy," he said, tightness in his voice.

That's enough, Scott wanted to say. *Let's just make him promise he won't do this again.* But the words didn't come out fast enough. Before he could pose another play, Bobby threw a fist to the side of Jesse's face with such impact that both Ty and Scott's jaws dropped. Scott heard the contact with bone and he watched in horror at the immediate swelling of Jesse's eye. The kid's glasses shattered.

What the hell is Bobby thinking? Scott bit down on his lip hard as he watched the kid crumble to the ground.

"Let's not," Scott said. "He's already going home now with his eye swollen shut. If his dad sees that, he's going to press charges ...."

Bobby threw him a look of disgust. "We've talked about this already. This kid is stubborn, and it's gonna take more than a knock to the ground to teach him not to mess with us."

Jesse groaned and lifted his hand to the tender swelling of his face. He attempted to sit, but when he did, Bobby crouched down and said, "You think it's over, don't you?" He shook his head, and his blue eyes were wild and uncaged. "It's gonna take a little more to teach you a lesson."

Jesse moaned. "No . . . no . . . I won't say anything. Please . . . ."

"Did you hear that?" Scott yelled. "He's not going to rat you out again, Bobby. Let's take him home."

Though Ty opened his mouth, Bobby was already shaking his head angrily. "You forget that he's made us sit out two games and cost us a few wins and who knows what else."

Scott threw Ty an exasperated look over his shoulder. *Let's get this done quickly then*, he thought to himself.

Bobby gave a quick nod. Ty stepped forward to grab the left side of Jesse's body and Scott took over the right. Since the kid couldn't have weighed more than 140 pounds, it wasn't hard to get a clamp on him. Jesse started screaming, "Help me! Help! Let me go."

For what he lacked in strength, Jesse made up for in precise kicks. Bobby raced to the car to pop the trunk. Then he dashed to the driver's seat to turn the key in the ignition. Jesse was putting up more of a fight than Scott had imagined.

It wasn't easy to toss Jesse in the trunk. While they held him down, Jesse did what he still could, thrashing with his legs, butting blindly with his head.

"His book bag's still out there, on the ground," Ty said, gesturing toward the empty school parking lot.

Bobby cursed. He was the only one in the position to scramble back over there and collect the fallen items. Anyone who knew Jesse Sander would realize there was no way he'd leave the contents of his book bag strewn on the pavement.

"Just close the trunk," Bobby muttered, dashing from the driver's seat to retrieve the satchel and the contents that spilled from it.

"You don't have to do this," Jesse said, sounding hoarse and close to tears. "You really don't. I won't make any trouble."

"You already have," Ty said, a ripple of anger breaking through his otherwise stoic resolve.

"Look . . . you won't be in here for long," Scott said, as if it was any consolation. He saw in his mind Jesse's terrified eyes and sought to deaden his own conscience. The kid was petrified, murmuring, "no, no, no" like a prayer.

Scott felt pressure at his temples as he and Ty slammed the trunk with Jesse inside.

"Get in," Bobby thundered without missing a beat, tossing the kid's satchel on the floor of the passenger seat.

Ty and Scott climbed in silently. Scott took the back, wanting to be as far away from the quarterback as possible. Bobby backed up the car, throwing gravel as he reversed and then lurched the vehicle forward.

Scott had to relieve himself so badly by now that the mere suggestion of a creek had the power to make him squirm. He clamped his knees together and closed his eyes; it's all he could do to keep it together. *It's almost over,* he told himself. *Before long you'll retrace your steps, and it will be as if none of this ever happened.*

5

Elli's Intuition

*E*lli glimpsed a familiar red Chevelle near the school parking lot right as she said goodbye to Jesse. A quick scan of the premises showed no trace of its owner, Bobby Minter. Perhaps practice had run late today. Coach Johnston could still be out on the field breaking down a drill, determined to drive his team to a win this Friday night after their two recent losses. But it still took her aback to see his car parked near the swimming pool. She wasn't anxious to run into him after their last encounter. The wheels of her mind turning, she took a long time setting her bag on the back seat of her sister's car.

"Come on, Elli. Won't you hurry up?" Nicole said, smacking her gum so loudly that it popped. She wore a mini jean skirt and a blue ribbed sweater. A peace symbol dangled from her rearview mirror, as customary as tie-dyed shirts, bongs, and war protest signs in Seattle. Elli still hadn't opened the passenger door. Nicole let out an exasperated sigh. "Why don't you get your own license? There are places I'd rather be than the Peninsula High School parking lot at four in the afternoon."

"Sorry, I was thinking about something," Elli said.

"Why do you spend so much time with a boy like that?" Nicole asked, turning the radio up a beat as a new Rolling Stones song came on. "Hand of Fate."

"A boy like what?" Elli asked, feigning misunderstanding.

Nicole shook her head. "A recluse. Someone who doesn't fit in. Don't pretend that you don't understand what I'm talking about." She smoothed strands of hair from her dark eyes. "I thought he might be queer at first, but he spends a lot of time with you . . . ."

Elli wanted to call out her sister's judgments, but she let the remark slide. There was an uneasiness in the pit of her stomach. She was still troubled over seeing Bobby's car, but she knew better than to bring it to her sister's attention. Nicole had graduated last year and said she could go a lifetime without returning to the premises and risking a chance encounter with him. Still, Elli couldn't keep her mind off the cheating in the science lab and the possibility that it could get worse for Jesse. She picked at her pink nail polish after settling into the front seat.

"Maybe he doesn't fit in because everyone else is the loser," she said as she clicked her seatbelt into place. She glanced over her shoulder as they careened out of the parking lot, but she didn't see any sign of Bobby or the guys he hung out with.

Let it go, Elli, she told herself. *Don't let your overactive imagination get the better of you.*

·⟨⇥⟩·

"Bobby, you gotta pull over," Scott said, desperate. "I need you to pull over or I'm gonna pee my pants."

Bobby threw him a disbelieving look in the rearview mirror. They were close to their destination, but Scott's nerves were in full gear. It didn't help that he had to pee so bad that he might just wet himself. He saw Ty shake his head out of the corner of his eye, but he didn't care about his teammates' irritation with him right now. He needed out of the cursed car.

Bobby jerked the car angrily to the side of the road even though there wasn't much of a shoulder. "Get out then."

Scott leaped out, feeling his head throb. It was starting to rain. He took a couple of steps away from the vehicle and with shaking hands, started pulling down his zipper. But instead of feeling instant relief as he faced the trees' cover, all Scott could think was that the worst wasn't over. Pounding thuds came from the trunk—the kid was trying to kick out the taillights. If they took much longer and Bobby found any damage on his car, it would be all the worse for Jesse.

Should he dart through the close-growing trees, away from any involvement in this risky scheme? He doubted that Ty or Bobby would stall their plan in order to chase him through the woods on foot. Bobby couldn't drive through those trees and brush.

As his mind raced through either/or scenarios, Scott noticed a yellow sign posted to a tree in front of him. Stepping closer to it, he saw that the sign was not only boarded to one tree, but to several before it. The message was clear and undeniable: PRIVATE PROPERTY, it said in bold black lettering. ALL TRESPASSERS WILL BE PROSECUTED TO THE FULL EXTENT OF THE LAW.

The signs were new; a few days ago, there were no notices in sight. The yellow farmhouse had sat vacant for years; deep green moss was overtaking the roof, and some of the windows were broken out and boarded. Scott felt chills at the back of his neck. Could this save them from a stupid prank? Bobby had assured them that this acreage belonged to no one, that it'd been vacant for years.

"Come on! What's taking so long?!" Bobby yelled out the window. Rain slanted from the sky, no longer just a steady trickle. He laid on the horn.

Scott stiffened. Couldn't Bobby read the obvious signs surrounding them? Why would he even consider using his horn? Was he trying to signal their presence to the new property owners? Scott pointed to the first of many signs, and Bobby finally paused long enough to drink the message in. His lips started twitching, disbelief taking over his features. He cursed beneath his breath and said something about getting in the bloody car. He barely waited for Scott to close the car door before laying on the gas.

Scott and Ty exchanged wary looks.

"Did you read the signs?" Scott asked finally. Didn't "*full extent of the law*" mean anything to him?

"Of course, I saw them," Bobby said, turning on his wipers. "Along with new windows at that farmhouse back there. It just means we need to get this over with a lot faster." His eyes gleamed like polished glass in the rearview mirror. "This property's been up for sale since I was a kid. How was I to know it would sell in the last few days?" He shook his head, dumbfounded.

"Maybe we should take him somewhere else," Scott said.

Or nowhere at all, he thought.

Bobby struck the steering wheel and gave an adamant no. "We've already come this far," he argued. "And I seriously doubt that whoever bought this property *moved* out here. They probably don't even live on the Peninsula."

No one said anything for a long, drawn-out moment. But the thuds coming from the trunk had not let up, and Ty couldn't refrain from saying anything any longer.

"You hear that?" he asked, his eyes incredulous. "He's gonna kick your taillights out."

Bobby gritted his teeth. "We're almost there."

"So what are you gonna do, beat him up some more and leave him out there until . . . ."

"We already talked about this," Bobby said, frustrated. "We don't come back for the kid until tomorrow morning. My sources tell me that his daddy, the traveling doc, doesn't get back until tomorrow night, so that gives us plenty of time."

Scott looked out his window, raised his eyes to the ever-deepening sky and watched as the rain shook down from the trees. "We need to hurry," he said, unable to dissolve the metallic taste from his mouth or the pulsing at his temples.

We need to hurry so I can come back for him before it's completely dark. Before this situation gets a lot worse than any of us wanted.

·❦·

"I shouldn't have left him alone."

"What?" They were almost home. Nicole popped a pink bubble before turning to look at her. "That boy you were talking to outside when I picked you up? Why? He being bullied?" She popped her gum again. "Really, El, you could do so much better." She reached over and tugged on the corner of Elli's cranberry-colored sweater. "But you might want to change your fashion sense if you want to catch anyone's eye."

"I don't want to catch the anyone's eye. And what's it to anyone what I'm wearing!" Elli said, beginning to fume. "That's not what's important right now . . . ." The frustration in her voice startled even herself. Nicole turned down her radio and tilted her head toward her, waiting for Elli to explain.

"Look," Elli said, "I think he might be in danger." The lump in her throat was so pronounced that it took pains to speak again. "I don't know what it is, but I have this bad feeling in my gut. I saw Bobby's car parked in the lower lot after school, and a little over two weeks ago Jesse and I turned him in for cheating . . . ."

Elli hadn't intended to say Bobby's name to her sister, but she uttered it now, knowing that if nothing else demanded Nicole's attention, this would. Her tactic worked. Nicole swallowed deeply, perhaps even losing her gum.

"What do *you* think you can do to stop Bobby if he really had it out for Jesse snitching on him?"

"Can we turn back and see if Jesse is on his way home?"

"And if we don't see him out walking in the rain . . . ?" Nicole said, holding out her palm, waiting for more of a plan.

"Then we wait at his house for a little while to make sure he gets there," Elli said impatiently. "And if there's no sign of him . . . ."

"You're getting ahead of yourself," Nicole said, though she was already putting her car in reverse. "Chances are Bobby stayed late to practice and his car there has nothing to do with Jesse."

Elli nodded, allowing that. She didn't mention the unusual placement of the red Chevelle again. It was enough to know they were retracing Jesse's steps. Why hadn't she asked Nicole if they could give him a ride home earlier?

·⟨⇔⟩·

The miles had felt endless. Countless turns and curves in the road, countless trees. But finally they'd reached their destination, and Scott felt relieved that there was no farther to go. They hadn't yet dealt with Jesse. There was no relief there. He hated the idea of the struggle that would ensue. How would he manage to make it back to the boat later on his own? What was his alibi for missing dinner? What reason could he give for borrowing his dad's truck so suddenly and on such a rainy night? He couldn't so easily say he was running a play with the guys or out walking along the Harbor. His folks might be easier to deceive, but he could see his older sister Connie looking up from her studies to give him a long, hard look. He'd have to bribe her for silence. How would he get her off his back?

Scott's throat tightened as Bobby set his foot on the brake and cut the ignition. "Let's do this," he said. Rain fell in veils as Bobby pointed to the site; the abandoned steel cabin cruiser had been there since they were kids. It rested, old and tattered amid an ancient lumber camp. It was anyone's guess why the boat had been carted up to the woods and left behind.

Scott used to imagine any number of stories about it when he was younger. Maybe a gift to a wife who hated the water? Or perhaps tragedy struck and someone was lost to the depths of the sea? Or maybe it was merely a collectible, an auction purchase bought on a moment's impulse. He'd probably never know. But the boat had always been a welcome sight until this moment. This day would mark a permanent before/after in his mind. They were forfeiting favorite memories and landmarks for *this*.

The nearest place, that little yellow farmhouse, was at least a mile down the road. Out here there were only trees—tall and disquieting as they tossed in the wind. Assuredly the new owners, who probably didn't even live in the Harbor, would not be out on a night like this one. No need to worry about those trespassing signs, not before the new owners had made more of their presence known in these parts.

"Come on. What are you two waiting for?" Bobby asked, the first to open his car door. "Let's get on with it."

·⟷·

The remains of a lumber camp still lingered in this part of the woods. Along the forested ground, one might glimpse a tool left behind from long ago, a forgotten hammer, a stray nail. But it was the rusted blue boat that made this patch of woods distinct for the boys. Bobby had discovered it the summer they were eleven. After building a series of forts with the neighbor boys, Bobby had said he'd ventured far from his own limited backyard. He'd been seeking the perfect site—the right soil for molding, an expansive tree for a support wall, space for different rooms. He'd told Scott that he hadn't expected to walk this far or stumble across the abandoned boat. There it had lodged beneath the flimsy corrugated steel cover. The boat was decades old, with chipping paint, and moss growing on the hull. But the interior was still in mint condition, though a bit musty.

As kids, Scott and his friends ran around outdoors for hours on end. It was only if they didn't return by nightfall that their mothers became concerned about their whereabouts. But Bobby had even more freedom than the others. He was often outdoors from sunup to sundown. His mother had a drunken husband to contend with at home, which made her less worried about her son's tendencies to wander.

Scott's mother furrowed her brow whenever Bobby Minter's name entered conversation. He caught her exchanging a wary glance more than once with his father, who finally looked up from his fork once to say, "Your mother and I . . . we don't want you playing inside their house . . . outdoors is fine, but we're . . . not in agreement with how the Minters run their household."

Scott gave his father a puzzled look and repeated back to him, "How they run their household . . . ?"

His father let out an exasperated sigh, but his older sister Connie stepped in and said, "Drugs and booze, Scotty. What else do you think?"

"That'll be enough," their mother said, wiping the corners of her mouth with her dinner napkin. "But yes, that's what we're concerned about in that house. It's unfortunate . . . because it's not those boys' fault."

Scott sat back, wondering why it had taken his older sister's bold statement for him to figure it out. Perhaps he didn't want to believe that Bobby's household struggled under such weighty issues. A little anger, a little beer was one thing, but it seemed the Minter's vices ran deeper.

As they grew older, Bobby confided that he wanted his father back the way he was *before*—before his speech started slurring, before he spent so many hours sprawled on the sofa taking out his aggression on the nightly news. Before he broke his back doing construction and went on permanent disability. He'd really started drowning his frustrations in the bottle then, and hadn't improved over the years—his waking hours spent reclining on the couch, serving as armchair general. With the Vietnam War raging, he yammered on about how he would have fought at the Tet Offensive, how he would have been an asset to Westmoreland, were it not for his cursed back. Never mind the fact that he knew nothing about warfare and might have dodged the draft if he were sober.

Bobby had pretended to thrive in his newfound freedom, but his clothes were often dirty, and his cheeks looked gaunt. More often than not, Scott's mother invited him in for a meal, and Bobby shamelessly helped himself to a large heaping and sometimes seconds. Bobby hadn't said much to Ty or Scott about his boat-fort until eighth grade when they'd had the freedom to go there with him. He'd spoken of it only to a select few. They knew this landmark was more sacred than church to him. What would happen now that the property was sold, Scott wondered? It was one more unanswered question.

· ☙ ·

"We don't need to tie him up," Scott said as soon as the three of them scrambled out of the red Chevelle.

"Fine. We won't tie him up," Bobby said. "He'll be scared out his wits when he sees where he is anyway."

Ty groaned. "Can't we just get this over with? I've got a lot on my mind right now."

Bobby snapped at him. "What do you have going tonight, anyway? Marianne waiting for you in a parking lot somewhere?"

Ty grimaced, and Scott could have sworn his teammate's face paled at the suggestion.

Without waiting for an answer, Bobby launched into drill sergeant mode. "Scott, you take his left side. Ty, you take his right. I'll make sure he doesn't get free."

"Shouldn't you go open the door to the hold before we let him out?" Ty asked Bobby, glancing at the trunk warily.

Bobby laughed. "Do you know how many times I've been out here? All you do is turn the hatch. Now, let's go."

Bobby unlocked the trunk in a hurry. Jesse was anything but wilted and spent. He came out swinging a tire iron, and they all had to duck to avoid being struck by the tool Bobby had carelessly forgotten.

"You've gotta be kidding me," Scott murmured as Bobby pried the instrument out of Jesse's hands and threw open the car door to toss it inside.

"Come on, guys," Bobby said, his breath hindered from fending off the kid's unexpected aggression. "Help me out."

Ty wrapped his arms around Jesse's scrambling frame to stop him running. He discarded him on the muddy ground like a sack of potatoes, pressed a shoe down on his back so he couldn't move.

Jesse's forehead was wet with perspiration and his left eye was swollen shut. He still wore his shattered glasses, useless as they were. His hands were raw from his attempts to escape and he grasped at the dirt as he raised his chin to his captors. "Let me go," he pleaded, voice faint.

"Grab him," Bobby said, undeterred from his initial plan. "Don't say another word, kid. We're gonna do what we're gonna do."

Darts of rain branded their skin, and lashes of interwoven mud and dirt struck their clothes. Jesse wasn't a match for their physicality, but the water made their fingers slick and less secure. He flailed like a salmon in their hands.

"Got him?" Bobby asked as he neared the boat, its blue tint indecipherable from black in the rain. Their next move would be the toughest—boosting Jesse up the ladder and on to the boat.

Scott could see the sheen of water in Jesse's good eye. "Please," he said hoarsely, "don't do this to me. Don't do this . . . ."

Scott heard Ty draw in his breath and he wondered if his teammate was having second thoughts about this prank as well. But Ty took the next step and pushed the boy up the first rung. Jesse tried scrambling, his jerky movements threatening to upend them both. "You don't want to do that," he said tightly.

The wait for Bobby to open the hull seemed eternal even though he was only some ten feet in front of them. Rain poured down, unrelenting. How quickly the sky would bleed its blue, making Scott's chances of finding this exact site all the harder when he came back. Jesse twisted and turned, far scrappier than any of them expected. There was a fight in him incongruent with his looks, and they hadn't even hoisted him up the side of the boat yet. Why was it taking so long for Bobby to give them the word to bring him on up? He raised his head and saw the look of confusion and fury spread across Bobby's face. He jerked on the door repeatedly, but it wouldn't budge.

"You gotta be freaking kidding me," Bobby said, beginning to seethe in his anger. "Some moron chained the door."

Scott was on the brink of laughter from the absurdity of it all. What were they to do with Jesse Sander now? He wished someone would pinch him and wake him from their self-made nightmare, but it was real. Real enough for him to replay these events for the next few decades of his life.

6

The Hold

Elli's stomach tangled into vines as Nicole drove the meandering, dark Sherman Drive to Jesse's house. It frustrated her that she was jumping to worst-case scenarios when she so commonly maintained the upper hand of her emotions.

But she'd seen the sociopathic glare Bobby had given Jesse upon being outed on those exams, and it had chilled her. She'd heard Bobby warn Jesse—*You'll pay for this.* His reaction gave her enough pause to get her thinking—*Who is guy, and what is he capable of?* He'd dropped her older sister cold, but she'd filed that behavior under "immature boy with bad intentions." But then he'd found her in the quiet library and cornered her, laid a large hand on her shoulder and pressed down so she couldn't move. Tears had burned at the backs of her eyes, and she still hadn't told anyone of the quarterback's threats to her.

This unsettled feeling about Jesse's safety was overshadowing her, and she didn't know how to quiet her increasingly panicked mind.

Nicole set the car in park when they arrived at the Sander's driveway and switched through radio stations distractedly, seeming not to understand Elli's urgency. The green house sat lonely and isolated in the rain. There wasn't a car in sight, but she hadn't expected to see one. Jesse had mentioned to her that his father wouldn't be home until Thursday night. But there were no lights on, and she thought that he would have at least turned a lamp on in the living room if he'd made it all the way home.

She stepped on the rickety deck, almost slipping on an uneven board. She caught herself from falling forward and wasted no time in ringing the doorbell. A few seconds brought no answer, and she raised a fist to knock. Perhaps the doorbell didn't work.

She waited: nothing. She quickly moved over to peer into all the hazy windows she could find. But the curtains were mostly closed and there were no lights left on to provide clarity. She was about to run back to her sister's car when she heard movement from the back yard and remembered that Jesse had an blue heeler, Lou, that must be anxiously waiting for his owner's return.

Elli brushed loose strands of hair from her forehead and headed to the car, more determined than ever. She clicked her seat belt back into place and stated the obvious. "He's not here."

"Where should we go next?" Nicole asked. "If Bobby has any involvement in this, it's gonna be difficult to get in the middle. He's so stubborn."

"What do you know about the places Bobby goes?" Elli asked, tired of hiding the obvious—that her older sister had been closely involved with the notorious quarterback not so long ago.

Nicole's expression remained mostly unchanged, but Elli hoped her directness wouldn't cause her to lose the help she desperately needed.

Last spring Elli had feigned ignorance when Nicole made a habit of sneaking across the downstairs deck at all hours of the night. Elli recalled with disdain how oblivious her parents had been about Nicole's midnight trespasses until almost the end of her and Bobby's shenanigans. So many nights Elli was woken to the hum of an engine near their driveway and the sound of Nicole's suppressed laughter against the spring air. Their parents' bedroom was at the other side of the upstairs, but still . . . . She didn't understand how that idling car never woke them at least once. How the dark circles beneath her sister's eyes didn't give her away.

More than a few times, Elli had pressed her face against her bedroom window to watch Nicole skip out the sliding door in the basement. She'd seen her sister's bare feet dance across the grass until she reached that bold red car sounding out in the distance. She couldn't do anything to stop her sister's indiscretions, so Elli had kept her mouth shut and hadn't asked Nicole what she was doing. Nor had she said anything to her parents about it.

Why hadn't Nicole seen what that boy was all about? It was well known on the school campus that Bobby Minter lacked a moral compass. Somehow Elli had known last spring that if she started asking questions, a thread of judgment would enter her voice. She was careful not to show her irritation over the matter now. She wanted her older sister's insight on this quest to return Jesse home safe.

"Why is Bobby going after a science nerd anyway?" Nicole asked, driving slowly along Sherman Drive.

Elli could feel the frustration build in her throat. "Bobby started cheating off his chemistry tests a few weeks ago, and Jesse and I reported him."

"And let me guess," Nicole said, turning up her window wipers. "Bobby has to sit out a few critical games his senior year."

Elli nodded glumly. "He already has, but he can't let it go."

Nicole laughed and shook her head. "How entirely predictable. I heard the Seahawks lost the last few games."

"I take it you don't like him anymore," Elli said, measuring up her sister's expression, one of bemusement at the fact the boys had lost.

"You could say that," was all Nicole said, but her voice trailed off in the saddest way.

·◑·

"I thought you said it was easy to open," Ty called out, incredulity pitching his voice. His blond hair was darkened by rain, and rivulets streamed down his red and black checkered flannel. The boys were struggling to maintain hold of Jesse, who was still writhing in their arms like a fish.

"Some moron put a blasted chain over the hasp," Bobby said, dumbfounded.

Scott closed his eyes. "Let's just take the kid home. This isn't working, and he knows better than to tell on us again." He released his grip on Jesse, but only a little. "Right?"

"Please let me go," Jesse said earnestly. "It's not worth it . . . ."

"Shut up," Bobby shouted, yanking at the chain with his bare hands. Within such a short time, the new owners had claimed their place, locking him out after more than seven years of visits here.

Ty and Scott dropped to their knees to pin Jesse to the deck of the boat. It was too hard maintaining their hold on him while standing. The chain to the hold refused to give—it didn't matter how aggressively Bobby pulled on it—and he began to scan the area for an object that would forcefully open it. It took him awhile to think of something strong enough to break the hasp.

"Don't move," he said as he leaped down from the boat and returned to his car and yanked the door open. Scott tried to keep his clutch on Jesse secure, but his hands kept slipping. They were already this invested. It would be disastrous for them both if he or Ty fumbled now.

Bobby returned with the tire iron, and after several forceful strikes the chain broke free. The door of the hold opened for him with a familiar groan. Bobby pulled a flashlight out of his pocket and motioned for Scott and Ty to carry Jesse over.

Deadening his conscience, Scott took hold of Jesse's left side. Tears coursed down the boy's face and the snot trickled from his nose. He so desperately wished there was another way to teach him a lesson. "It won't be for long," he whispered—his feeble attempt to soothe the kid, give him a shred of hope that this wouldn't be forever. They weren't monsters, no matter what the kid thought. *Were they?*

It was dark inside the hold. Bobby followed behind, and as he shone his flashlight over the back wall, it revealed bright pink graffiti. Someone who had it in for Bobby had been there, according to the angry script. They deposited Jesse near the wall under the pink letters. Jesse tried to buck forward, attempting to inch closer to the entrance, but his efforts against the three were futile.

Bobby left the hold first, with Scott close behind. The interior of the boat gave him the creeps; it was so confining. Absorbed in these thoughts, Scott reached for the ladder, lost his footing, and tumbled down to his side on the hard earth. His knee struck against the ground, and he could feel his jeans tear as small rocks embedded into his skin. Blood was visible before he felt the pain. Ty was still up top.

"What's taking him so long?" Bobby asked, bent over with his hands on his knees.

Scott could hear Ty yelling at the kid to stay put as he curbed the flow of blood on his knees with his palm. Ty finally slammed the door behind him and wiped his hands on the front of his pants. And with that final, decisive slam, they left him. Like the unsuspecting Fortunato in Poe's story, Scott thought, cast into the depths. He was irritated with himself for thinking of literary allusions at a time like this. He shut his eyes, trying with all his might to dissociate from what Jesse was going through. He didn't want to imagine how it must feel being sealed in tight corridors, without a soul to hear, no matter how loud he cried out for help. What could define cruelty any better than what they'd just done? He had to break him out. He couldn't leave him like this for the amount of time Scott had planned.

7

Retracing Steps

*N*o more than ten minutes later, Elli and Nicole were back at their starting point—Peninsula High School.

"I don't see the sense in scanning the school grounds." Nicole said. "Maybe Jesse ran an errand after school?"

But Elli bolted from the car as soon as Nicole put her foot on the brake, even though she had a premonition Jesse wasn't here. On their way out of the science lab less than an hour ago, Jesse had set his textbook down and said he was having trouble focusing.

It was uncharacteristic of him. For the last few weeks they'd been inseparable, and though she hadn't thought of him like *that*, something had shifted within her the last week or so. Along with his intellectual insights, his blue-gray eyes had a wistful beauty to them, even behind his glasses.

She glanced at him. "What do you have going on tonight?"

He shrugged, and she couldn't help noticing a melancholy sweep over the slope of his brows. It dimmed the light in his eyes. "I don't have any plans . . . . My dad's out of town until tomorrow . . . not that we talk much anyway."

She didn't know why she pressed him more, but her questions continued. "Why did you move here if you really don't get along with your dad?"

Jesse frowned before looking at her again. She immediately regretted her question but couldn't think of how to take it back.

"I wanted to give him a try." Jesse started to answer, but didn't stop there. "He was over in Vietnam, you know, working as a medic. Dad's always been quiet, so it's not surprising that he won't talk about it much, what he saw there. I don't think my mom had the patience to stay with him . . . . She's remarried now and has a new baby to take care of," Jesse glanced down at the open textbook before looking back at her. "I don't really know where I should be."

"Where do you want to be?" Elli asked, peering into his serious eyes. Really, if he didn't wear those thick, brown-framed glasses he might be even nicer to look at.

Jesse shrugged. "I still don't know. Half the time I feel like I'm in my dad's way. I mean . . . he's gone a lot, but when he is home, I can tell he likes having his space so he can read the newspaper or take a nap without worrying about getting me something for dinner."

Elli risked placing a hand on his shoulder. He hadn't asked for her empathy—he'd just told her about the dynamics between him and his father—but the reality of his family life tore at her. He didn't shrink from her touch, but he didn't have anything to add to the discussion either. His hands trembled as he homed in on one last equation before admitting he didn't have the concentration to finish it now. She let go of the conversation as they moved out to the parking lot, and she drew her cranberry sweater close her frame. She noticed how heavy the clouds were overhead, but didn't want to mention something as trite, as impersonal, as the weather.

"Hey, what are you listening to these days?" she asked him instead. She'd caught Jesse humming to himself more than once when they worked together.

He dug his hands into the pockets of his jacket, looking deep in thought. Was he thinking of a response that might impress her?

"Fleetwood Mac," Jesse said suddenly, a satisfied smile playing around his lips.

Elli turned to him and smiled. "I like them too," she said easily. "Do you have their new album yet?"

"*Heroes Are Hard to Find*?" Jesse shook his head and said, "Not yet. I spend almost everything I have on art supplies."

She shrugged her shoulders and said, "I don't have it yet either, but I think I'll buy it soon. After I do some filing for my dad."

Their conversation had been cut short as Nicole had driven up and motioned for Elli to come in a hurry. Elli had frowned at her sister's sheer impatience. It had been totally unnecessary for her to lay on her horn when she was just seconds from leaving Jesse.

Now that they were back in the school parking lot, her thoughts turned to the precarious angle at which Bobby Minter's car had been parked. She narrowed her eyes and scanned the nearby huckleberry bushes. Could he possibly have been waiting for her to leave the premises so he could get back at Jesse for ratting him out on those chemistry tests? And if so, why hadn't she thought of that before?

It had been less than an hour since she and Jesse parted ways, though it seemed much longer. The rain fell forcefully, and brittle leaves scurried at her feet, their beauty faded. A world of hurt could have befallen him in the minutes they had been apart. Elli ran to the school and tugged on the closest door, which was still unlocked. She had no key to the science lab, but she tried peering through the fraction of glass in the upper right corner of the door. She knocked, even though she was almost certain Jesse hadn't returned. The lights were out, and all she could see were stacked chairs, the periodic table on the wall, the skeletal frames of small animals, eerie in the pallor of the silent room.

Elli sighed heavily and began making her way back toward the running car. As she did, she glimpsed something tossing in the wind—a stray piece of notebook paper. She bent down to pick it up. The rain had smeared the vast majority of the answers, but it was clearly Jesse's homework assignment—the one he'd told her he was too tired to finish in the lab earlier. This was no accident; she had watched Jesse fold this paper carefully into the front of his binder before they'd left the science lab. There was no reason for it to be lying here.

Elli had every conviction that Jesse was the victim of foul play, and that Bobby was the one leading the charge. She raced back to her sister's blue Cadillac and breathlessly waved the paper before Nicole, who stared at it in confusion.

"What is it?" Nicole asked, her eyebrows furrowing. "Why are you carrying that soggy piece of paper?"

"It's Jesse's," Elli managed to answer, willing her panic to subside. She couldn't help Jesse if she wasn't thinking clearly.

"Elli, I don't know what you want me to do, but getting worked up about some wet piece of paper that a science nerd left behind . . . ."

"He wouldn't have just left it behind," Elli interrupted, eyes fixated on the smudged ink. "He's not that careless. I was with him when he left the lab, and I watched him put that assignment in the front of his binder. It wouldn't have just fallen out."

"Alright then. So you think Bobby and his teammates may have jumped Jesse as soon as we left and took him on a joyride? What are you and I supposed to do? We can't even prove it. We didn't see anyone in this parking lot when we left."

"You don't like Bobby anymore, right?"

Nicole rolled her eyes and said dryly. "I don't see what that has . . . ."

"If you don't like him," Elli said desperately, "why don't you help me track him down? You were out and about with him all last spring. So where did he take you? Where might he take Jesse? If we get within a short distance of them, we don't have to intervene. We can call the police, and Bobby can get what he deserves." Elli stopped talking mid-sentence, noticing that her sister's skin was starting to pale to a shade lighter than ivory.

"I know of one place they might have taken him . . . if they have him at all . . . but we have to take the back roads to get there. I wish it wasn't raining so hard. I'd fasten my seat belt if I were you."

8

Thwarted Plans

*J*esse sat with his hands pressing into the crude floor of the boat's hold. It was only moments since they'd left him. *What now?* His head throbbed from the aftermath of Bobby's blow. His left eye was swollen shut, and his clothes were soaked through with the scent of fear. What was worse was that he'd wet himself a little. It happened the moment they pulled the door shut. There was no internal lever to open the hold, and he realized with panic that it must have broken off over time. The gravity of the situation and what this meant for him washed over him and made his blood rush to his ears.

God, help me, he prayed, hoping the Creator wouldn't care that he was more of a foxhole believer than anything. He needed some divine intervention to work on his behalf.

The cramped ride in the trunk and the dark boat had snapped him right back to his childhood terror: the time the babysitter got fed up with him for asking too many questions and locked him in a stuffy closet for half the night. He'd never forgotten the pounding of his heart, the resistant doorknob, the complete absence of light.

It felt just as harrowing now that his vision was blurred, and he was straining to see in the dark hold.

Hot tears burned his face, but he backhanded them. Why had he thought he could get away with telling on someone as powerful as Bobby Minter? Even with Elli Grayson there, insisting that it was the right thing to do, he should have known better.

Panic threatened to take over, lead him down that long dark corridor he'd felt before. He breathed deeply. This wasn't the end of the road.

Was there a possible escape route? He wouldn't wait for their condescending faces to loom over him once they finally decided to unlock the door and take him home. It still made him shudder to think of his babysitter's sardonic grin on the other side of the closet door when she'd said, "*Come out, Silly. Did you really think I wouldn't open the door? Why so scared?*"

Jesse wanted nothing done on their terms. Their time was over, and his must begin. If only he could find a way to start breaking out.

·⊷·

"That wasn't so difficult now, was it boys?" Bobby said, grinning into the rearview mirror. His smile, wide though it was, wasn't convincing.

Ty was nonplussed. "It took longer than I expected, especially since someone chained the door."

Not now, Scott thought, disgusted with Bobby's nonchalance. He slumped down into his seat, longing to be free from the red Chevelle. This was the last time he would ever put himself in this situation with Bobby at the wheel. It was stifling in the car and surprisingly humid, considering the chill rainstorm outside. He kept drinking in recycled nicotine air. How his teammates could smoke that stuff and still have full lung capacity on the playing field was beyond him.

"It didn't take me long to unlock it," Bobby retorted.

"Yeah," Ty said shortly, raking a hand through blond streaks that were standing up from the rain. "But you were just lucky. What if you hadn't had that tire iron?"

"Who cares about the what-ifs?" Scott asked, frustrated. "It happened, didn't it? The kid is in the boat just like *he* wanted."

Too late Scott heard the he instead of the communal *we*.

"What do you mean *he*?" Bobby shouted, his eyes flashing in the rearview mirror. "All three of us wanted this to happen. All three of us wanted that kid to pay."

The car picked up speed as it wound down the hill and sent the tires skidding.

Ty clutched onto the armrest to steady himself. "Will you watch what you're doing, Bobby?! And stop pretending like you weren't involved in this, Scott."

"Who's pretending?!" Scott cried out. "Didn't I do my fair share? Didn't we lock him in there without a way to escape? What more could you want?!"

Feeling sick to his stomach, Scott leaned forward, unable to contain his thoughts any longer. "You know what I think? I think all three of us should turn around and get him out of there now."

He looked out the partially fogged-up window and felt the rain was almost as heavy as his remorse. He didn't expect either Ty or Bobby to agree with him, but it was too late to care that he had, in a sense, betrayed his follow-up scheme.

"You think he doesn't deserve it?" Bobby asked, his blue eyes brewing as he locked eyes with Scott in the rearview mirror. With his vision off the road, the tires lost their traction and skidded dangerously near the edge of the slight precipice going down the hill.

Scott felt his stomach drop. He hadn't known the traction was this far gone.

"Jeez," Ty sputtered. "Will you watch what you're doing? Do you even have your lights on . . . because you really should. It's getting really dark . . . ."

"I *am* watching," Bobby insisted, whipping his head back toward the road in front of him, which Scott could no longer see. There were no streetlamps, no lines, no speed bumps. Only the dirt road and its disregard for lighting their way.

"No, you're . . . ." Ty began, but it was too late.

The headlights of an oncoming car rushed toward them. There was no time to correct course or turn the wheels in the opposite direction. Bobby was traveling too fast down the hill. It was all at once horribly inevitable, a house of cards falling fast out of everyone's hands.

Scott drew in his breath; not even a yell escaped his mouth, so stunned was he with the slow-motion scene of which he was a part. Time ceased as each three-thousand-pound bullet collided with the other, filling their ears with the unstoppable sound of crunching metal. All Scott could remember was the silent *no* that lodged in his mouth as the world went completely dark around him.

9

Christmastime

1999

All these years had passed. Scott Brighton still had to pinch himself over the fact he'd returned to the Harbor. He never thought he would after the fiasco of his senior year in high school, but he thought the time was right. His father had suffered a recent stroke and lost much mobility on his left side, so this return to the Harbor was out of necessity more than anything. It was a forced retirement, and Scott knew that he couldn't let the doors to his father's business shutter. His mother, a slight woman who couldn't possibly do all the lifting, was adamant about his father not staying long in a rehabilitation center. Scott gave notice at his insurance firm in Bend, Oregon and moved his family back to his hometown.

His plan to move "home" had set off ripples of hesitation in his wife and his kids, but it had gone as well as he could have hoped. The first month had been a flurry: enrolling his daughter Sadie at Harbor Ridge Middle School, his son Jared at Peninsula, growing accustomed to the business operations, co-signing the lease on Charlotte's home goods boutique downtown. Scott, for one, hadn't realized how much he'd missed the small fishing community of his youth. He loved taking it in—the light green of the Narrows Bridge, the boats along the marina, the plunging blue water beneath, the stunning view of Mt. Rainier when skies were clear. There were still old haunts to visit: the Gig Harbor Broiler, the Athletic Club, the bowling alley.

But after four months back, he had to admit that the move hadn't been seamless for him or his family. There were growing pains that came with settling in, becoming part of a community, even one he'd once belonged to.

Just when discouragement threatened to knock, he told himself it was normal to feel that he didn't quite have his footing. That he was treated as more of a transplant in need of consulting with someone who'd actually lived this side of the Narrows. He gave himself more than one pep talk on the way to work, telling himself he, Charlotte, Jared, and Sadie could thrive here.

But here he was now, parked out in front of Peninsula High School to pick up his son who reminded him a lot of the boy he'd once mistreated. It wasn't a reminder of the past that he welcomed. It also wasn't the first time that Scott had returned to his alma mater, but the unease at being here gave him a deep-seated pain in his gut. His thoughts were already taking a deep dive through the past, retracing the events of some twenty-five years before. The dark blue of Jesse's satchel that had fallen to the sidewalk. How badly he had needed to pee that day. How his concentration had been more on where he could relieve himself than on what they were about to do.

The details of that fateful afternoon pressed into his mind so clearly that Scott had to stop himself.

Why now?

Hadn't he found it within himself back then to keep on at Peninsula without being plagued endlessly with memories of the prank gone awry? So many times he had walked over to that same spot in the parking lot where they'd taken Jesse by surprise. Why was his mind forcing him to recollect his crime now? Was it his conscience speaking to him, or perhaps even God reminding him that the passage of time didn't blot out his sins if he hadn't sought forgiveness for them?

·⟷·

Jared knocked his fist loudly on the passenger window, simultaneously irritating and startling Scott. Scott had forgotten to unlock the door and hadn't even noticed the steady stream of players exiting the gym. Scott abandoned his plaguing thoughts and turned his Christmas tunes down a notch on the car radio. He leaned over the seat to unlock the door and watched Jared lower himself into the passenger seat. "Hi Bud. How was your day?"

Jared didn't turn to meet his father's eyes. "Don't wanna talk about it," he mumbled. Jared's expression carried marked defeat as he steadied his hands in his lap.

Scott struggled to find the right words. He didn't want to start in and immediately put his son on the defensive, but he also didn't want to pretend that he couldn't sense his son's discouragement. He'd have to be comatose not to feel it.

"Would you like to stop for a hot chocolate?"

Jared almost choked. He rustled a hand through his sticky hair and said, "Does it look like I want a hot chocolate?"

The retort riled Scott. He couldn't win. Was it his fault that back in the day he'd been a strong running back and that his son was struggling on the junior varsity team for basketball? He'd left his contracts on his desk, forgone phone calls to come and pick his son up from school, and the only interaction he received from Jared was blatant hostility.

"Why are you so upset?" Scott asked, hearing the bite in his tone before he could stop it. The winter sun slanted cruelly in his eyes. He glanced over at Jared and couldn't help but see Jesse Sander. The odd comparison aggravated him. Jesse hadn't ever tried out for a sports team, but they carried themselves the same. "It's not as if you just lost a game."

There were other responses at the tip of Scott's tongue. Words to try to force his son out of his lowly posture toward the world. *You're too sensitive. Toughen up, or the world's going to eat you for lunch.*

Unbidden, his mind turned back to Jesse. These were thoughts that had crossed his mind about his classmate back in the day, and they flooded him now with such immediacy he might have thought he was back in high school. It frustrated Scott to no end that he was thinking about how much Jesse got to him. That escapade was the pesky mosquito that managed to emerge from the fly swatter. Every time.

"Not as if I've lost a game?" Jared repeated back slowly. His brow furrowed, and his mouth tilted down as he looked at his father, reproach in his eyes. "Thanks for the show of support. You act like you never had a bad practice a day in your life." He shook his head and muttered beneath his breath, "Maybe you haven't, but those days are long over for you."

Scott's head thudded with sudden indignation, and he reached out, squeezed his son's left arm hard enough to leave red marks. "Who do you think you're talking to?" he asked tightly, watching Jared's eyes widen over this sudden show of aggression. "You think you're talking to me, kid?" He gave Jared's arm one more squeeze to show him he meant business.

"Get your hands off me," Jared yelled. "Don't freaking touch me!"

Scott was suddenly attuned to their surroundings: how they still took up a spot in the pickup line, how others might wonder why they weren't moving, how Jared's chest was starting to heave.

He forced his hands back to the wheel, where they should have stayed, and he whispered before he was even ready. "I won't ... I won't do that again."

Jared turned to his father and said, "Stop the car. I'm not riding home with you." Scott hadn't started accelerating, but the declaration still took him aback. Jared was opening the car door before he could convince him otherwise.

"What the hell are you doing?" Scott cried, his eyes flashing. *If he was going to be that defiant* .... Scott paused his thoughts and rolled down the window, attempting to stop him.

"I'll see you at home," Jared said hoarsely, his breath coming out in white plumes around him. "I'm not getting back in the car with you."

Scott was about to tell his son, "Like hell you're not," but his words died in his throat when he saw Jared's coach out of the corner of his eye, walking out to his Ford Taurus. Scott did his best to give an appreciative smile, but knew it was forced. His son had just made a show of exiting his car.

Scott glanced in the rearview mirror and saw there were other cars behind him, kind enough not to honk at the holdup. He'd had it in his mind to try persuading Jared to take a seat, but the threat of a public display warded him off. "You want to walk five miles, that's fine with me," Scott said out the window. "Why don't you pay your grandparents a visit while you're at it? Maybe they can teach you a thing or two about respect."

Before he made it out of the high school parking lot, Scott's eyes started burning. What was that all about? Why hadn't his son been able to bounce back from whatever frustration he had on the basketball court easier? And why was *he* having such a hard time separating himself from past angst? He'd been out of high school for twenty-five years, but he felt like he was reliving the worst of those days right now. Comparing his son to Jesse

Sander of all people. He caught Jared in the rearview mirror, his shaggy hair tilted to the ground, arms swinging in his oversize Seahawks sweatshirt, seriousness etched into his brow. Or was that determination?

Scott began to find his breath again. Wasn't it obvious that Jared was beating himself up for his perceived performance? It hadn't been so long ago that a similar strain of competition had pumped through his veins. Though he never worried about making the final cut, Scott knew all too well the biting disappointment that followed a missed pass or a team defeat. He hadn't experienced this much in high school, but playing for Oregon State University had sobered him up in no time. He wasn't the only contender on the team. Other guys were as fast as him. And faster.

He was no mind reader, but he could see how the offer of a hot chocolate hadn't come at the right moment. Scott caught his reflection in the rearview mirror. His dark eyes were intense and sad. He quickly looked away, not liking what he saw.

10

What Nicole Knew

1973

"*Tell* me about this place you think they might have taken Jesse," Elli said, releasing her hair from her unraveling braid.

"We don't even know if he has Jesse," Nicole said, straining to see the road in between strikes of the wipers.

"But imagine that he does . . . Where do you think he might have taken him?" Elli turned toward her, desperate for a lead.

"I don't know if this is the best idea, going there with the rain pouring down as hard as it is. It's getting hard to see. "

"We have to," Elli resolved. "Jesse should have made it home by now, and the fact that we found his homework on the pavement tells us that something's not right."

"Fine," Nicole said, though she sounded none too happy about it. "There's this abandoned boat out in the woods that Bobby's been going to since he was a kid . . . . He still goes there sometimes. I think he went there a lot to escape his dad . . . . It's off Brooks Drive on this abandoned property . . . ."

"Oh, I know where Brooks Drive is," Elli said. "There's this quaint yellow farmhouse nearby."

"That's the place," Nicole said dryly. "Last time I was out there Wendy and I took spray-paint and left some lovely artwork on the interior of Bobby's hangout . . . . Don't look at me like that, Elli. He so deserved it. I have no regrets."

She might have laughed at her older sister's antics if she wasn't so desperate to find Jesse.

Some ten minutes later, as they approached the dirt road that led to the old boat, Elli saw a yellow sign with black lettering posted to a tree. She spotted several more, their message partially hidden and directed Nicole's attention to one—PRIVATE PROPERTY.

"I don't believe it. Someone finally bought this place."

Nicole let out a sigh. "If I know Bobby at all, that wouldn't stop him for anything."

Elli said, "We can't let it stop us either. There are some things worth being prosecuted over." Not wanting to lose her sister's attention, she added. "We can feign ignorance if anyone questions us."

Nicole unclenched her jaw. "Alright, but if we get stopped by some aggressive property owner who wants to slap us with a fee, you're paying it." A half-smile edged its way onto Nicole's face. "I admit it makes me happy that Bobby's beloved boat is no longer his. From now on he could be penalized for returning to his little marijuana hut. His precious make-out hideaway. Hahaha!"

Elli kept her eyes fixed on the road ahead. Her hands were clasped tightly on her lap. It was raining so hard that it was hard to see the road before them, and yet she didn't think they could afford to turn back now.

"It wouldn't surprise me if that's where they took him. Bobby doesn't possess one kind bone in his bo . . . ." Her words were cut short. Her stomach lurched. "My God," Nicole said, her hands going bone white in their desperate grasp of the wheel.

Through the torrential downpour Elli took in a blue Mercury rolled helplessly on its side, its front wheels spinning slowly as if it wanted to right itself. Crumpled into the ditch was the same red Chevelle she'd seen in the lower school parking lot only an hour before. The metal frame was bashed in at places, and a smoky haze rose from it. Her stomach clenched.

"No," Elli said, the word barely audible. She turned to see that her sister's face had gone pale as a sheet. Mud had spewed onto the window from the hard stop. Nicole almost forgot to put her car in park before reaching for the door.

"Oh God," Nicole said, her voice bled thin. She stepped out of the car, trance-like. Elli yanked herself loose from her own seatbelt, opened the door and ran to where her sister stood. Nicole put a hand to her mouth. Elli watched as Nicole sank to her knees, and she began to grow faint herself. Desperate to evade the freefall of panic, Elli tried to detach from the lure of helplessness.

"We need to find help fast," she said, reaching down to pull her sister back up. "I'm going to see how many are injured, and then you're going to need to drive back down to that yellow house to ask for help."

Nicole nodded, still kneeling on the ground, acting oblivious to the gravel embedded in her knees. "Yes, I want to help," she said, looking like she was forcing herself to remain in the present. Elli helped lift her with a forceful grasp. Nicole looked down at her mud-caked knees, but made no effort to clear them off.

"Lord, help us," Elli murmured, as she left her sister and stepped toward the hopeless scene of crushed metal and acrid smoke.

They could only have been minutes away from the impact. The high front wheel of the Mercury still spun. Elli trudged across the mud-soaked ground, careless about the damage to her boots. Her heart caught in her throat; she tried to prepare herself for the worst.

The driver of the blue Mercury was stumbling on his way down the embankment to reach the red Chevelle—a man who appeared in his mid-thirties, clutching his forehead and looking dazed. A red stream trickled through his hands, and he struggled to stanch its flow. At the sound of Elli's footsteps, he turned to face her, desperation washing his features. They stood less than ten feet apart. She removed her cranberry sweater and handed it to him. "For your forehead," she said. "To stop the bleeding."

The man accepted her offering and raised the soft fabric to his forehead. "You just drove up?" he said, confusion knitting his brow.

"Yes, my sister and I," Elli said, breathless before moving past him. She ran over to see the totaled red car in the ditch, the shattered glass that had burst from the windshield, and the faint movement of some of the passengers inside.

"Please," he said, desperation driving his tone. "Please drive back down the hill and stop at the yellow house. Ask my wife to call an ambulance right away." He quickly turned to the red car down the embankment.

Nicole was at her shoulder, ghost pale, and she hadn't even seen the worst of it yet. It was one thing for Elli to maintain her calm, another entirely for her to coax her sister through this shock. She tried to reach for her sister's hand. "We need to drive back to the yellow house and call an ambulance . . . ."

But Nicole's gaze was fixed on the front of the red vehicle. Before Elli could stop her, she ran down the embankment and peered in the driver's side of the crumpled Chevelle. A sickness waged war in Elli's stomach as they got closer and saw that the driver wasn't there. He lay still, on his back, some way in front of the vehicle—surrounded by shattered glass, drenched in his own blood.

"Bobby!" Nicole screamed, landing on her knees once more. She sought his wrist and moments later said, "He still has a pulse, but it's faint." She then lowered her head to his chest and tilted his head back, placing her mouth over his own.

The driver of the blue Mercury sank down to his knees beside her, oblivious to anything else that might be happening around them. "Please be okay," he said to himself or anyone who would listen. Elli wasn't sure which. "You've gotta be okay."

Elli dashed back to Bobby's car and prepared to look in the windows as best she could. Unspoken prayers welled up within her. A car door eerily swung open just as she reached for it, and she steadied herself against a slide in the mud. A boy in the passenger seat, groaned and clutched his side. "My God, this hurts," he said.

She recognized him as soon as he turned to look at her. "Ty, are you okay? I'm so sorry," she whispered as he continued to wince. "We'll get you some help soon."

She tore her attention from him to peruse the rest of the vehicle. She recognized Scott in the back seat as soon as her eyes fell on a lock of his dark hair. He lay still, and she couldn't see the rise and fall of his chest.

"Oh God," she gasped. "Scott, can you hear me?"

Despite his own pain, Ty turned around and leaned over the seat and grasped his teammate's wrist. The wait for Scott's pulse felt eternal. She forgot her disappointment in him. She forgot her disgust for his recent behavior. Seeing him like this made her heart ache, and she prayed silently on the behalf of them all.

Ty turned toward her. "He's passed out, but still breathing." He tapped his teammate on the shoulder. "Come on, Scott. Wake up, man."

Elli's breath spiraled around her in a long exhalation. She'd been holding it in. Tears struck her eyes, but held, and she somehow ventured back to the original narrative. "I thought Jesse Sander might be with you."

Ty clutched at his ribs and winced. "Yeah," he said, his breathing staggered. "He was . . . ."

"Where is he now?" Elli demanded, suddenly indignant despite their real time crisis.

"The *Linnea*," Ty said, biting down on his lower lip. "Please go for help," he managed, watery blue eyes pleading with her. "Then get Jesse out without telling the police. Please. Bobby's suffered enough."

Elli frowned. "The *Linnea*? What's the *Linnea*?"

"The boat," Ty said, closing his eyes again, as if she should know that already. "The abandoned boat. You'll go get someone to help us, right?"

She nodded. "Yes. I will."

But how could she get anywhere? Nicole lay sobbing over Bobby's broken form. She was in no shape to drive back down the hill. Elli paused on the embankment above the stranger and Nicole before descending. She could hear them pleading with him to hang on.

"I need the keys," Elli said, standing over her sister, not wanting to repeat herself. "I need to go for help."

"But you don't drive."

"I know how, and I will" Elli said, unwavering. "We don't have time to spare. They need an ambulance up here now."

The driver of the blue Mercury looked at her, his face already aged a good ten years from the last few minutes. "Go down to the house—the yellow one. My wife's there—Leah. If she doesn't answer at first, keep knocking. Tell her to call an ambulance and send them up the hill until they see us."

Elli assented. She'd take care of the boys first. And then she'd find her way to Jesse.

·⟷·

Jesse wiped his nose with the back of his hand and felt an unconventional defiance take over. The time for squeezing his eyes shut and wishing it all away was behind him. Bobby Minter wouldn't have the final say. He willed himself to stop catastrophizing. What had it ever done for him but made him feel weak and defenseless?

With only one clear eye, his depth perception was lacking, making it even more difficult to see in the dark. The only light he could decipher made its way in dimly through the cracks from the wood panels placed over the outside of the windows. As he moved about cautiously, something hard and circular rolled at his feet. He reached down to the planked floor and grasped at it, his fingers already straining in the cold.

It was a flashlight, and relief flooded over him when the first click illuminated the prison he found himself in. He was far from an escape, yet this beam was an answered prayer. "Thank you, God," he murmured, again wiping the back of his nose with his sleeve. "Please show me how to get out of here."

Jesse cast his newfound light all over the walls, and dust mites rose all around him, spinning like brush across back country roads. Miscellaneous items ranged about, here and there. A faded jump rope, a baseball mitt, twenty-pound dumbbells, a tattered copy of *Playboy* magazine, discarded beer bottles rolling here and there, a Swiss army knife. A glimmer of hope passed through him; the items might be old, but they were evidence that humans came here. His light came to a stop on the back wall. It illuminated a scrawl of intermingled pink and black graffiti. "*BOBBY'S AN ARRO-GANT PRICK,*" it read.

"You don't say," Jesse murmured. So this was Bobby's hangout. No hope after all. These cast-off items represented the various stages of his life. Someone else had been here recently though, someone who was angry enough to spit nails at him. If he wasn't so bruised, he could have laughed out loud. Had truer words ever been spoken about the notorious quarterback?

But as it stood, his expectations that someone, anyone, would rescue him were futile. If he was to escape from this predicament, it was going to have to be by his own tenacity and effort. His Swiss army knife was still in his jeans pocket. Jesse's hand closed around it. He held it like a promise, but didn't know if it was enough to break out of there. The interior of the structure was dark, despite the flashlight's beam, and the handicap of one good eye limited him. He studied the boat for exits. He looked at the door his captors had shut. He looked to the windows, covered with boards on the outside. Two-by-fours spanned the window casings with bolts passing through to secure the wood from the outside. He groaned, tasting the strenuous nature of this task ahead.

It would be a considerable effort to escape. He tilted his head and analyzed the window. He might as well try kicking them out. And soon. Before dark. Was it even possible at all?

11

Winter's Plight

1999

*T*he sky had a wintry silver-blue tone and the radio landed on "Merry Christmas, Darling" by the Carpenters. Scott's mind, however, was further from the holiday spirit than it had ever been. He knew he'd have some explaining to do when he pulled into the driveway without his son in tow. He so rarely was the one to pick Jared up from school, and now he hadn't managed to pull it off at all. He thought about stopping for something warm to drink himself. It might buy him some time before having to tell Charlotte what had gone wrong.

He doubted that his son had taken his last-minute advice to stop in at his parents'. More and more lately, Scott resorted to bribery to make the visits happen, and it was starting to make him weary. Jared complained that his grandpa had changed since the stroke and that he didn't seem interested in teaching him how to do things anymore. He didn't show Jared his sailboat collection anymore. Didn't want to work on cars together out in the garage. Only wanted to watch sports reruns on TV, and the kid had too much energy for that. Could he blame Jared? It was difficult to watch his father's health decline so rapidly, to see his mother wait on him hand and foot.

He hadn't been over there himself in nearly a week. But he didn't want to swing by in the middle of a fallout with his son. His mom might be consumed with his father's care, but she could still take Scott's emotional temperature from a mile away.

Jared had at least five miles to walk. A coffee run wasn't going to save Scott from relaying to Charlotte what had happened. If he knew his wife, she'd come out of the home office to greet him right away. Still, he stopped and ordered a hazelnut latte for himself figuring it was a better route than a litter of beer.

Minutes later, their earthen colored house finally announced itself through the trees. He turned off the ignition and reached for his jacket on the back seat. As he clutched the latte in his other hand, the liquid spilled over the top and scalded his fingers. He cursed under his breath. Why had he thought that now was an appropriate time to stop for caffeine?

Sadie was already peering out the living room window, looking anxious to tell him about her school day. His daughter bounded down the front steps before he was even out of the car. Her face brightened at the sight of him and he was amazed at how closely she was beginning to resemble her mother. Her hair was a few shades darker, not Charlotte's sun-kissed blond, but her blue eyes were replicas of her mother's.

"Hi Daddy," Sadie said brightly. She wore a navy track suit, her signature attire. Sadie was the one who'd inherited his natural athleticism. She was apt to run around at recess and climb all over playground structures. Both he and Charlotte had recognized it when she was a toddler, but they were careful how they worded it around their children.

"Hi hon," Scott said, willing a smile on his face. He didn't want to be downtrodden for her. "What are you up to?"

Just then, Charlotte emerged from the house, her expression expectant as she moved down the stairs. She wore a gray wool sweater that fell slightly off her shoulders. Despite its natural warmth, she crossed her arms over her chest, bracing herself against the chill in the air.

"I thought you were picking Jared up today so I could stay home and place some orders."

Scott swallowed quickly. He looked down at the coffee on his hands, feeling awkwardly misplaced, unsuccessful in the singular task she'd given him.

"Yeah, well, I did go to pick him up, but something upset him at practice. He wouldn't talk to me and decided to walk home before I had the chance—"

Charlotte's frown deepened, and with it, small lines in her forehead were more pronounced. "He's walking the entire way?" she said slowly. "While you stopped for coffee on the way home?"

"He's fine," Scott persisted, trying not to get too defensive. "I noticed he was down. So I asked him if he wanted a hot chocolate, and that's what set him off."

Charlotte narrowed her eyes, and all kindness left her expression. "You didn't even ask him what happened, Scott? You just agreed to let him walk out there? In this weather!?"

Scott gripped his hands tighter around his drink. He hadn't tasted it yet and didn't know if he'd bother now. Charlotte had already told him he wasn't himself during this Christmas season— said he was acting world-weary, as if he was on the verge of an existential crisis. He didn't want to give her more fuel. But still he said, "No, I didn't ask him. I could already see it didn't go well by looking at him. Ask him, don't ask him. It's a no-win situation when it comes to that kid." Scott stopped cold. He'd just referenced his son as "that kid." It was a mere slip of the tongue. But it touched a nerve for Scott, and his breathing immediately went shallow. The blood rushed to his head. He didn't know why for the life of him he'd begun to draw comparisons between Jared and Jesse. Why did his mind keep reinforcing their minor commonalities: the way they doubted themselves, how they sometimes carried lowly spirits over their slumped shoulders, how they were susceptible targets to those considered more powerful?

Scott knew he'd lost Charlotte for the moment. She took a step back and said, "I'm expecting a call from a vendor. I think you should go back out there and pick him up."

He set his latte down on a step and raked a hand through his tousled hair. He needed a haircut, even though his dark curls allowed for a longer length between cuts. Sadie remained at his shoulder, her sunny disposition giving over to seriousness. He wished that she'd give him time to himself, but didn't know how to ask without having her disappointed in him too.

Charlotte paused on the top step and turned back to look at him. "You brewed a whole pot of coffee this morning and forgot to touch it. That's not like you, Scott. Are you sure you're alright? You seem really keyed up." But before letting him answer, she headed toward the front door. Sadie remained planted on a lower stair, peering up at her father. Perhaps it was helpful that she hadn't left him as well. It was harder to get lost in the tangle of negative thoughts with his daughter calling him to the present.

"So, Dad, I have a question for you," she began, perhaps hoping to gain his attention and distract him from trifling matters, like another one of Jared's upsets.

Though now wasn't the most opportune time, Scott looked at her and said, "Ask away," as brightly as he could muster.

"Since you used to go to Peninsula, did you ever hear about a boy that was shut up in an abandoned boat when you were there?" She'd tilted her head, inquiring, but there was no accusation in her eyes.

Still, the question caught him off guard, and he sought an explanation as he lowered himself to one of the porch steps. He moved the too-hot latte to another stair and accidentally knocked it over. This clearly wasn't his afternoon.

"Probably not," Sadie prattled on, filling the uncomfortable silence with her own imaginings. "I only asked because I go to school with this girl, Linny, whose grandparents live in this old yellow farmhouse on Brooks Drive. She told me her grandparents inherited the property. It used to belong to some of the first residents in Gig Harbor, but it sat empty for years. Dad, why are you looking at me like that? Is this a story that you've heard before or something?"

He realized he was probably losing his color before her eyes, but he didn't know how to stop it. What might he say to his sweet, unsuspecting daughter who still thought he painted the stars? Who saw a greatness in him that didn't exist? He racked his brain, trying to unearth any hidden agenda in his daughter knowing this information. Had someone found his daughter on purpose? Was someone trying to confront him with the sins of the past, wanting him to own up in a way he never had?

The family belonging to the yellow house had left the property untouched for some time following the collision all those years ago. They'd refurbished it a year later. Spadoni brothers had graded and graveled the rain-mudded roads, put guardrails up near the embankment where Bobby's car had flipped over, and secured a gate near the front entrance so trespassers couldn't so easily enter. The family had learned of the reason Bobby and his teammates were trespassing on their property that gloomy afternoon. Yet Scott had heard rumors over the years that the new owners had left the *Linnea* in her place beneath the corrugated metal covering.

"Daddy," Sadie said, catching Scott's attention once again. How he hated when his mind veered off course and he found himself lost in "what-had-been" thoughts. They did nothing to change what had actually happened.

He placed a trembling hand to her knee; it was still scabbed over from a recent fall off the monkey-bars. She winced, and immediately he removed his grasp.

"Sorry," he murmured. "You need to keep putting Neosporin on that."

Sadie nodded, disinterested. She turned the conversation back to what she wanted to know. "So you still haven't told me," she continued, "whether you know anything about the boy that was shut in the boat."

He'd had no intention of telling either of his kids what he'd done in the past. He'd never even told his wife. Even now, it would be so much easier to say the entire Peninsula had heard of the unfortunate incident. That though that time was a dark chapter in the school's history, the students learned so much through that past cruelty, and he hoped nothing like it would happen again.

But that would be a bold-faced lie, and Sadie was smart enough to detect inaccuracies miles away. Rather than holding back a moment longer, he looked into her kindly blue eyes.

"I know about that story," he said. I know because I played a part in it . . . . I'm not proud of it and wish I could go back and undo it. To this day, it's the greatest regret of my life."

12

Mind Over Matter

1973

*R*ain fell in sheets outside the boat while Jesse stared at his chosen exit. He took a deep breath and kicked the two-by-four blocking the window for a second time. Then he preceded to kick it again and again.

He tried shoving the broken shards from the windows as he worked, but it was impossible to move all the small fragments as they littered the ground. His legs gave out and he worked to loosen the nuts wedged in the board as much as he could with the Swiss army knife. The effort wrenched his hands, but he refused to think about his discomfort. If he went down that rabbit hole, he would lose his momentum.

But it was so impossibly hard not to listen to his thundering thoughts. When the nuts barely had any give, he used a weaker part in the board to his advantage, trying to force the two-by-four to give way. And little by little, it began to work in his favor.

"I'm out of here," Jesse repeated beneath his breath. His legs were leaden not only from kicking the boat windows, but from trying to kick out the taillights of Bobby's rig earlier.

Jesse began to pray again. He'd had little enough practice since his parents split up and the words sounded feeble. "Please help me get outta here sooner rather than later," he said, the lump in his throat painful.

God didn't always deliver on human timelines or expectations. His father, man of few words though he was, had driven this point home. So many men he'd helped on the operating table went back into the world different. Forever altered. They might appear restored, and yet they emerged with battle wounds. Some were physical, but others were psychological and spiritual. He wouldn't liken this stupid revenge ploy to a war and yet, a thought crossed his mind and settled there. Would he emerge from this the same?

The thought threatened to immobilize him, but there was no time to consider the aftermath. Jesse drew upon a strength that wasn't his own and kicked some more at the window he'd started on. And then more. And more. With the burst of hope in his chest, desperation and helplessness began to edge their way out of his body. The pain he felt was evidence he was on his way out, and that's all that mattered, escaping the prison they'd created for him.

·⇔·

Elli approached the yellow farmhouse and steeled herself for the task ahead. She had little time to steady herself and find her voice. *Scott will fully recover*, she told herself, an attempt to maintain a calm she didn't feel. He hadn't opened his eyes in her presence, but his breathing was even, and he still looked like himself, if a little worse for wear. But it was hard to stop thinking of Bobby Minter, his body twisted on the ground. Would he recover from such a harsh collision? She shook her head, unable to entertain such possibilities. She set the car in park, jumped out and ran to the front door.

Her knock was urgent. She chose her fist over the doorbell, whose inflections she couldn't control. It didn't take long for the driver's wife to surface and open the front door. Immediately, worry flickered in her large green eyes. Elli shivered, missing the warmth of her sweater, and crossed her arms over her chest.

"We need to call an ambulance right away," Elli panted. "Your husband sent me here. He was in a car accident just up the road, but he's gonna be alright." She saw the relief pool in the woman's eyes. "He's not as bad as the others, but we need help here fast."

The woman's face was filled with strain, but she motioned for Elli to come inside. Elli closed the door behind her just in time to hear a little girl's voice from around the corner.

"Mama, who's here? Is Daddy coming?" The girl, looking about eight or nine, bounded toward the front entrance, and her expression sobered upon seeing a stranger. She righted her glasses and peered up at Elli, in open curiosity.

"Hello, I'm Elli," she managed, even as her heart was hammering. If this were a regular visit, she might have attempted more conversation or paid more note to the elegant nature of the interior of the home, but all her mind sought right now was evidence of a telephone. There was one on the living room side table.

The woman spoke clearly to the dispatcher, but she looked ready to wilt right there on the floral rug. She moved the long, coiled extension through her fingers. "And how long do you think it will take them to cross the bridge?" she asked the dispatcher. "My name is Leah, and my husband, Jake Halvorson, was in the accident."

After hanging up the phone, Leah went to her daughter and crouched down to her eye level. "Eva, I need you to go to your room so I can have an adult conversation." Eva's lip jutted out and Leah stood to her feet. "Now! I don't have time to argue with you. Come on; listen to me, sweetie."

"Yes, Mama, but I want to help you bring Daddy back home right now."

Leah closed her eyes. "We will," she said, squeezing her daughter's hand. "That's what I'm going to talk with this young lady about right now. The best way you can help right now is to let us talk for a few minutes alone."

As soon as Eva left them, Elli blurted out with, "I didn't see the accident. My sister and I drove up here because we ... we suspected a few guys from school were locking a friend of mine in the old boat on your property." She took a breath. "We didn't make it to the boat since we saw the accident first. It looked like the other car was on its way back, but it ended down in the ravine and ...."

Leah set the phone cord down and walked over to Elli. "Was anyone ... badly hurt?" she'd lowered her voice, perhaps fearing the answer.

Elli nodded wordlessly, then looked into Leah's green eyes. "Bobby Minter ... it looks like he went through the windshield. He's still breathing, but it looks bad." Tears fell down Elli's cheeks, but her voice remained level. "The other two boys ... they were breathing, but one of them was still passed out when I left."

Leah started to shake, but she didn't freeze or give in to panic. "I'm going to drive up there ... will you please stay with my daughter?" She bit down on her lip. "It's best that she doesn't go."

As if sensing that her mother was going to leave, Eva clamored down the steep and narrow wooden stairs. Her little glasses were lopsided on her face, but she seemed too distressed to consider straightening them.

Dropping to her daughter's eye level and righting the frames, Leah braced her little girl by the shoulders. "I'm going to go see Daddy. I want you to say a prayer for him and whoever else was in the accident. I'll be back as soon as I can, sweetheart. Understand?"

Eva nodded, mustering courage, even as her eyes watered. Rising back to her feet, Leah looked at Elli. "You should call your parents and tell them where you are. I don't know how long I'll be. But they shouldn't have to worry about you on a night like this."

"I'll call them, but before I go home, I need to check on Jesse ... the boy I think was locked in the boat ...." She couldn't forget that he was the entire reason she'd come out here in the first place.

"I'll help you with whatever you need once I'm back," Leah said. She reached for a coat in the closet, kissed the top of her daughter's head, and rushed out the front door.

Elli forced herself to remain present with Eva. She held on to Leah's assurance that she'd help her check on Jesse once she returned.

"Your daddy was the one who told me to come here," she said, wanting to give this young girl a burst of hope. "They'll take care of him ... the doctors will."

She was careful not to add that she'd seen one boy that was possibly beyond a doctor's healing hand.

·⟨⟩·

It was a far from seamless effort to remove the screws from the board in the window, and it left Jesse's hands torn and raw. There were slivers embedded in his palms that he tried to suck out. In the process, he'd felt like banging his head against the wall more than once. He had only the Swiss army knife to get the job done. Sweat beaded the back of his neck despite the chill in the air. His intensity heightened. As he worked, he grew more and more irate. He rode on the wave of his rage as long as he could.

The more the board moved, the more he began to realize that none of those guys would have handled the situation any better. Imagine the tables turned. *If it was Bobby Minter bruised and*

bloodied and locked inside, he'd probably be too stunned to think
straight. Would he calm down enough to put his hands to work? How
would he do when the rusted screws bent and broke?

Jesse began to surprise himself, even pitying the ones who had
done this to him. What did a jock like Bobby really have going
for him at the end of the day? He was a quarterback for one more
year; he would be replaced by next season. His grades were shoddy,
the girls he mesmerized later turned on him, and it was no secret
that his father was the town drunk.

Still, Bobby's unpromising prospects didn't lessen Jesse's aggravation toward him. It didn't change the fact that Bobby and his
posse had set out to humiliate him. But as the last of the screws
fell loose from the board, his discomfort was replaced with a
determination he didn't know he possessed.

The board dropped to the ground. Relief coursed through his
body. Tears pooled at the back of his eyes, but he couldn't embrace
a victory too soon.

His gaze fell upon the sodden ground, a litter of fir needles that
looked almost black in the late afternoon light. He deliberately
slowed himself down even though he wanted to cannonball out
of the boat and hit the ground running. Wisdom demanded that
he choose slower movements, that he might avoid cutting himself
on broken glass or giving himself even more splinters from the
shattered wood.

But there was nothing more liberating than the wind at his
back when he stood once more in the open air, delivered from the
prison they'd created for him. He let out a yell of triumph. Such
a time called for it. It didn't matter that no one was there to hear
him. Never again would he let himself fall defenseless to their
aggression. If Bobby or any of his cronies so much as pressed a
finger to his back, he'd be ready. They had overpowered him this
once, but he determined it would be the only time. He might not

be a physical match for any of them, but he could out-strategize the lot of them any day of the week. They would live to regret they'd ever done this to him.

13

Finding Jesse

*M*inutes beat on and Elli grew restless waiting in the old yellow farmhouse for Leah Halvorson to return. The old grandfather clock in the living room startled her every half hour with the cheery timbre of its chime. She tried to avoid catching her reflection in the rectangular mirror on the wall, not wanting to see desperation leaping from her eyes. She struggled through another round of Candy Land, lifting Eva's piece instead of her own in one round. Eva looked questioningly at her and Elli admitted she needed a break. "Your parents are fine, sweetie. I'm just worried about my friends, is all."

Why did the telephone sit so idle? And why had she given Ty assurance that she wouldn't call the police? She felt like kicking herself for giving her word when she didn't even know if Jesse was safe. She resolved to do right by Jesse, no matter the additional consequences the boys might face.

"*Mom*," she suddenly said aloud. While she and Nicole were given to dilly-dallying after school—often stopping for a snack or to socialize—it was well past the time they should have been home.

Their mom would be especially worried about them driving in this onslaught of rain after sundown.

Elli reached for the living room phone, wrapped the plastic cord around her fingers and braced herself for a frenzy. Her mom would answer her phone in no time, but she would not be pleased Elli had taken so long to call her. She'd probably snap into "fix it" mode, although there were some things even Elli's capable mother couldn't resolve.

A flash of recollection overtook her—a clear image of Bobby laying bloodied on the ground, and she ground her teeth.

She set the cold plastic receiver against her ear and spun her fingers over the familiar numbers. Her mother answered on the first ring, intensity already present in her tone.

"Mom," she said, recognizing the panicked pitch that was taking over her own voice. "Mom, Nicole and I are fine, but there's been an accident. Not with us, but one that we came across soon after it happened, and Nicole's too shaken up to drive."

"Elli, where are you?" Mrs. Grayson interrupted. "I'm coming there now."

Address? Did she even know? She rummaged through the mail left on the table with the phone but couldn't find the number. "It's off Brooks Drive. That little yellow farmhouse that sat abandoned for so long . . . . Nic and I thought these boys were up to a revenge stunt and they were, but . . . there was an accident and we had to call an ambulance and . . . ."

"Elli, could you go look at the front door? See if there are any numbers listed? I think I know the house, but Elli? Can you hear me? . . . Phone is staticky, and you're breaking up. Elli . . . ."

"Don't drive out in this craziness, Mom. I'll get a ride home. I just wanted to let you know where—"

The call ended, and Elli stared at the receiver, dumbfounded. There was no dial tone. Perhaps a tree had crossed a wire and tripped it up. It was unbelievable and beyond frustrating that nothing was going seamlessly.

Elli placed a hand to her temples, not certain how much more pressure she could take. Her mom ought to know where this yellow farmhouse was, but it didn't look yellow in the dark. It wasn't so different from the other scattered farmhouses out on these quiet roads when the sun left the sky.

Moments later the front door opened and set Elli's heart pounding again. Mrs. Halvorson burst in the room, her heightened state evident in her quick glance across the room and her urgent reach for her daughter.

"Eva, Eva honey . . . come with Mama. Elli, you can come with me too. I have your sister out in my car, and I can drive you both home. It took a longer time than expected for the ambulance to get here." She closed her eyes. "The wait seemed endless. They were coming from Tacoma, and there was a backup on the bridge . . . . The medics . . . they asked my husband to ride over there too, to see if there's any internal damage. They wanted me to stay with . . . with your sister."

"My sister . . . ." Elli started in, not knowing what information she was searching for. Nicole wasn't the one of the forefront of her mind, but she was relieved Mrs. Halvorson had her out in the car.

"She was inconsolable until they put that young man on the stretcher. She stayed on the ground and wouldn't get up until I told her I'd bring her to you. Deputy Morgan took down her statement about what she'd seen and why she followed the boys onto private property."

"So the deputy knows about Jesse," Elli said, grateful that this responsibility wasn't only bearing weight on her shoulders. Now Jesse would be rescued from that boat and delivered home before the night was over. Maybe that was the day's only saving grace.

Had she followed her own gut instinct, she might have insisted

Jesse ride home with them today. It was so hard not to blame herself. What if she had convinced Nicole to stop at the initial sighting of the red Chevelle? Had they waited beside it, they might have caught the boys off guard, and derailed their entire stupid plan. Instead, she was left hoping that no one was dead.

Elli and Eva buckled up in the back of Mrs. Halvorson's black Ford Bronco. Nicole sat in the passenger seat, statuesque and pale. She didn't acknowledge her sister's presence at first. The November rain no longer poured down in sheets, but the trees still bent and swayed with such force that Elli thought a branch might shatter the windshield any moment.

"I tried to tell Mom where we were," Elli said after an initial pause. "Described it as the yellow farmhouse we used to pass all the time, but the phone lines are down. Hope we don't miss each other on the road."

Mrs. Halvorson groaned. "I might need to borrow your parents' phone when we get there. I don't want to miss Jake's call if he needs me. Man, I could really use a smoke right now." With one hand she searched through her purse for a cigarette and half-laughed as she came away with one. "So much for giving these up this month. Nicole, will you give me a light?"

Nicole fished for the lighter from Mrs. Halvorson's purse. She'd barely spoken since Elli had gotten in the car. Was it grief or shock rendering her silent? Or simply the lack of anything appropriate to say? They drove on in the uncomfortable quiet, Elli calling out street names and places to turn.

Nicole suddenly straightened back up in her seat and pressed against the headrest. "We shouldn't go home quite yet."

Mrs. Halvorson turned toward her quickly. "What do you mean, Nicole? I'm sure your parents are starting to worry where you are. Your mom might even be on the road, so we should all keep an eye out for her."

"I didn't . . . I didn't tell Deputy Morgan about Jesse and the boat," she said, her voice clear and confessional.

Silence filled the car as they all considered these words and their implication.

After a few moments' pause, Elli asked, "What do you mean?" There was a harsh quality to her tone, but she couldn't undo it.

"I didn't want them to get in any more trouble than they were in . . . so I didn't mention anything about carrying through on their plan," Nicole said, her voice unapologetic.

"You didn't tell the deputy that Jesse is likely locked in that boat?"

She felt like reaching her hands around the front seat and giving her sister an intense shake, but she stopped herself, knowing that Nicole was in a fragile state. And what good would it do? What good did shaking someone so insanely frustrating ever really do?

If Mrs. Halvorson was upset by the sudden change in plans, she kept her thoughts to herself. But she did pull over to the shoulder and rest her hands on the steering wheel. "To tell you the truth, I'm not entirely sure where the abandoned boat is," she said, her voice heavy. "My husband tried to point it out when he was showing me the property, but I didn't really notice. I think I was looking through a catalog at the time." She rolled her window down to exhale the smoke. "Jake said he found some items in the boat. He didn't have the heart to throw it all out, but he did put a chain on the door to discourage teenagers from coming back."

"That was Bobby's place over the years," Nicole said, sounding faraway. "He was the one with the most injuries. A chain on a door wouldn't stop him. I'm sorry, Elli, but if you think he brought Jesse there, we should probably turn around."

"So you know where it is," Mrs. Halvorson said, in a matter of fact tone.

"Yes," Nicole said. "I've been there more than a few times."

Elli's anger finally settled down a bit. The only way to move forward was to take a light approach with her sister. "We need to get out there as soon as possible," she said.

·⟨⇒⟩·

Jesse only let himself rest on the sodden dirt floor for a minute after he freed himself from the window of the cursed boat. No longer confined, he felt sweet relief course through his veins. It didn't immediately occur to him that he was only halfway home— he might have escaped the confines of a structure, but he was left in the thick of undecipherable woods to fend for himself. He studied a splinter in his palm, sucked it out despite the pain, and spit it on the ground. Then he stood to his feet and took in his unfamiliar surroundings. He was grateful the rain had settled to a drizzle and wasn't obstructing his view, but the only breadcrumbs left to lead him out of this clearing were the tire tracks Bobby and his posse had left behind.

Too late he remembered that he'd left his green vest behind in the boat, but he'd rather suffer in the cold than spend another moment revisiting Bobby's hideaway. He shivered under his long sleeve flannel shirt and his muddied jeans, ripped and smeared with blood from his banged-up knees. The left side of his face throbbed where Bobby's knuckles had struck him, but he couldn't afford to think of his injuries. He needed to find his way out of this forested maze and get home before darkness took over the sky.

He followed the muddy tracks the tires had left for him, wishing there was another route apart from this cruel reminder of how he'd gotten here. Before long he was practically running down the hill, away from the old boat, watching his feet lest he trip and start flying through the air. It wasn't time to play around. So he kept his vision on the tire tracks and their imprint down the hill. He wouldn't give in to the blistering rage at what they'd done. He turned his thoughts to his father and attempted to draw upon some of his old man's calm right here, right now. *You can do this. You can do this. Remember who you are.* He said it over and over to himself like a mantra.

The air filling his lungs was fir-scented and no longer the stale confinement of urine and beer and dust from the boat. Jesse almost smiled. *You're a Sander and this is far from over. Those boys have so much to answer for, and they'll live to regret it.* Once he had worried that turning them in for cheating them would threaten their play time, but he no longer cared if they never played a game again. That wasn't his problem. He hadn't asked for any of this.

There were no rails along the road and the descent over the edges of the pathway were stark and steep. Though trees rested at either side of the road, they weren't close enough to his footsteps to break a fall. Jesse slowed his pace.

Moments later, the scent of burnt rubber blotted out the woodsy aroma. His eyes darted around the trees, looking for the source. When his gaze drifted down and to the right, he was unprepared for the carnage there. Yellow caution tape marked out a space around two damaged vehicles. Bobby's red Chevelle—demolished and left sputtering on its side, the shattered glass littering the ground with violent abandon—and an unknown blue Mercury. Jesse clutched his stomach, thinking he might hurl.

The compulsion to vomit was too strong to overcome. Didn't matter that there was barely anything in his stomach. He bent over with his hands on his knees and expelled mostly bile and saliva.

He didn't want to look again—not at all—but what if anyone was still in the vehicles? He had to see with his own eyes that no one was forgotten there. He lowered himself down the precipice to do what his conscience told him he must. When he reached the wreckage, he saw that the yellow tape had not lied—the area was devoid of any human life save his.

Jesse suddenly heard the spinning of wheels approaching fast. His heart raced, and he cowered like an animal, but he felt relieved that he wasn't alone. A green truck pulled up next to the embankment. The driver rolled down his window and let out a puff from his cigarette. Dusky embers littered the ground. Words rushed out like a waterfall.

"Hey, you look like you need a ride. Why don't you get in—I'll take you wherever you need to go."

Jesse, wound up from the wreckage, turned and pointed toward the scene, where some of the vehicle remained visible from the driver's vantage point on the road.

"No one's here anymore . . . ." The young man shook his head, his eyes red-rimmed and his voice sounding ragged.

Jesse furrowed his brow. "I . . . I don't understand," he said, finally, pressing the heel of his hand to his almost-shut eye. "Why did you come back up if they were all taken?"

"Let's get you home," the driver said, sounding a little terse. "You look like you've been put through the wringer. What happened?"

Jesse looked at the ground, wouldn't meet the driver's eye. "I tripped and fell is all. The rain and the mud didn't help any."

The ragged-looking driver bit his lower lip and looked at him straight-on, forgoing any probing questions, perhaps for Jesse's sake more than his own. "You have a black eye, but I get you not wanting to talk. Here, let me pull a u–turn. Let's get you home."

Jesse thrust his hands into his pockets and waited on the driver, letting out the breath he'd been holding. He caught sight of an American flag bumper sticker and the new mud splashed on the body of the truck as it drove forward. Once the truck pulled around, Jesse reached for the handle of the passenger door and climbed up into the cab. He hoped he didn't smell too much of sweat and urine, but what could he do? He had to believe this guy had his best interest at heart, or he wouldn't be offering him a ride on such a windblown day, right? He wouldn't gain any leverage by remaining in a suspended state where he distrusted everything around him. Worst-case scenario, this guy meant him harm. He still had the Swiss army knife in his back pocket. Hitchhiking was reckless, but his gut told him the worst was over.

The driver moved cautiously down the hill, drew a cigarette back to his lips, and inhaled for a long while. Jesse tried to glance at him without staring. In the seconds he let his attention linger, he gathered that the driver was a few years past high school, though his energy felt ages beyond.

A couple of dog tags hung from the rearview mirror, tobacco canisters littered the floor, empty beer cans gathered at his feet. The driver made no comment about the mess, but instead let out a sigh and a spiral of smoke. "Where we headed?" he asked, turning toward Jesse.

Jesse gave him the address and thrust his face into his hands. His head throbbed, and his vision was blurred from the stress of it all. The driver adjusted his bandanna and steeled his eyes straight ahead.

"H-how bad was it, the accident?" Jesse asked, thinking of how he'd dry-heaved on the gravel. He hoped new waves of nausea wouldn't overtake him now.

The driver didn't take his eyes from the road. In the most stoic of tones he said, "Bad is a relative term for me now. They're all alive. I heard the paramedics say that much." He let out his breath, and the tobacco assaulted Jesse's senses.

"You know," the driver said, taking a quick look at Jesse, "you'll be alright. Some guys . . . they run inside at the first pelt of enemy fire. They freeze and have to be summoned back to the land of the living. But you, I can see the fighter in you. It doesn't have to be coaxed out much. It's already there. Yeah, you'll be alright."

Like you're alright? Jesse felt compelled to ask, but he didn't.

The words of the rugged driver gave him new life and yet Jesse could see the aftermath of the war in him. The violence the guy had seen hadn't made him unkind—no. But his boyish smile was probably gone, and in its place an abiding restlessness, long-stained fingers that itched for tobacco. He'd undoubtedly picked up other habits to get by too, to dilute what he'd seen or what he'd been forced to do.

There was a don't-mess-with-me strength settled into the driver's shoulders, and yet it didn't seem he'd allowed the world to chisel him into a vacant statue. The fidgeting, the suspicious twitch in his eye—these adaptations from the war hadn't undone him. Jesse wanted to hold on to this evidence of a young man who had weathered so much, but come through not entirely broken.

·❦·

In the twelve or so minutes it took to reach the road to the old boat, barely a word was exchanged. Eva, as if sensing the importance of this mission, kept quiet. As they passed the Halvorson's property, a truck pulled out of the dirt road, it's taillights glowing ahead of them. Elli's heart somersaulted. They were edging up to a dark Ford pickup. She could see the outline of a driver. He had broad shoulders, but she was much too far away to notice any other defining traits about him. The tires whirred, as it picked up speed. The only bumper sticker was of a nondescript American flag. The truck was gone down Brooks Drive before Elli could so much as skim the license plate.

"I can't believe it," Mrs. Halvorson said, her breathing shallow. "Why are people coming here? In the middle of a storm? Some help those "Private Property" signs turned out to be."

"Maybe he was just turning around," Nicole said, giving the driver of the green truck the benefit of the doubt.

"Maybe. On another night, I might take his license plate number and call it in, but this day has had enough trouble of its own." She paused, rested her foot on the brake. "Jake and I will have to invest in some better security measures." She played with the beads on a homemade bracelet at her wrist. Elli mustered a smile for her. Her stomach turned into tighter knots as they drove past the now vacant red Chevelle. The blue Mercury, which was easier to access, had not yet been towed from the property. Glass littered the ground. Up the hill they continued, well beyond the unsettling scene of the accident.

The outline of the *Linnea* came into sight as the headlights shone upon it. "There it is!" Nicole said. Mrs. Halvorson slowed the vehicle to a stop, and Elli reached for the door latch.

"Wait a minute while I look for a flashlight in the glove compartment." Mrs. Halvorson sure enough located one and handed it to her in the back seat.

Elli burst free from the back door and sprinted to the steel boat. Despite the beam that shone from her light, it loomed dark before her, eerily silent. She could feel her heart thumping in her throat. Mrs. Halvorson followed at her heels, leaping across teaming puddles, ignoring branches that were snapping beneath her black boots. Small splinters of glass littered the ground and Elli felt her heart lurch.

She began climbing the old rickety ladder up the boat without looking back. It was a struggle, balancing the flashlight in one hand and directing it to illuminate not only her path, but Mrs. Halvorson's. Once aboard, she took in the somber quiet of the cruiser. Her discerning eyes swept over the disarray left on deck, though none of the empty cans or curled magazines told tales of Jesse's presence here. She narrowed in on the boat's cabin and sucked in her breath. The door was closed, and she couldn't hear any sounds of life within.

It took several concerted attempts to open it. Though this day had already presented several distressing events to her, she wasn't prepared for the signs of struggle she found inside. The remains of the window. The splintered wood scraps that littered the floor, lingering in all their protest. She felt the draft of cold air descend upon her skin, and it sent shivers up and down her spine.

"Jesse," she whispered as her eyes traveled down to the dirty floor and she saw the bent and broken glasses he'd left behind. His green vest rested over the kitchen counter, streaked with mud and rain. She sensed his desperation, and it sent tears to the back of her eyes. "You've broken out, but where are you now?"

14

A Waking Nightmare

When Scott came to after the accident, his throat was dry and burning. He didn't know where he was or who was around, but he murmured something about needing water. A pretty young woman dressed in a white uniform left a glass for him at a nearby table. Her shoes squeaked on the linoleum floor, generating more questions about his whereabouts. He propped himself up on his elbows and studied the room. The dire situation he'd found himself in only hours ago flooded him with immediate dread. He felt the terror of it enter his bloodstream. He wished he'd kept his eyes closed.

He still hadn't regained all his mental capacity when he began to drink in the details of his surroundings: sterile walls, off-white floor, IV pulsing through his arm. He looked to his left and saw his mother sitting there, anxiously awaiting this moment. The lines around her eyes were more apparent than usual in the harsh light.

"Scott," she said, moving forward to place a hand on his arm. Blood rushed to his head, and he felt his uneven breathing starting to rev up before he could get his bearings.

He started replaying the collision in his mind. He recalled the last seconds before—begging Bobby to turn his lights on and telling him to keep his eyes on the road. Then the blunt force as they'd gone over the ravine. And then, nothing.

"You're going to be just fine," his mother said, the first tears beginning to spill down her colorless cheeks.

Scott winced and reached for his ribs, which he found were tightly bandaged. "You sure about that, Mom?" he asked.

"You were unconscious for a few hours. It took a while for the ambulance to cross the bridge," she told him. She clasped a hand over her heart. "Such a terrible feeling as a mother." She cleared her throat. "The medics told us that you broke some ribs and have some bruising, but you're otherwise okay." She reached for his hand. He couldn't remember the last time she'd done that. "You're so fortunate. A guardian angel was looking out for you."

Scott had a pervading sense that despite this relief his mother promised, all was not well. There was a thick sense of doom that clung to him. He couldn't accept for a minute that he was going to walk away from this accident intact and whole. The nightmare of what had happened washed over Scott with sudden clarity. His mind raced relentlessly at all that had spun so quickly out of control. But the image that plagued him now was not of Bobby losing command of the wheel. He could replay the collision frames later, one-by-one. Right now all he could see was the forsaken look in Jesse's eyes just before they left him in the hold of the boat. He hadn't run back to let Jesse out.

He hadn't made it back at all.

And now, Lord only knew how many hours Jesse had been locked in there without food and water, surrounded by the darkness. Such panic rushed through Scott's being that he could barely stand the physical restraints; he yanked at the wires he was attached to, and his mother tried to stop him, alarmed. He settled back on

the bed and shook his head, dumbstruck. *No. This can't be real.*
In this moment, he imagined he felt a semblance of how trapped
Jesse was. "Jesse," he said, though he hadn't intended to speak a
word of what he'd done.

His mother heard him, but confusion spread across her face.

"What time is it?!" he asked, bolting upright and wincing from
the sudden movement he'd inflicted on his ribs.

"It's a little past nine at night," she said, frowning. "You were out
for a couple hours, but you're with us now."

Past nine at night? he thought. Panic stole his voice, and his
mother took a seat in the stiff chair provided for the hospital's
visitors. "I know," she said soothingly.

But she couldn't know unless Bobby or Ty had given testimony
to their involvement in Jesse Sander's current captivity. He severely
doubted that either of them had said anything despite any level
of injury they were suffering in the rooms nearby. Wait, was Bobby
even . . .

"Bobby," Scott said, squinting against the pain. In any other
situation, he would have pushed the button and demanded medication to take the edge off. But on this occasion, he knew he
deserved to feel everything, every pang, every welt, every bruise.
Immense fear flooded him, and he felt he might pass out, but he
needed to ask these questions. He needed to know.

Scott met his mother's gaze and saw there was trouble brewing
behind her eyes. She couldn't hide her tears behind the Kleenex
she'd found on the bedside table. "Bobby is severely injured," she
said gravely. "His life isn't going to . . . be the same."

His throat felt like gravel. This was so unreal; it just couldn't
be happening. "W-what?" he stammered, raising his head from
the pillow that provided anything but comfort. It felt like a bag
of sand behind his neck.

"Bobby still hasn't . . . woken up," his mother said.

Before he could respond, Scott's father entered the room. His silver hair was tousled, his face flushed, and he was jingling loose change in his khaki pockets—a habit he couldn't seem to shake, especially now.

"Barb," he said, glancing from his wife to his newly awakened son, "Why didn't you come get me? Why didn't you tell me he was awake?!"

His father planted himself on the edge of the bed and gripped Scott by the shoulders. His face had become a canvas of emotion. Relief flooded his dark blue eyes, and he let out his breath. "My God. I wish I could take your place. Hate to see you lying here, son. Just hate it."

But Scott couldn't enjoy his reunion with his parents or taste relief that he'd been spared lasting harm. He had just been told that his teammate hadn't woken, but his foremost thoughts still lodged to Jesse Sander, alone in the abandoned boat. The *Linnea*. He couldn't still be there, could he?

Ironically, Scott had thought of his own thirst when waking up. How naturally his first inclination was about his own bodily discomfort. He still hadn't said a word to his father, whose eyes were swimming with unshed tears.

As if Scott couldn't hear what he was saying, his father turned to his mother and said, "Are you sure he's with it? Barb, why isn't he talking to us?"

"I just told him about Bobby not waking up yet," his mother answered, her gaze lowered to the floor. "I think he's just shocked." She rose from her chair and reached forward to pat his hand again, but Scott clenched it in a fist.

His mother's face flushed, and Scott willed himself speak. "I'm sorry, Mama. It's not you." Since he didn't know how else to tell them that he wanted to be left alone, he raised his eyes to the ceiling.

"Ty came through this well," his dad said, patting Scott's shoulder with a calloused hand. "He actually didn't break as many ribs as you, and he's already been released from the hospital."

Scott nodded solemnly, not knowing how to tell his father he had more concerns than his teammates. Although it was a relief to know that Ty had walked away from the collision with less injuries and that he hadn't been dealt a blow like Bobby, who was still unconscious. "Do you know who was driving the other car?" Scott asked, fastening his eyes on his father's flannel shirt more than his face. He felt enough intensity without needing to absorb any from his father too.

"It was the man who owns the property and the boat out there. He's not physically injured. But he's in a bad way emotionally." He paused, as if not wanting to burden his son with the toll this had taken on so many already. "Seems his wife called him at work to tell him there were trespassers on the property, so he was taking a drive up the hill to see what was going on when this happened."

"I need to get out of here," Scott said, sitting up and throwing the stark white covers from his body. His ribs were bandaged and did they ever ache. He was certain that beneath the bandaging his lower torso was purple and bruised. Still, he wanted up. He looked down to see he was in a hospital gown, the type that stayed open at the back, but he didn't much care about modesty right now.

"You're not ready yet," his mother said, rising to her feet and trying to reason with him. "They need to check your vitals. They might not want you to leave until the morning since you were unconscious for a few hours, hon."

"You don't understand," he said, looking to his mother tearfully. "I need to check on one of my classmates. To make sure he's alright."

His mother reached for his hand and said, "Everyone who was in Bobby's car was accounted for, hon. And you're all alive."

The intensity in Scott's eyes wouldn't let up. "No. Listen to me. Listen. This isn't over. I won't know unless you let me leave this hospital room that everything is alright ... not everyone was in that car."

15

An Unlikely Escape

Elli hardly blinked as she took in the scene Jesse left behind. It took little effort to uncover the truth. The hateful words on the back wall of the hold she only momentarily glanced over with the flashlight. The discarded, broken glasses, the green vest, and the pried-open window told her what she needed to know.

"They brought your friend here," Mrs. Halvorson said, breath staggered, "and shut him inside?"

"But he found a way to escape," Elli finished, tears of sadness and awe melded together in the corners of her eyes. "I don't think he could be too far away right now." She couldn't explain why she sensed this. It wasn't as if she could detect Jesse's scent of sweat and evergreen. But she had a premonition that he wasn't far from this place.

Elli and Mrs. Halvorson walked toward the back of the boat, attention focused on the ladder. There wasn't any further reason for them to linger. Elli motioned for Mrs. Halvorson to go down first. She directed the beam of the flashlight down and waited as patiently as she could, though she wanted nothing more than to tear through the woods right now in search of her friend. Once back on solid ground, Elli scanned around the tree trunks for any sign of Jesse. She started listening for his footsteps now that the downpour had let up. She only heard twigs and leaves crunching beneath her own boots. After a few minutes of seeing nothing out of the ordinary, Mrs. Halvorson suggested that they go back to the shelter of her vehicle and drive slowly back toward her house, taking measured glances for any sight of the boy.

But all they saw as they progressed down the hill were the shards of glass from the accident. There was no young man in sight. Elli was certain they would have seen him if he was anywhere on the dirt road. He'd be depleted after being restrained by the three guys and exhausted from escaping the boat.

"He could have taken a shortcut through the woods instead of the main road," Mrs. Halvorson said. "It would have been harder, but he might have taken that route, rather than risk the guys seeing him again."

A well of frustration springing inside her, Elli said, "I felt like he was nearby. It would take him a while to leave your property, even if he was running, which I don't think he'd have the energy to do."

Nicole spoke up. "Isn't it enough to know he escaped? If this boy is as smart as you insist, he'll make it home."

"It's not enough. I need to know that he's made it safely home. And what if he walked this way and sees the glass and Bobby's car? What will he think? She turned to Mrs. Halvorson. "Is it alright if we take the road back to Jesse's house? He might be somewhere along the way, and I think it would help to check on him."

"Of course," Mrs. Halvorson said before Nicole could insert her opinion. "I'd feel better knowing that he made it home safely too."

Mrs. Halvorson edged up to the main road. They all kept their eyes watchful for a boy who looked weathered and tattered.

"He's wearing light jeans, blue flannel, and Converse sneakers.

He had on a dark green vest, but he left that behind at the boat." Elli said.

Little Eva, growing restless in the back seat, tried to draw Elli's attention away, saying that her beaded bracelet was coming loose. "Could you hold it for a few more minutes, hon?" Elli asked, unwilling to take her eyes from the road. She perused both sides as rapidly as she could, knowing that no one else in this car was as desperate to find Jesse as she was.

As Mrs. Halvorson drove up to the Sander's house, Elli's heart began to sink. It looked no different than when she and Nicole had first been there a few hours before—curtains closed, no porch lights on, no sign of movement inside behind the heavy curtains. Where could Jesse have gone if not here? There were no grocery stores and gas stations between the Halvorson's farmhouse and the Sander's secluded residence.

It troubled her that there were no further clues to his whereabouts. How could any of them know he was safer than when he'd been tossed inside the hold of the boat? He may have broken out only to find himself in an equally dangerous situation. Perhaps he was disoriented and lost, soaking wet from the rain. He might be more intelligent than most, but anyone could get lost in dark woods.

·⟷·

Even in the solitude, long after his parents had left his bedside for the night, Scott had trouble falling asleep. As much as he'd wanted to go home, the staff at St. Joseph Hospital had insisted on keeping him for observation since he'd been unconscious for so long.

He had a splitting headache but didn't know if it was from hitting the seat in front of him during the crash or because of what he remembered upon waking. The emotional shield he'd placed over his actions—telling himself that he'd be the one to rescue Jesse—had slipped and he was exposed for the jerk that he was.

He'd been about to confess his misdeed to his parents in part, but the pretty young nurse came back in and said she needed to check his vitals. His parents dismissed his murmurings about Jesse. Everyone in the accident was accounted for; they'd met the parents of the other boys in the waiting room those first panicked minutes. They might have thought he was delirious from taking so much impact to the head.

Over four hours had passed since the accident, and he knew nothing of Jesse's condition. If someone didn't make it out to the old cruiser, Dr. Sander would eventually arrive home from his travels to discover his son was missing. From thereon out, it wouldn't take long before an investigation was underway, and that could mean disaster for him and his teammates. Someone was sure to put two and two together . . . like sharp-witted Elli Grayson.

It hurt beyond words to sit up, but Scott winced through the pain and reached for the telephone on the side table. He needed to call Ty, and quick. Ty had been released from the hospital hours ago—Ty would have to be the one to correct the error of their ways. He picked the receiver up. What was the number? He couldn't remember. Not only that, there was no Gig Harbor phonebook in the bedside drawer. He was at the mercy of the operator.

His mouth was parched, but it was hardly an excuse to lay his head back on his pillow and will this scenario away. He needed to act, and fast. Hands shaking and heart beating loudly, he sought the operator's support, praying that he would be able to beckon to her sympathy.

A minute later, as predicted—"I'm sorry, Sir. We don't give out unlisted phone numbers. You'll have to reach someone who already has the Parsons' phone number to convey your message."

"I don't have time," Scott said, closing his eyes. "With all due respect, this is an emergency. Ty Parsons and I were in the same car crash tonight, and I need to talk with him right now about the damaged vehicle. So his parents aren't left believing it was all his fault." Scott winced at the white lie, but didn't know how to ramp up the desperation without divulging they'd trapped a kid in an abandoned boat and needed to get him out.

She sighed, sounding resigned. "This is a long-distance number. You'll have to call collect."

"I know," Scott said, undeterred.

Two minutes later he was greeted by a brisk hello on the third ring. Ty's mother, no doubt.

"Hello Mrs. Parsons," he said, clearing his throat. "This is Scott Brighton. May I please speak with Ty?" His urgency was so great, he didn't think to apologize for calling on her dime.

"Oh, Scotty, we're so sorry about what happened. Our heads are still spinning, and we did get the chance to speak with your parents a bit, you know . . . . We wanted to come see you, but Ty was so eager to come home and rest." She paused while Scott tried to think of a way to get her to hand the phone over to Ty. "It might be best to reach him in the morning. He's exhausted right now."

We all are, he thought. "It can't wait," he said aloud, knowing his frustration was etched into those words. "I'm sorry, Mrs. Parsons. I know it's past 10 o'clock, but I wouldn't call unless I really needed to speak with him."

"I understand," she said. "I'll have him answer the phone in the hallway."

Scott imagined the effort it would take Ty to get out of bed to speak with him on the phone: propping himself up, taking hold of the bedpost, leaning on his crutches for support. But Ty shouldn't rest comfortably, knowing they'd left Jesse Sander out there, defenseless and alone. Ty finally reached the phone, his voice low and gravelly. "Scott?" he said, simply. Scott thought he heard a crutch clamor against the wall.

"Ty," Scott jumped in as soon as the sound faded. "What are we gonna do about Jesse?"

A twinge of relief hit Scott now that he wasn't the only one bearing this burden. But Ty didn't say anything in response for a long while, and Scott could feel himself begin to sweat through his hospital gown. Had Ty even given the locked-up boy any thought?

"We have to do something," Scott said, feeling a bead of sweat drop from the back of his neck. "I'm stuck here. The hospital won't let me go home yet, and I've broken most of my ribs."

"Yeah, well, I'm kind of stuck too," Ty retorted. "If you hadn't heard, I was sent home with a broken leg."

It was becoming evident to him that Ty didn't have a conscience anywhere close to his own when held to the fire. He resented the blanket defeat of his teammate and wished they could change places—Ty stuck in a hospital bed and Scott hobbling out in the woods to do the only humane thing there was left.

"Do you have any idea what will happen if we don't do something tonight? What happens when Jesse's dad comes home? What if he files a missing persons report? And if they find him so close to the scene of the accident, you think Deputy Morgan won't put two and two together?" Scott could scarcely catch his breath for fear that Ty would hang up on him. "Even if Elli did ride home with her sister after school, did you ever consider the possibility of her seeing Bobby's car? I could swear I saw her looking at it a few times before she left with her sister."

"I left him a Swiss army knife," Ty said, sounding reluctant to share this bit of insight. "That kid is smart enough to break out one of those boarded windows .... I scouted out the boat a few days before we took him out there and thought that would be the fastest way to make an escape."

Scott pressed a hand to his forehead. "You did what? You left him a Swiss army knife? How? When?"

"I was the last one to leave the boat," Ty said, as if Scott should have already realized this. "I tossed it on the floor near his feet before closing the door on him."

This detail altered the trajectory of everything.

But had it worked? No matter how smart Jesse was, fear could shut down the most rational of brains. And what if he'd escaped from the old boat, but found himself lost and overwhelmed in the Gig Harbor woods?

"We need to do more," Scott insisted. "It's going to be so much worse for us if we don't find someone loyal enough to Bobby to go out there for us. We don't have any other choice. We have to take care of this before something really bad happens, before the kid dies or something."

Ty sighed heavily and whispered. "My mom's out in the hallway, staring me down ... okay ... she's gone now. Didn't you hear me tell you that I gave him that knife to escape?"

"And didn't you hear me tell you that it's not enough? We need to make sure that he got out of there. We're the ones who did this to him."

"I've got this handled," Ty said, sounding weathered and worn, this time for real. No matter how callous he pretended to be, Scott could tell that Ty's apathy was dislodging.

"How?"

"Don't worry. I've got this taken care of," Ty said, resolutely.

Scott was shaking his head disbelievingly, though Ty couldn't see him. "It would help to know what you had in mind ... I mean, it's not like Bobby's around to ...."

"Don't talk about him," Ty said sharply. "I didn't expect Bobby to be ... so bad off. When I saw him go through the windshield ...."

"You saw that?!" Scott asked, immediately pained. Who knew

he'd find himself thanking God he'd been so quickly knocked unconscious? The fact that his teammate had witnessed Bobby flying through the glass was enough to soften his attitude toward the numbness Ty clung to now.

"I don't want to talk about it, but yes. I saw it all," Ty said.

Half expecting his teammate to slam the phone down, Scott took his chance at a last question. "Are you really going to be able to find someone who . . . ."

"Yes. Just leave this to me."

·⟨⟩·

Mrs. Halvorson tapped her hands on the wheel as the car idled in the Sander's driveway. "What should we do next?"

As she spoke, Elli caught a shadow near the back gate of Jesse's house. She saw the Sander's blue heeler first. His tail was wagging energetically as a dark form helped him to the water hose. Elli narrowed her eyes, trying to pinpoint who was giving the dog the drink, and then she saw with a catch in her throat.

It was Jesse.

Elli threw her door open and stumbled in the dark to reach her friend, splashing more mud on her pants than she had the entire rain-dashed afternoon. "Jesse!" she yelled, her calm restraint gone. Her glasses almost fell to the murky ground. "Jesse! We've been looking all over for you."

She thought she saw him shrink into himself as his name was called, but she couldn't be certain. He was standing sideways, and it was only reluctantly that his eyes met hers, as if he was willing himself to become invisible. His clothes were tattered and damp, his light wash jeans torn at both knees. Strands of hair clung to his forehead, and his left eye was decidedly swollen shut. *Maybe Bobby deserved what happened to him,* she thought angrily before casting the thought down. She didn't want that vengeance, that low grade darkness coming from her.

"Well, I'm here. You can go home now," he said flatly, resting a hand on his dog's head. "Thank you, Elli, but I'll be alright." Before she could respond to his dismissiveness, he winced, took his hand away from the dog and started working on a splinter in his palm.

Mrs. Halvorson, stepping outside of the car now that she realized Jesse was here, drew closer to them, though Elli wished she'd be intuitive enough to remain beyond the wheel. Couldn't she see how overwhelmed Jesse was right now, how ashamed he felt to be seen in this condition?

Instead, she walked closer and without introducing herself, said, "I'm so sorry, honey. You don't deserve any of this. Do you want us to take you to a doctor? That eye of yours looks awfully . . . ."

"No," Jesse said, cutting her off, perhaps harsher than he meant. "My dad's a doctor. He'll be home tomorrow, and he'll have plenty to say about how I look, I'm sure." His laugh was sardonic, but he swallowed it so fast Elli wondered if she'd only imagined it.

"We need to report this to the police," Mrs. Halvorson said, looking toward her running car. "You see, it happened on my property, and it's a criminal act."

Jesse shook his head adamantly. "That's the last thing I want," he said. "Please . . . on my way home, I saw Bobby's car in the ditch. No one was inside, but that's enough. He's paid more than enough." He bent his head toward his muddy shoes. "Please tell me," he said, panicked eyes raising to Elli. "Is everyone going to be alright?"

Elli gave a slow nod but left out the part about Bobby's condition. He didn't need to absorb any of that weight, especially now when his own wounds were fresh. Jesse leaned over, rested his hands on the torn knees of his jeans and let out the breath he'd been holding so long.

Mrs. Halvorson looked as if she wanted to speak some more, but she bit down on her lip. If the rest hadn't happened today—if those boys hadn't paid so severely—Elli didn't think she'd be able to honor his request.

"We can't leave you here like this, hon," Mrs. Halvorson said, eying the darkened windows of Jesse's house. "What time are your parents coming home?"

Jesse turned his focus back to his blue heeler, who was most attentive to him. "My dad's traveling, and he should be back sometime tomorrow," he said, answering because he had to. "I'll be fine," he added as Mrs. Halvorson started pacing. "I'm used to being on my own. Thanks . . . for checking on me."

With those words, Elli watched him remove the spare key from beneath a flowerpot that hadn't seen a bloom for quite some time. He hugged his arms close to his body, waiting for them to go. Elli had no idea what he'd do with the rest of his evening or how he'd shake off the heaviness of what he'd endured. For all she knew, he might slip into the house and drown out the loneliness with chemistry equations. *But he can't do that*, Elli reminded herself, thinking of the washed away paper she'd found on the pavement.

As they walked back to the vehicle, Elli made a decision. "I'm going to stay here awhile with Jesse," she said, looking determinedly at Mrs. Halvorson.

"Are you sure that's the best idea?" Mrs. Halvorson asked, her eyes pools of empathy. "I'm sure the two of you are close friends, but it seems like he wants to be left alone for a while." She lowered her voice to a whisper. "I think this humiliated him."

"Yes, I'm sure," Elli said, already running over to the passenger window to speak to Nicole.

She anticipated her sister's hesitant response. "Don't you see that he's already gone inside and closed the door behind him?"

"He's been through a lot, and I want to be here for him . . . in case he needs help getting through it," Elli said, undeterred. "I'll call Mom and have her pick me up later tonight." She didn't mention the faulty phone lines, hoping they would be back in order when she needed them.

Nicole let out a sigh of resignation. "You're a good friend," she said at last. "I hope he accepts your company. He might not want it, and if he doesn't, you can't take that personally, all right?"

16

Jesse and Elli

He'd been inside the house for less than two minutes when he heard her knock. A knock he'd recognize anywhere. Decisive, three beats, fast. Her fist fell the same no matter where they were—visiting a teacher after hours, wanting to be let into the school library, interviewing a source for the school newspaper. She was precise, and she didn't apologize for it.

Jesse only hoped she wasn't wanting him to account for the last few hours. He'd turned on a lamp in the living room and moved a pile of mail from his father's chair to the kitchen counter—that's all he had time to accomplish before going to the door to undo the double bolt.

Jesse opened the door a smidge. "You don't have to check up on me, Elli. Honest." But before he finished those words, he knew he'd let her inside.

Her hair was damp around her shoulders, having unraveled from her braid, her teeth chattered in the wind. There was a smudge of dirt on the left lens of her glasses. He saw that she'd lost the cranberry sweater she'd been wearing earlier in the day and only had an oatmeal-colored cotton long sleeve shirt now. He felt a shiver rush down his spine and remembered he'd lost his outer layer too. The puffy green vest, his unspoken nod to school spirit. *Go, Seahawks!* Wordlessly, he held the door open for her.

The wheels of Mrs. Halvorson's small four-wheel drive turned as soon as he made the gesture. They'd made no arrangements to pick her up. He supposed that's what the telephone was for. Once he allowed her inside, Jesse shut the door firmly behind her and latched it at the top. Medical books, articles, and newspaper clippings cluttered the living room, but he couldn't be bothered by the mess now. He finished clearing off a seat on the gray couch and guided her over to it. Handed her a green Afghan to rest on her lap. Tried to calm his blue heeler, Lou, who leaped at her, licking her cheek.

"How did you know to look for me?" Jesse asked, taking a seat on a blue chair opposite her. He rested his hands on the torn knees of his jeans. "That boat's out in the middle of nowhere."

"I saw Bobby's car near school grounds right after school. I didn't think anything of it until Nicole was driving us home. I just had this hunch something wasn't right," Elli said, threading her fingers through the well-loved blanket he'd given her. "I made her turn around, and we tried to find you. We even came here, to your house, but you weren't home."

Jesse furrowed his brows, still not comprehending. "But how would you have known to look on that property?"

Elli shook her head, "I suppose it's one silver lining of my sister dating Bobby last spring. She knew about his hangout. She thought he might have taken you there if he was going to pull any sort of stunt. If she hadn't, I never would have known where to look."

Jesse raked a hand through his disheveled hair. "And now we can't even put this behind us . . . not with the accident." He looked down at the green-colored carpet. "There's no way they all could have escaped that unharmed."

"I'm sorry I lied," she said, looking down at her lap. She wavered for only a moment before lifting her eyes. "Bobby isn't okay . . . . He went through the windshield, and his body looked broken," she said, weaving the ends of the blanket through her restless fingers. Her pale pink polish had chipped even more. "The other two boys have broken ribs, but nothing as serious. Not even close."

"What do you mean he looked broken?" Jesse asked, his mind reeling. He stood to his feet, blinking fast. The floorboards creaked their protest beneath the carpet. He rocked back on his heels and braced himself, arms over his chest.

He followed her crestfallen expression until he couldn't any longer. "No," was the only word he could summon. The unconcentrated horror of this truth struck him. He'd spent the earlier part of the afternoon telling his fear to flee. He even trusted God was guiding him out. What was he supposed to do with this awful revelation? "I can't believe it," he said, not only once. "I never would have wanted this . . . . It's only been a few hours since the accident. Maybe he's better than . . . ." His voice drifted off, and he remembered the sickening sensation in his stomach as he'd peered over the precipice . . . just as a green truck had stopped, and the driver had rolled down his window in an effort to distract him.

"I was there a few minutes after the accident," Elli said, tears trailing down her cheeks now that it was over. "I saw Bobby on the ground. The other boys were in the car. Ty . . . he was awake in the front seat. Scott was knocked out, but I've heard he's come to now from the lady who dropped me off. They own the property. Her husband was the driver of the other car."

Jesse shook his head, forgetting his own pain and the fact that his left eye was swollen shut. "That's horrible, that you saw the scene of the accident," he said. "How do we make this better?"

"You weren't involved in the crash. Jesse, you need to remember that kidnapping you and taking you out to the *Linnea* was completely on them. You didn't ask for it." She threw the Afghan over the back of the easy chair and went to him. She rested a hand on his shoulder, but he shrank away. He wasn't ready to be comforted or feel human touch.

"I'm sorry," he said, wary of offending her. "I . . . I . . . just don't understand why it happened. They could have learned their lesson another way." He leaped to his feet, turned the light off in the kitchen and paced down the hall, Elli close at his heels. If nothing else, he needed to take himself out of the center of this wayward plot. Elli was right—he hadn't wanted any part of it, and he was incapable of stopping an accident he'd never have wished on anyone. "I have to shower," Jesse said, feeling the intense discomfort of the clothes he had made his escape in. Clothes he was still wearing and would never put on again. "I'll be fast. Do you want to . . . listen to some music in my room?"

Her lips turned up in a smile, and he couldn't help wondering if it was strange of him to mention music at a time like now. Still, he pushed his bedroom door open and let her follow him in. It was the only place in the house with much color. He tried to see it through Elli's eyes—the bright green of the walls, the carefully selected posters of concerts he'd never been to, but still dreamed of. There were models on his shelves of buildings he'd imagined. He pulled out the chair at his desk and invited her to take a seat. Below her fingertips were unfinished sketches, colored pencils, lead sharpened and awaiting his next session.

"I don't need any music," Elli said, "It's enough for me to just sit here and look around." Her gaze swept over the structures he'd built and displayed. "These are really stunning." He could tell that she meant it, her attention transfixed on his creations. "Would you mind if I looked at your sketches?"

"I don't mind," he said, without giving himself the opportunity to second guess his unfinished efforts. Her appraisal of his work would normally have frazzled him, but he couldn't summon the necessary emotion after a night like this one.

He opened his dresser drawers and grabbed the first clothes he could find. At first, he hadn't wanted her to see him like this, but now he was relieved she'd felt led to come back. After the isolation of the boat's hold, he didn't want to be alone for long. Even though the shower helped drain away the mud and dirt, he didn't like being subject to his inner monologue. Perhaps Elli's presence here was another nod from above. Even with her beauty, she was so incredibly real and comforting.

A few minutes later, his hair still damp, Jesse returned to his room dressed in washed jeans and a flannel shirt. He planted himself at the edge of his bed. *Kiln House* lay to one side of him on the top of a few albums.

Elli got up from the chair and walked over to him, laid a gentle hand to the side of his face that was bruised. Her touch lingered on his skin, and he found kindness and understanding in her deep brown eyes.

"Tell me," she said softly, sitting down beside him on his twin mattress, "how did you break out of the hold? And how did you manage to get home so quickly?"

He bit down on his lip and said, "I found a Swiss army knife on the floor . . . . It helped me get the screws off the boards. And as for getting home so quickly, the strangest thing happened, Elli—I didn't walk very far at all. Someone drove up at just the right time and gave me a ride home. I was convinced that the knife and the driver were both sent by God, but now I can't be certain . . . not with finding out about the accident and how that went . . . ."

"They were still sent from God," Elli said, reaching and taking up his trembling hand in her own. "Tell me. Was the guy who brought you home driving a Ford truck? I only saw him in the car, so I doubt that . . . ."

Jesse gave her a wry smile. "Yes, Elli. I was resting my head in my hands on the ride home, so you wouldn't have been able to see me. But how did you know?"

"We weren't very far behind you. We came up to the dirt road as you left. I imagine you didn't turn around. I imagine you wanted to put everything from the afternoon behind you. Tell me, though. Who was that guy? How did he know to pick you up?"

"I've never seen him before. He's an army veteran, looks in his early twenties," Jesse said. "I kept asking him how he knew to find me, but he didn't tell me. Didn't want to talk very much about himself. Just wanted to make sure I was okay."

Elli's surprise showed on her face. "Did he . . . did he know about the accident? He must have seen Bobby's totaled car on the property as he drove by. I mean . . . how did he know to find you?"

Jesse shook his head, still perplexed. "That was the strangest thing. I thought it was practically a miracle that I escaped. It was even more surreal to have this guy that I've never met drive up to me and roll down his window, tell me to hurry up and get in. I thought maybe he got turned around on the property. You know how these back roads are—it's so easy to lose your way."

Elli shoved a strand of hair behind her ear. "But for him to drive that far up . . . I don't think it's a coincidence. There are other, much easier turnaround points on the property. He must have known that something was up."

"He told me that he'd heard about the accident from a local , but he didn't say anything more about it. No names—nothing,," Jesse said. "I was glad he showed up when he did. Elli, the car was so terrible to see. I thought I was practically in the clear, despite not knowing my exact way, but I would have fallen over if I had to keep going."

Elli stared at him intently and righted her glasses. "Kidnapping you was supposed to be secret I imagine, but someone obviously talked. Seems like the guy who wouldn't give you his name knew he would find you."

"Either that or he wanted to see the accident."

"But he didn't want to get out of his truck," Elli said, holding out her palm. "Look, I don't think this guy was there because he had a sudden inkling that someone was left behind. I think he was up there looking for you because someone had told him *exactly* what was going to happen to you. And anyone with half a conscience wouldn't be at peace sitting on their hands with that knowledge."

Jesse shrugged. "So one of those guys had half a conscience. Are we supposed to be grateful for that?"

Elli shook her head and tightened her grasp on his hand without worrying about his response. "No," she said, face set. "I think we can thank God that you got out of there, but those guys get no credit for decency. Anyone with half a heart wouldn't have done what they did to you."

17

Reflection

Winter of 1999

*S*cott watched the light go out of Sadie as he recounted what he still considered his gravest mistake. He didn't know what possessed him to tell her of his direct involvement, but minimizing and denying his role in it over the past decades hadn't done anything to blunt his guilt.

At first, he was afraid he'd see Sadie's eyes shimmer with tears. When Scott analyzed his daughter's response, though, he saw she was not about to cry. She didn't look at her father with reproach, but there was an undisguised sadness that etched its way onto her features. "I haven't even told your mother about this," he said, debating whether to ask her to keep this condemning insight confidential.

"Have you ever apologized to Jesse, Dad?" she asked quietly. Her innocence prompted a small smile on his face.

This same question coming from anyone other than his daughter would have provoked frustration within him. Did others realize just how meaningless an apology might be to the likes of Jesse Sander? Jesse had possessed enough willpower to extract himself from the prison they'd stuck him in. That had said something about his determination. He had been a lot scrappier than any of them had given him credit for.

Perhaps as a result, Jesse had believed in himself more, knowing that he was resourceful when the odds were stacked against him. Scott thought about his own experience—being trapped in Bobby's car and waking to find he'd lost hours he couldn't remember, the persistent fear he had developed of elevators in quiet buildings, caves, tunnels, pretty much any enclosed space. Had Jesse been able to shrug all that off?

Or—and Scott's heart panged at the possibility of this—had Jesse crumbled under the weight of their bullying? He was a successful architect to the outside world, but had that single November day punctured his armor, made him terrified of confined spaces, and left him walking with his chin down to the world?

Why, in either scenario, should Scott feel he had the right to quiet his conscience through offering a years-late apology? Both might be worse off for it . . . . Scott because he knew he had no right, Jesse because he'd be forced to revisit forgiving someone long after he'd determined to move on.

Sadie hadn't taken her concentration from her father. She was solutions-focused, and it was a trait he normally loved about her. He looked her directly in the eyes. "No, I never told him I was sorry."

Sadie hunched her shoulders forward, as if looking for a way to give her dad another chance. "But you are sorry, aren't you?"

Scott nodded, though he couldn't find words to make her understand. In the days following the accident he had walked around hollow-eyed, devoid of most emotion except when he stopped by Bobby's hospital room.

He'd expected Minter to lash out at him for having the audacity to darken his room in an uninjured state—he'd heard the Bobby might never walk again—but Bobby's eyes had filled upon seeing him and he'd said, "I'm glad that you and Ty aren't like this. That you won't be like me." Those moments had surprised and troubled him. They still haunted him.

So he'd looked for ways to offset the sludge of guilt that clung to him in the days that followed. Academics, athletics, working with his father on his Mustang. He'd barricaded himself in his room and blasted his music, letting the noise drown out his internal monologue. On the point of a remembrance or on finding a hint of laughter again, he had faltered.

Scott'd had no option to change schools for the rest of senior or senior year, so he'd bore down and studied the way he always should have. Classmates hadn't so easily been able to ask him questions about Bobby Minter's absence while his head was bent over a chapter on the Constitution. In the absence of a textbook, he'd taken notes so furiously that his pen had bled through to the next page. He'd already taken a shine to English, but now he memorized lines from the Fireside Poets without distraction. He felt a sense of nostalgia and loss as he presented "The Barefoot Boy" before his Honors English class. And when he wasn't taking scrupulous notes, he'd practiced out on the field as football gave way to baseball season. Their quarterback had opted to work from home the rest of his senior year, and it had gone without saying that he'd never play a sport again.

Sadie was still waiting for him to explain himself as he recounted the end of his regrettable high school years.

Scott drew his attention back to her and said, "I might not have had the right response, sweetheart, but I never felt that Jesse would benefit from my apology. He stopped coming to school right after the boat incident and we were in different classes when he came back. I haven't seen him until recently. The Christmas party the other night—that was the first time our paths have crossed in *years*."

A frown darkened her face, showing that she didn't find his answer justifiable. "But why shouldn't you apologize? You often talk to me about being guilty by association. Bobby might have been the one driving the car, but the plan wouldn't have gone on without you and that other boy."

The expression he had taught her acted as a ruler striking down on his own wrist. He didn't want to minimize this principle or tell her in a self-defensive manner that she couldn't understand the pride that grown men had to contend with.

"Maybe you're right," he allowed. "I don't know if Jesse has any interest in speaking with me, but I can at least pray about what I'm meant to do next. Truth is, I don't know what I'm meant to say . . . or not say. So much time has passed."

Sadie smiled up at him, so eager to stand in the cracks and offer him the grace he didn't deserve.

Scott rested a hand on his daughter's shoulder and said, "Let's go on in, Sade. It's too cold to be talking out here." He was about to add that he could make her a hot chocolate with marshmallows if she'd like, but his tongue caught on those words, reminding him how flat the offer had been for his son. He felt half tempted to get back in his car now, find Jared meandering somewhere along the five-mile walkway, and insist on driving him home. Jared might be hotheaded at times, but Scott was certain his son's aggravation had simmered down after the first fifteen to twenty minutes. He'd never been one to stay angry long.

"Do you think Jared will come straight home?" Sadie asked, as if reading his thoughts. Her voice exposed a blend of curiosity and concern.

Scott gave a short nod. "Yes. His sweatshirt will only keep him warm so long, and he doesn't have anywhere else to go. I doubt he'll stop at your grandparents' house when he's this upset with me."

Sadie wrinkled her nose, as if unconvinced that going inside was the best idea. "Do you think . . . maybe you should drive back out there and pick him up? He could still have a consequence. Be grounded, even. But maybe you should still pick him up."

Scott shook his head, though he hated to think of his son's discomfort. His parents wouldn't have softened a blow of his own creation. Besides, Jared lived only five miles from the school. It wasn't as if he'd left his son to cover marathon distance in a rainstorm. He rested a guiding hand to his daughter's back and said, "He needs time to clear his head. It won't take him much more than an hour, less if he runs partway. Come on inside."

18

The Aftermath

1973

*J*esse scooted up near the headboard of his bed, the water from the shower still clinging to his hair. He could still smell the evergreen of the woods and the mothballs from the old boat, despite rinsing off. Wordlessly, Elli moved beside him and propped up her head with one of his pillows. It wasn't typical for them to run out of words with each other. But now, after the heaviness of the day had seeped into their bones, they settled into a rare silence. Any other night, he would have been unnerved by her close proximity, by her warm breath that brushed his shoulder. He would have worried about what she thought of his cluttered house, his too eclectic room, his lanky form so close to hers . . . .

But after spending all his efforts, he had no capacity left for awkwardness and felt stripped down to his barest form, his most real self. There was still vulnerability in that, but he felt safe. Like coming home and finding the lights were on and smoke was spiraling from the chimney.

Elli leaned her head toward him and pressed her face against his shoulder. She rested a gentle hand on his arm. He'd been drawn to

Elli since he met her the second week of sophomore year, but he'd already set a guard around his heart. She shone so bright though, that sometimes flashes of her spirit still got past his shield. He knew he was in love with her that night, when she understood what he needed without the use of words.

"I won't let them overtake me again," he said, exhaling against her tangled dark hair, long ago fallen loose from its braid. He rather liked the dark curtain it had become, though he told himself not to ruin this moment by raising a hand to it. "I know I'm no fight for them physically, but I'll keep a knife on me from now on and threaten anyone who ever tries to lay a hand on me again."

"Jess . . . do you really think that's for the best?" she murmured against his shoulder. "I know you want to defend yourself, but you could get yourself suspended if someone caught wind and found it on you after all that's happened."

"It wouldn't matter as long as it stopped them." He ruffled his hands through his uncombed hair. "I don't want to be helpless again." He recalled how claustrophobic he'd felt in the trunk of the car and how it had propelled him right back to the time was a little kid, locked in that stifling closet. He had hated the power-lessness of it. It hadn't been fun to resort to a mantra of—*Bobby isn't going to let you die*—as a reminder he would somehow live.

"After what happened tonight, I don't think that any of those guys will ever lay a finger on you again."

Jesse shrugged, knowing she was probably right. "If not them, other guys on the team might. I'm what you might call an "easy target," and I don't want to be anymore."

"They're jealous of you, Jesse," Elli said, looking at him intensely. "No, really, they are. You might not have a place on their football team, but you're going to lap them all someday because you're smart. You're a gifted architect already. It comes so naturally, and most people would be tripping over themselves to do what you do."

He typically wouldn't have accepted such a compliment, but his heart was primed after being pelted with ugliness and lies. Elli's words were both the balm and warmth he needed, and he drew them close. He didn't shrink away when she rested her arm around his shoulder. He let it remain there as the minutes melted away.

He must have fallen asleep, for the next thing he knew, Elli was bolting up beside him. "I heard the front door open," she said, sounding scared.

Jesse sat up quickly and reached for the baseball bat he kept just under his bed. His heart hammered in his chest. How could he have left the front door unlocked after all he'd been through? Hadn't he latched it at the top and made sure all the curtains were closed on the off chance that someone else on the team would retaliate against him, blaming him for the accident too? Lou wasn't barking though and he let his breath go.

"My dad's home early," he said, matter of fact, rising to his feet.

Elli managed to leap over to Jesse's desk and plant herself in the wooden chair just as they heard Dr. Sander call down the hall, "Hel-lo, Jesse, I'm ho—"

Jesse's dad threw the door open and was blinking fast, adjusting his glasses as he looked from his son standing awkwardly, to the unexpected girl sitting at Jesse's desk. Jesse had never invited anyone over before, though his father had told him he was welcome to have friends at their place. Jesse imagined the last person his father expected to see was a beautiful girl like Elli keeping him company this time of night.

Jesse glanced over at Elli. Though she was a little windblown, given the events of the afternoon, her prim glasses still rested on the bridge of her nose, and she had a fierce intensity, even as she pretended to analyze his sketches for the first time. But Dr. Sander's attention didn't linger with her long, not once he got a good look at his son's face.

"What happened, Son?" he asked, dropping his surprise and exchanging it for the medic mode he was well acquainted with. He took two steps across the room to Jesse's side, inspecting the bruising and his swollen left eye. The skin was mottled purple and blue, an unseemly expression of the ordinarily pleasing colors.

"Who did this to you?" he asked, stepping back. His dad's nostrils flared and his breath became staggered. "And why? You don't antagonize anyone. You keep to yourself." His eyes watered before his question could even be answered. "I don't . . . I don't understand."

Jesse shook his head, not having the reserves to give his father a full account of the afternoon. He already felt years older than he had when he and Elli had parted in the parking lot after working on their chemistry assignment.

Elli, as if sensing his reluctance to revisit the heaviness, turned her chair in Dr. Sander's direction and said, "Hi. I'm Elli Grayson. One of Jesse's friends." She adjusted her glasses as she stood to her feet. "And you're right. Jesse doesn't antagonize anyone, and he's the last one to deserve this. His only crime was turning in a few classmates for cheating off him. And though one of the boys hit him hard, things ended a lot worse for them, so . . . ."

The narrative came to a stop. Elli turned to meet Jesse's gaze with apologies beating in her dark eyes. Jesse might not want his father to know all the particulars. She'd taken his chance to spin a story from him and realized this too late. But Jesse's expression didn't change. He hadn't thought of diluting what had happened much. His father knew he wasn't likely to pick a fight with anyone. He was the little kid who'd carried spiders to safety so they could scramble away in the shrubbery. He made no attempt to enter the story, so Elli resumed.

Dr. Sander crossed his arms over his chest, listening intently as she told him the events of the afternoon—how she'd had suspicions that something was off upon seeing Bobby's car, how her sister had a premonition that the cabin cruiser was where they'd taken him, how they'd stumbled upon the terrifying collision, and how they'd made it back to the boat and discovered Jesse had broken out on his own.

His father's face had gone immovable as stone by the end of the telling. Jesse could see that he struggled to digest the part about the boat, lowering his eyes to the ground, as any parent would.

Having endured the chaos of war, his father had learned to keep his composure amidst shock and sadness. But that didn't mean he wasn't visibly moved to learn that his own flesh and blood had been trapped in a hold of a boat. Jesse could tell his dad wanted to draw him near, but he couldn't afford to be hugged when that so rarely, if ever happened, in normal life. Jesse was trying to maintain his composure with everything he had left in him.

"I'm proud of you, Son," his father said, eyes watering. "That took a lot to force your way out and make your escape. Shows what you're made of."

"I'd like to think Someone was looking out for me," Jesse said, his smile small but true. "Because of . . . the knife and the flashlight. Because Elli figured out where I was. And because a truck pulled up alongside me on the way home, so I didn't have to walk the entire way. It wasn't all my doing."

His father said nothing, perhaps struggling to accept his son's immediate tilt toward optimism when this was the sort of situation that ignited a parent's rage.

"I don't want to go back to Peninsula," Jesse said in a determined whisper. "This is not something I want to hear about in the halls or be questioned about from teachers or students. It'd be awful."

Elli's back straightened up right away, and he felt a twinge of guilt for not telling her he felt this way. He said he'd never let himself be overtaken by those guys again. He hadn't said he meant to avoid trouble by attending a different school entirely.

His dad's nostrils flared. "Those dimwits can find another school. Not you! Don't you talk about going somewhere else. They don't get to commit a crime and go back to their charmed little lives. I'm going in there first thing tomorrow morning and making sure they answer for this as soon as they're back there."

Jesse hung his head, too fatigued to say anything to him about why that approach would cause further resentment from those three boys. There were no easy answers.

"I wasn't shut up on school grounds, so I don't know what the school could really do," Jesse said, sounding weary.

"Except that it did start on school grounds," Elli interrupted, turning to Jesse. "They were waiting in the bushes nearby for you, and that's when they captured you. It doesn't matter that they finished the job somewhere else."

His dad directed his attention to Elli. "Exactly. And those self-important hotshots are going to pay for it in more than one way."

"Understood," Elli said, though her tone was quiet.

Jesse said nothing.

Mr. Sander spoke up again. "Thank you for being here for Jesse. I've heard a thing or two about my son's brilliant science partner."

He attempted a smile, and Jesse felt himself redden even now, when he thought he had no emotions left.

"You're more than welcome to crash on the couch, but if you need a ride home . . . ."

"I was going to have my mom pick me up, but if you're able to take me, that's even better," she told his dad. "It's only a five-minute drive."

"I'll give you a couple minutes to get ready then," he told her, his eyes kind despite the gruff quality of his voice. He exited Jesse's room and left the door almost closed behind him.

Jesse mustered a smile, but he felt the idea of her absence move through him like an abrasive wind. He lost so much if he took a break from school, but he didn't see a way around it—especially because of the accident. He needed time to collect himself before walking back into the fray.

As if she hadn't surprised him enough for one day, she took two steps across the carpet to enfold herself in his arms. "If you go I'll miss you as my science partner, Jesse, but I understand . . . . Remember, I'm only a five-minute drive away. Or a long walk. Until we can drive."

·⟨↔⟩·

Visiting Bobby in the hospital was one of the hardest things Scott had ever done. He lacked the acting chops to maintain a stoic expression. What was worse, he didn't know how Bobby would respond to him. Would he be seething about his injuries, that Scott and Ty would recover and live ordinary lives while he would be physically marred by this mistake the rest of his life?

He was thrown off-kilter by the quarterback's reception as soon as he set foot in the hospital room.

"You and Ty will be alright," Bobby had started out, his voice choked by uncharacteristic emotion. "I should have been watching the road, should have turned my lights on like you asked. I'm so sorry. But my God, am I relieved that you're both walking and that you're not . . . ." He feigned a laugh. "That you didn't suffer a worse fate. And Ty . . . he called me and told me he was making sure that Jesse got out of the hold. That just leaves me . . . dealing with this."

The green balloons and yellow flowers did little to stave off the reality of the beeping machines and tubes monitoring Bobby all the while.

"It's so soon," Scott said. "Doctors can do so much more these days, and you never know how much progress you might make."

Bobby's Adam's apple moved in his throat, making Scott think his words might have been a step too far. Perhaps best-case scenarios were too much for him right now.

"You never know," Bobby said, but without much hope. A few tears escaped his eyes and traced their way down his cheek. A substantial lump grew in Scott's own throat. He fumbled, not knowing how to respond. He couldn't tell Bobby he shouldn't cry when his teammate had every reason in the world to.

But Bobby spoke first. He smiled through his tears. "I'm not crying for me right now. I'm just crying that any of this happened. It wasn't worth it, it just wasn't."

·⟨⟩·

Scott didn't return to school until the new term, and the return was as boulder-heavy as he'd imagined. The local news had come to the school to interview faculty and students about Bobby's accident. Scott couldn't imagine much worse than this type of limelight.

"He was on fire," Coach Johnston had said, looking a little misty around the eyes. "Bobby was an exceptional player, so quick-thinking and fast on his feet. It's devastating to hear about his accident. My heartfelt prayers are with him and his family."

Bobby's accident spurred an outpouring of support even from students who had never exchanged a word with the quarterback before. Many showed up at the Minter's chain link fence and showered the front lawn with well-wishes. Letters, flowers, and candles mounted up on the property. Mr. Minter's towering outline was sometimes seen against the lamplight of the front window. Sometimes he'd lift a hand in gratitude. Word had it that Bobby's old man was so overcome with grief that he'd stopped drinking for several days.

"We should bring the Minters something too," Scott's mother said one night over a dinner of lasagna and Caesar salad. "A meal like this, perhaps." It was typically Scott's favorite, but his appetite had declined lately. It was hard to enjoy food when the world had gone gray and dull around him. He felt like a spectator, looking in on the window of his own life. He wasn't feeling at home in his own being. Was this what it meant to grow up?

"What good would it do to bring them anything?" Scott asked his mother, sounding harsher than he'd intended.

He could see his mother trying not to look hurt. Her coal-dark eyes were earnest as she set her elbows on the table and leaned toward Scott. "If not a meal, then what would you suggest?"

"This dinner's perfect," his little brother Charlie said, beginning to smile. "I could even help you make some fudge brownies."

"None of these gifts are going to make Bobby better," Scott said, rising to his feet so fast that his dinner plate spun. "I bet his freezer is stocked with casseroles already. Enough food to forever remind him people are feeling sorry for him."

Scott's older sister Connie paused her fork mid-bite. "Sometimes it's the thought that counts," she said, searching out her brother's eyes, as if hoping he'd come to the same understanding. "Everyone knows you can't will this situation away."

"Your sister's right," Scott's father said, twisting his wedding ring in a circle around his finger. "We're all sorry about what happened. Whatever we can do to support Bobby and his family, we should do."

Scott softened, realizing that he didn't need to take out his anger on his whole family. They'd done nothing wrong except champion his recovery and treat him like a returned hero of sorts. He closed his eyes and nodded, hearing nothing but the quiet, consistent ticking of the grandfather clock and the Everly Brothers playing softly in the background. He willed the normal, predictable sounds of his childhood home to soothe him back to equilibrium.

How could he explain to his family that it wasn't so much Bobby's accident that was tearing him apart—heavy as that was—as his wrongdoing against an innocent classmate? The reality of what he had done sank its teeth into him, reminding him that he should have acted according to his conscience in the first place. Now he was paying.

Two questions stared him in the face—could he ever escape the clutches of his sin? And if so, what would be required of him?

19

The Light Shines Brighter

1974

*J*esse startled awake, feeling phantom fists pummel him. The slam of the trunk and the darkness of the hold engulfed him. He bolted up in bed, having sweat through his sheets, and cursed under his breath. "Not again." Still, the remnants of that time were fading as the months passed.

Apart from these occasional night terrors, he didn't dwell on the bad memories. He directed his mind to the glimmers of hope he'd had: the flashlight near his sneakers, the pocketknife on the floor, the recollection of his father's soldier stories, telling him that he too could rise out of the mire and emerge stronger.

He'd decided to dwell on the aftermath—the fact that he hadn't been overtaken, the fact that he wasn't limited to what a small group of guys had to say about him. He did his coursework at home for a few months, and then returned to Peninsula High School with the new term.

Within a short time, he settled into his speaking voice, learned how to dress in clothes that fit him, and filled out a little more. While still scrappy, he no longer felt like a scrawny science nerd.

When Jesse caught his reflection in the mirror now, he didn't scoff or avert his eyes in disgust. He met his own blue-gray gaze and saw an undercurrent there, the glint of someone who possessed his own strength. There was no reason to shrink away when he had done his best. His identity was not limited to what a few vengeful boys thought about him.

Still, life wasn't without its struggles. Jesse longed to recapture the ease of his afternoons with Elli in the science lab, but they were assigned to different classes the following semester. True to her word, she did bike over to visit him and Lou on occasion. But then she got busy with academic demands and a role in the school play during the winter months.

January and February loomed long and cold without her presence, and he hadn't known how to recapture the rapport they'd shared as lab partners. It had been so much simpler when they had the same deadlines and problems to solve. There was still a kindness and a mutual respect between them, but the simple reason for coming together was gone, and in its place was a greater recognition that continued time together might mean they were more than friends.

While he missed Elli's constant companionship, Jesse saw a promising change in his father since that November night. Dr. Sander became a lot more guarded with his time. He didn't take as many shifts out of town, and he started taking real interest his son. At first it felt awkward to have him home so much.

But Jesse grew accustomed to his father's distractibility: how he read select portions of *The Peninsula Gateway*, *The Seattle Post Intelligencer*, and *The New York Times* and left the issues scattered on the couches and counters. He was used to his dad clicking through TV channels and unwinding with a bowl of chocolate chip mint ice cream on his lap. He wasn't so used to him spending more time on dinners, making conversation with Jesse about *his* interests, or asking him to join him on the occasional weekend fishing trip.

Jesse wished his dad's bids for attention were easier for him to accept. Truth was, he'd gotten used to their stagnant roles, and their new relationship was taking him some extra time to get used to. But he decided to go along with it, knowing that in time his exchanges with his dad would be more natural.

"I want things to be different," his dad had said, throwing open the dark blue curtains to let the light in through the windows. "I've made us live too small and routine, and it doesn't help either of us. Life isn't easy, but that doesn't mean we can't chase a little joy sometimes."

One early spring day after Jesse had finished his homework and was about to help himself to a peanut butter and jelly sandwich in the kitchen, he found a letter waiting for him on the counter. Unless it was an architectural magazine, it was rare for him to receive anything personally addressed to him. He didn't recognize the penmanship.

With curious fingers, Jesse tore the top of the envelope open and let the lined paper fall open in his hands. He stared down at the page, taking in the unfamiliar handwriting. He forced himself to read the words without instantly scanning for the signature.

Dear Jesse, he read.

I've been wondering how you're doing ever since that night I gave you a ride home. You wondered who I was and how I knew you were out there on the yellow house property. I didn't think it would help to tell you after so much heaviness in one day. But I thought about it some more and think you have the right to know.

My name is Bradley Parsons, and I'm Ty's big brother. I knew about their dumb plan because I overheard my brother talking about

*it to Scott and Bobby shortly before it happened. I told Ty it was a
stupid idea, but I wish I'd done more to stop it and am sorry I didn't.*

*My little brother called from the hospital, but you were already
on your way home. I'm glad you let me drive you the rest of the way.
I don't know why seeing you all bloodied and beaten hit me for so
long—I was in Vietnam, in case you hadn't heard—but I really hope
you've found a path forward. My brother and those kids were losers
for doing that to you.*

*Drop me a message when you get the chance. I hope you're doing
a whole lot better. Also hope your eye is good as new.*

Take care,

Bradley Parsons

It was a lot to absorb. He hadn't known Bradley was Ty's older
brother, and yet, did it change what Bradley had done for him?
Bradley and Ty—they were not one and the same. It wouldn't be
fair to treat them as if they were.

This letter from Bradley was the medicine he needed for his
bruised soul, and yet he hadn't realized it. He had Elli Grayson on
his side. His distant father was starting to come around and look
for activities the two of them could do together. They had even
been attending Chapel Hill Presbyterian Church. While these were
undeniable gifts, it was so much to adjust to and accept. And now
the guy who'd driven him home was writing him a personal letter.

He tossed the letter back in its envelope and brought it to his
room, shoved it in the back of his desk, not certain he wanted
to respond. The house was still, save for the creaking branches
outside his window. In moments like these, he could almost hear
his enemies' taunts again. And he was tempted to chide himself
for being so reactive to the tests they'd cheated on. If only he'd

let it go and told Ellie he didn't want to pursue it. Those guys wouldn't have been able to fool college entrance exams anyway.

But he forced himself to shake those oppressive thoughts—that he was any way responsible for the way in which they'd treated him. Just the same, all his decisions had begun to take on a new significance. Answering the letter from Bradley Parsons would be the decent thing to do.

The sight of Elli Grayson approaching his front door threw his concentration—her black boots quick and determined, her hands deep in the pockets of her cream-colored jacket, the end of her braid escaping the caramel pompom hat that rested on the top of her head. Her cheeks were rosy, and her eyes lit up as Lou approached her.

"Lou," she laughed, tamping the dog's head down as Jesse opened the front door to usher her inside. Lou knew better but liked to leap up and leave his pawprints on the people he favored most.

Elli gave Jesse an elusive smile as soon as she was indoors and said, "I haven't heard from you in a while. I thought we could catch up. Talk about our latest records . . . or you know, chemistry."

"Thanks for stopping by," he said, elated she'd thought of him. He was losing her to more play rehearsals and performances lately. He didn't want to risk changing the natural ease between the two of them and so didn't pursue her company the way he wanted to. Let other things fall away if they must. His relationship with Elli was not something he was willing to compromise with a few compliments that might unsettle the ground beneath them. No, what he had with her already was beautiful; it was intact and true.

He led her down the hallway to his room, and turned over his shoulder to smile at her. "Let's talk records, Elli. I'm not so sure how exciting chem—"

The words were scarcely out of his lips before she'd bridged the gap between them and encircled herself in his arms. She was so close, he could feel her heart beat and smell the apple scent that clung to her hair. Instead of taking the risk of stumbling over words, he bent down and sought her mouth with his own. She tasted sweet—like she'd swallowed something laced with sugar—and he leaned in for more, feeling his pulse quicken.

He hadn't kissed a girl before, but meeting Elli's lips with his own felt so destined, so meant to be, that he didn't want to pull himself away from her wonder. Not so long ago she'd been Scott Brighton's girl. It was almost unfathomable to think that she was now turning her attention to him. But here she was, so present and so real. Lou gave a sudden bark and dashed toward the door. Jesse and Elli pulled apart. His dad must be home. Without the interruption, Jesse wouldn't have known how to break away from her embrace at all.

"My dad probably needs help unloading the groceries," he said. "I'll be back in a sec." He turned from her and worked his way down the hall. "Hey Dad," he said, not pausing to think of the gloss he was now wearing on his lips, "let me give you a hand."

His dad raised an eyebrow and said, "You've got company, I see." He smirked. "I've got it; I'll put it all away. It's not that much more. Tell Elli I said hi."

Jesse tried to keep the heat from flooding his face, but it was no use. He hadn't been successful in keeping anything from his old man before; why would he think he could start doing so now?

20

Not Too Late

While there was much to be grateful for, Jesse's struggles were far from over. The moment between classes became the worst stretch the of day. In the absence of lectures, notes, quizzes, and tests, he had the flurry of the hallway to contend with. Students he didn't even know felt at ease approaching him at his locker or at the drinking fountain, wanting to impart their own thoughts on the situation last fall. It was six months after the accident, and he was still dealing with the aftermath.

A pretty brunette, Caroline, tapped his shoulder and once she had his attention, turned her doe-eyes in his direction. "I'm so sorry that awful accident happened. I've been thinking about Bobby lately. How is he? Poor guy. Is it true he'll never walk again?" She leaned closer, and Jesse didn't try to hide his irritation. He took a step back and crossed his arms over his chest.

"If you're so interested in Bobby, why don't you drop by and talk to him? Make him some chicken noodle soup while you're at it?"

Even as he ridiculed her question, he hated how mean he sounded, but she'd unknowingly triggered his anger, and he couldn't contain it. Truth was, he didn't know what to tell her. Didn't she realize he was the one that had been wronged in the situation and that Bobby Minter had reaped the natural consequences, as dire as they were?

Caroline blinked quickly at him and shook her head. "I just asked you a simple question. You don't have to be such a jerk, Jesse."

He thought of pretending he couldn't hear her, but decided at the last minute to answer her. "I'm sorry. I'm the wrong person to ask. Bobby and I . . . maybe you didn't know . . . but we were never friends. I wasn't in the car with him when it crashed. I was the one . . . the guys locked up."

"But you won't hold that against him forever?" Caroline said, uncomprehending. "You found your way out, and you get to live the rest of your life normally and he . . . ."

He turned his back to her before she tried to reason with him anymore and left her staring after him, bewilderment undoubtedly knit across her brow.

The exchange bothered him for the rest of the afternoon and filled him with pent-up tension. Why did she assume that because he'd made it out with scratches instead of bone-deep injuries, he'd kindle a friendship with the ring reader of the guys who bullied him? He scratched his head, puzzled over the exchange well past the time he got home from school.

He didn't know why he thought of it now, but Jesse found himself reaching for the letter he'd shoved to the back drawer of his desk over a month ago. He didn't like to admit it aloud, but he still berated himself for not handling the cheating incident differently.

He removed the folded paper from the envelope in his hand. He felt he at least owed Bradley a response to the heartfelt words he'd written. Of course, he didn't pick up the phone. It wasn't in Jesse's nature to call strangers, even ones who had given him a ride home in his time of need. Instead, he wrote:

*I have to remind myself it wasn't my fault. I still feel
partially responsible. I could have spared them all the
consequences if I'd dealt with the cheating incident on
my own. I know these thoughts aren't helpful. It wasn't
my fault. But the thoughts still come. Thank you for
taking the time to write to me and tell me who you are.
It helps, knowing that someone wasn't ok with what
they were doing. Your words meant even more when I
read them the second time.*

He sealed and mailed the letter and his breath became noticeably
lighter.

· ⟷ ·

Jesse busied himself with other things—namely, drafting a potential design for a new restaurant along the Harbor shore that his
father's friend had mentioned he might try his hand at. They
would hire a professional architectural firm to design the official
plans, but there was a chance one of the team might look at his
renderings and see something promising in his vision. His father's
friend had said that if he wasn't offered an internship at a firm,
he could at the very least receive an endorsement from one of the
architects. And it was fun to at least pretend he was a consultant
on the project.

His designs kept him up late at night, far beyond typical hours
for a school night. He depended on a small lamp at his desk to
help hide the fact he was staying up until the sky lost its black
and faded to the first periwinkle shades of dawn. So consumed
was Jesse with his behind-the-scenes artistry that he forgot to
wonder if Bradley might respond to his letter, or if he was thinking of him at all.

He stepped into the kitchen to pour himself a glass of orange juice one late Saturday morning in spring, still blurry-eyed from lack of sleep. His father handed him an envelope with an inquisitive expression upon his face.

"Got yesterday's mail, and this one is for you. It says 'Parsons' in the return address. Isn't that the name of one of the kids who locked you . . . ." he began to say, already seething.

Jesse saw the familiar slant and he reached for it.

"It's Ty's brother—he drove me home that night." He retreated to the quiet of his room before his dad could ask any more questions.

His hands shook as he held the letter. His stomach knotted, and his breath quickened. Just why had he responded to Bradley Parsons again? And why was Bradley writing him back? The last thing he wanted was to read about flashes of the accident—scenes he didn't know about and could go the rest of his life without hearing about in vivid form. But the letter might not linger on the night that had brought them together. He might as well read it.

> *How are you doing, man? Just thinking of you and wanted to ask how life is treating you these days. Is your eye ok? How is school going? Thought maybe we could meet up for coffee or lunch—if that doesn't sound too weird.*

Bradley's one-liners spoke to him. They were rays of sun, in fact. But what would their interaction become if they saw each other and were expected to carry on a conversation? As much as he appreciated the words Bradley inscribed in this second letter, Jesse thought that their correspondence might best exist in written form. The two of them didn't run in the same circles. Jesse knew nothing of recovering from a war, lifting weights in his free time, or having an intact family life.

He shoved the second letter in the back of his desk drawer beneath some colored pencils as he'd done with the first and turned his focus to his renderings of the restaurant again. He made no mention of the invitation to his father, who expressed curiosity about the letter's contents.

Only trouble was, he couldn't put Bradley Parsons' offer to meet in person out of his mind. Over a month had passed between the first letter and the second, but for some reason he couldn't stop thinking about this one. He pondered the invitation extended to him. When he caught his reflection in the mirror, there was no lingering evidence of Bobby's blow. But he still winced as if feeling his fist and the bruising that followed it. How long would that reflex last?

He turned to what he could more directly control. He would answer Bradley's request to meet in person, even if their meeting fell flat. He would follow through on a request from the guy who cared enough to give him a ride home on an otherwise disastrous night. If they quickly ran out of words, his gratitude to Bradley Parsons would remain unchanged and he'd continue to respect the soldier from a distance.

·◐·

One Saturday several weeks later, Jesse met Bradley for lunch on Harborview Drive. Jesse stepped in the diner, feeling a little unsteady and uncertain about how this meeting would go, but he was soon put at ease. He glimpsed Bradley across the room, caught the unabashed smile on his face, and couldn't help but feel relief when Bradley pulled back a chair in welcome.

"Hey, hey. So glad you could make it."

Bradley seemed lighter than the day they'd met. He'd recently showered, his hair wasn't as overgrown and falling in his eyes—but it wasn't just that. He seemed more present. Less lost in the tangle of his own thoughts, more centered and hopeful. "Got a job at Patterson's Market . . . been getting some lifting in . . . going to church a little more and finding some community there. "

Jesse hadn't even glanced at the menu before Bradley filled the air energetic soundbites.

"But that's enough about me. Tell me about you, Jesse. What's new and exciting?"

Jesse balked at the question, uncertain how to proceed with that line of questioning. New and exciting? So often the days felt the same muted gray as the slate skies over the Harbor.

"I don't really know . . . Not too much lately. I'm working on some designs, which is fun, but other than that, I'm mostly just keeping to myself and getting by." He felt grateful when the waitress paused over their table to take their order and returned promptly with their drinks. His mouth was parched.

Bradley returned to their conversation, having read between the lines. "Don't let them keep getting to you," he said. "Those boys, my brother included, know they should have left you alone that night. I can see it in their faces. And the fact that they're paying for it now is not on you, Jesse. Don't think it is for one minute."

Bradley took a sip of his Coca-Cola. "You shouldn't shoulder what isn't yours to carry."

"Thanks for reminding me," Jesse said, taking a long drink of his coke before looking back to Bradley. "I just wish it was easier to let go sometimes."

He was immediately sober upon realizing he'd just spoken this to Bradley, of all people. There was a sudden gravity in Bradley's eyes, but the veteran didn't seize the moment to mention how what he'd endured was a million times harder, though it was.

"We all do," Bradley finally answered him. "But like anything, healing is a lot of work and a pretty involved process."

Jesse had heard enough stories of soldiers' returns home to garner that they often found healing through service projects—horseback-riding and therapy dogs and mentoring relationships. Lord knew these soldiers needed some peace and solace after the indifference and cruelty they often met after their return from people who'd never walked a mile in their combat boots. Never waded through a sweltering jungle with dead bodies all around.

Jesse knew without Bradley having to utter another word that his process toward wholeness was far from over. He credited the guy for showing up with a sunnier outlook than the one he'd had and felt a slight bloom of conviction. If this guy could go through such darkness and still show up with a smile on his face, his own world didn't have to remain one of oppressive clouds and rain.

"You have a lot going for you, Jesse," Bradley said, breaking from any possible thoughts of his own life's hurdles. "I see your drive and your purpose. I just hope you start to feel encouraged. Get some joy in your every day that matches what you have going on."

After their initial meeting, Jesse sometimes spied Bradley's truck parked in front of the Gig Harbor Athletic Club or out at Madrona Links Golf Course. And while he didn't stop what he was doing every time, he sometimes paused and went in to say hello, smiling to himself that this start to the unlikeliest of friendships was just what he needed to be lifted from the dreary aftermath of the past fall.

Jesse couldn't help feeling lighter, knowing that Bradley would greet him with a wide smile and a—*Hey, hey how you doing?*—every time.

· ⟷ ·

Only one thing made Jesse more nervous than seeing Bradley Parsons again, and that was knocking on Elli Grayson's front door.

Nothing more had come of their interrupted kiss. Even if there was a mutual knowing in their eyes, Elli did her best to keep a platonic air between them at school, and she moved at such a pace with her studies and her scripts that he didn't know how to ask her what it had meant to her—if anything at all.

But he had something he needed to show her, and he wouldn't allow a little trepidation to stand in his way. It was spring break, and he couldn't stand the thought of not sharing his work with her until school was back in session.

He silently prayed that her father wouldn't answer the door. Mr. Grayson wasn't unfriendly, but he habitually wore a stiff upper lip disrupted only by an occasional joke. And his jokes were so self-deprecating that it was hard for Jesse to know if he should laugh. But it was worth the risk of coming face-to-face with Elli's father to see her. He'd come today with a portfolio of his near-completed drawings of the restaurant.

Jesse sighed his relief when he saw Nicole on the other side of the door. Today she wore a blue velour tracksuit and less makeup than usual. It was a Nicole that seemed more down to earth, and didn't pop her trademark gum. She didn't quite smile at him, but he was grateful she didn't roll her eyes either—like she might have done before the afternoon of the abandoned boat.

"I'll go get Elli," she said, gesturing for him to come in.

He hesitated. She spoke in a pragmatic tone. "You don't have to be shy anymore. The entire world knows that you and Elli are practically together."

Jesse's sweater suddenly itched at his collar. Moments ago, he was outside in the brisk Pacific Northwest spring, grateful for the insulation of his sweater, but he felt instant heat upon entering the Grayson's home. He would probably stammer next, but how could he not say something? "Elli and I . . . we're good friends." He almost dropped his portfolio as he made that point clear and had to adjust it against his thigh, so he didn't drop it to the ground.

Nicole was kind enough to let his insistence and his fumble of the portfolio go. She merely smiled over her shoulder and left him standing at the grand entrance of the Grayson home. He told himself once again not to let himself become intimidated with the vaulted ceilings, the cherry-wood side tables that boasted tall ivory candles, and the flawless buttercream walls.

The first time he'd been here he had sensed Elli's discomfort with his fixation on her family's affluence and tried to steer his attention to what mattered: their shared music tastes, their chemistry class, her acting adventures, and his architectural designs.

Now he turned all his concentration to the portfolio. By the time Elli reached the front door, he was second-guessing his decision to bring it. His efforts were already feeling trivial and obsolete. But Elli smiled brightly at him, and his heart immediately felt lighter. She looked impossibly cute in a Coca-Cola T-shirt and dark-wash bell bottom jeans. A trademark braid held her dark hair, and small wisps escaped from it as they always did.

"Jesse," she said, the smile evident in her voice. "I'm so glad you're here." She searched his face and may have seen uncertainty flicker across his features. He knew that his color still hinted at a raspberry hue, but didn't want to tell her what her older sister had said about the two of them.

"Here, follow me," she said, leading him down the hallway and opening the door to the study, which her mother indicated was the most appropriate setting for gathering with a member of the opposite sex. He'd only glimpsed the interior of her room once, just enough to admire her posters of her favorite musicians when she'd run in to grab some colored pencils off her desk. The Beatles. Pink Floyd. Fleetwood Mac.

"My mother's protective of me since she's overcompensating for my older sister," Elli had told him, the only time he'd ever caught her on the edge of embarrassment. But he told her it was a sensible rule, that he understood it, and that he was all too happy that he could spend time with her at all.

They entered the study, where a large table awaited his portfolio. Right away she gave her undivided attention to it. "Are you finished already?" she asked, a hint of awe breaking into her voice.

"Yes," Jesse said, tasting a blend of sheepishness and excitement. "But it's not what the restaurant is going to do, of course. It's only my idea . . . what I'd do if it was my job."

Elli shrugged, showing him it made no difference. "You told me that your dad's friend is one of the architects at the firm and that he's going to at least take a look at your work."

He was laying the paper flat on the table so that she could see for herself the wraparound fish tank near the entrance, the appointment desk artfully staggered at an angle, the layout of the main floor with guests positioned far enough apart for intimate conversation. She took it all in. Her eyes harbored a dark glow that made his risk of vulnerability entirely worth it.

"They're going to love it, Jesse," she said, finally standing back and marveling over his creation of what could be. "I knew you were talented, but your drawings are truly amazing. Jesse, don't shake your head and get all humble on me. I mean it. This is what you're meant to be doing."

He instantly felt taller. There was no one's praise—not even the lead architect himself—whose words could mean more to him than Elli Grayson's. She saw him, had always seen him for who he was under his temporal awkwardness and insecurity. She'd never treated him like he operated at a disadvantage—the bumbling nerd with four eyes. He'd always felt intact and whole and more capable in her presence. So he rocked back on his heels and folded his arms across his chest. "I know this is what I should do . . . Thanks for seeing it . . . appreciating it, I mean."

"Appreciating it!" Elli said, throwing her arms up and on the cusp of laughter. She caught her sister walking by out of the corner of her eye. "Hey, Nicole, come here and take a look at Jesse's drawing for a new restaurant along the Harbor."

He was surprised when Nicole scooted into the study without additional coaxing. Her eyebrows were arched, and she said, "A new restaurant in the Harbor sounds promising. We could definitely use more options here so we're not driving to Sixth Avenue all the time."

"My dad's friend encouraged me to work on a design," Jesse clarified as Nicole peered over the table, "and if I'm lucky, the architects might borrow an idea or two. I can only hope they see something worth incorporating."

Nicole wrinkled her nose. "But it's brilliant," she said offhandedly. "Why wouldn't they take your exact plans? No one could do it better."

Jesse smiled but didn't know how to accept her compliment. He was quick to say, "It's missing a few things, but the general idea is there."

Nicole was already sold on his design. "You're going to be great," she said before walking out of the study room.

Elli brushed a hand on Jesse's shoulder, and he warmed at her presence. If he'd had more courage or stupidity, he might have turned toward her and given her another kiss. But Jesse was keenly aware that they were in the study of her parents' home. He didn't want to compromise his fragile standing here with something she might not want again.

Instead, he smiled sadly at the missed opportunity and turned to ask Elli something he'd been wondering—even if he ruined the magic of the moment. "So how has your sister been doing since the accident? I know she was at the scene with Bobby and that she had a tough time . . . ."

Elli dropped her hand from his shoulder and pursed her lips together. "She didn't come out of her room for the first few days, and she played the same record over and over. Didn't shower for days and wouldn't go to work. My dad eventually got her out with some tough love. Told her he was going to have an intervention counselor come to the house if she didn't come out of her room . . . . But it's been months now, and she's starting to act more like herself again, only softer. Mom . . . my mom found her a counselor and I think maybe some medication too. You know, to take the edge off. I think it's helping somewhat."

Jesse thought of Nicole and what she'd been forced to weather. He had seen evidence of this softening. The Nicole he'd known at the beginning of November was callous and removed. She wouldn't have said hello to him, much less decided to look at his work or complimented it. This new side of her was less guarded and not so myopic as the one he'd experienced before.

"She went to see Bobby once but hasn't been back to his house. It's not as if she needs to be there. He wasn't kind to her at the end of their relationship," Elli said. "She was traumatized when she saw him at the scene of the accident, though, and relieved that he didn't die. But the life he's now living is far from ideal."

Jesse could only imagine how it must feel for the once bright and shining quarterback not to have only his senior season taken away from him, but all hopes of future seasons seized from him too. There was no containing what was lost.

Jesse chewed on his lip, wishing he hadn't brought the conversation here. He hadn't want such a grave outcome for Bobby, but also didn't think he was meant to forget the way he'd been treated. He had nothing to say to his former classmate and found it troubling trying to reconcile the outpouring of love given for him after his injury. How much more *poor-Bobby-this* and *poor-Bobby-that* would he be forced to endure?

Elli, as if sensing his sudden discomfort, turned her attention back to the renderings spread over the broad oak table. "Someday I'll tell people I know this famous architect whose designs are found all throughout the state." Her smile shone, and he wished he had the enthusiasm to match it.

Someday. Would they be in each other's lives? As thrilled as he was to have such a friend in Elli, he could see her coming into her own—gaining the attention of more of their peers on the stage, no longer looked to as the quiet girl with her nose buried in textbooks. When would she realize her possibilities with the opposite sex and forget him?

Later, when she followed him out of her house and walked him down the porch steps, it struck him that they might be on borrowed time. Her smile was genuine and bright and yet his reasons for stopping by were dwindling. He'd taken it for granted, how easy it was to linger at the school after hours with her when they had pressing labs and exams looming before them.

He hadn't missed Mr. Grayson's arched eyebrow as he'd passed him in the hall on the way to the front door. His brief *Jesse Sander* by way of greeting. Elli's father knew their study sessions had come to a close too. He must wonder what he was doing over at the house.

All these things made it hard to tell Elli goodbye. For weeks he'd worked on his design of the restaurant, energized every time he thought of her reaction to his earnest work. Now that he had nothing else to show her, he wondered how many more of these visits would flow so seamlessly.

He clutched the portfolio beneath his shoulder this time, aware that the wind's tug could force it from him if he wasn't careful. For all the praise it had given him, he wished it wasn't so cumbersome to carry, when he only wanted to imprint these moments with Elli on his mind.

Sensing his struggle, Elli gave him a compassionate smile and said, "I'll let you go, Jesse, but only on one condition."

Curious now, he tilted his head to the side and appraised her. How beautiful she was with her hair falling messily free from her braid, her dark eyes constant and warm. "What's that?" he asked her.

"You enroll in a science class with me next year so we can be lab partners again," she said simply. "It's just not the same, you not being there." She smiled sadly. "I really miss you."

His heart stirred at this, and he set his portfolio down at his feet, daring it to scurry in the wind. He opened his arms to her, wrapped her inside and wished he didn't have to let her go. "Thank you for saying that," he said against dark hair that still smelled like apple and a hint of evergreen.

"It's the truth," she whispered against his shoulder.

She had lines from *Sense and Sensibility* to run and one of her parents might even be at the living room window, waiting for her to come back inside right now. But this moment was near perfection—finding it meant that much to her that they have more time together again.

He lowered his lips to hers, shaking a little in his shoes. He drew her closer to him and kissed her softly. She tasted sweet, a hint of berries on her lips. His heart beat wildly, but if Elli was surprised he wanted to kiss her again, she didn't show it. Her lips were warm, and she smiled against his mouth. It gave him such relief, acknowledgement that he hadn't misread her entirely and that he wasn't merely subjugated to the "friend" role.

Suddenly remembering their position—in view of the front windows and anyone who might happen to walk on by—Jesse took a step back and murmured an apology. He shoved a hand through his tousled hair, waiting for her response.

"Don't be sorry," she said, offering him one of her amused smiles. "It didn't take me by surprise. I know you like me, Jesse Sander.

Have known it for a while." In a rare show of shyness, she glanced down at her boots before glancing back up at him.

"I just don't want it to change anything between me and you," Jesse said. "Your friendship means the world to me, and I don't want it to—"

"Change," Elli said, finishing the thought for him. "I get it. I don't want it to change either. But I happen to like you, more than 'like you,' too."

"Really?"

"Yeah," Elli said, teasing back a strand of wayward hair. "But it doesn't mean we're ready for anything more . . . yet. You and I—we're so busy with our pursuits—that it would be best for us to continue as we are. At least for a while. So we don't change what we have."

Still caught up in the headiness of that second kiss, Jesse didn't have the wherewithal to challenge her notion that "just friends" was best. He reached for her hand, pressed his fingers against hers and said, "It makes sense for now, Elli. It really does. But I'd be lying if I didn't have greater hopes for you and me."

She stood on her tippy-toes and gave him another short kiss—more of a sendoff. "I better get in there before my dad comes looking for me," she said, eyes widening. "But time is on our side, Jess. We'll talk about this again. It's not too late."

21

Time's Consequence

*A*s they headed closer to the summer months, Scott could scarcely enjoy the regular rites of passage—final sports seasons, last dances, and senior speeches. There was a dullness cast over everything. He didn't saunter down the hall like a big man on campus. He only took up the space he needed. He became more of a recluse and kept his nose in his books far more than he ever had in all his high school years.

Just two weeks before the end of the school year, he sighted Ty Parsons standing at his open locker as he walked down the hall. He could probably count on one hand the number of true conversations he'd had with his teammate since last November. Sensing that he should probably acknowledge him, he paused and waited for Ty to look up from his locker.

Scott tried to swallow the lump of frustration that arose to tell him he wasn't over Ty's lackadaisical response to the accident. He leaned into a conversation despite the leftover discord he felt between them. "Hey, Ty," he said, adjusting the weight of his duffel bag on his shoulder.

"Oh hi," Ty said absently, revealing he was none too interested in conversing with him. He looked back into his locker quickly.

Scott was weary from his unsuccessful attempts to get his long-time friend to show emotion. It'd been absent when he'd dismissed Scott's concern over Bobby's scheme. It'd been absent when he'd brought his girlfriend along, as if he couldn't imagine why Scott would want a meeting with just the two of them. And it'd been absent when he left the hospital without saying a word to his teammates—especially Bobby. It was like trying to squeeze water from a radish—getting this guy to talk.

Sometimes he wondered if he was the only one who wanted to outrun what had happened. Sometimes the error of his ways caught up with him in the middle of the night and he awoke drenched in sweat, his heart taking on an unnatural rhythm. He replayed those moments he was waking up in the hospital and couldn't shake the helplessness that hovered even now, reminding him he had blacked out and lost time, lost control of everything.

Ty's fingers twitched and without having to ask, Scott knew he was craving a cigarette.

"I did my best that night, you know," Ty said, intensity snapping in his blue irises. It took a minute for Scott to grasp his intended meaning. "I left Jesse a knife and knew he could work his way out. It might not be enough for you, but it's what I could do at the time. I asked my brother to give him a ride home . . . even though I knew it meant Bradley would be mad as hell at me."

"Is he still?" Scott dared to ask, not having given their brotherly dynamic any thought.

"What do you think?" Ty asked, tilting his head to the side. "Look, I don't want to talk about it anymore. The kid got home, and he's probably able to move on easier than we are. He doesn't have to walk down these halls and fend off questions about being a bully every day of his life."

Out of the corner of his eye, Scott could see Marianne Prather staring their way. Only—was that Marianne? She didn't look like herself, save for those big hazel eyes. While she typically floated down the halls with a perfectly timed toss of her hair, her glossy demeanor was replaced with the somberness of a funeral procession. She wore a faded gray sweatshirt, oversize jeans and she clutched her textbooks close to her chest.

Ty averted his eyes from her and glanced back at Scott. Anger beat in his eyes. "If you want to know the truth, I was too worried about her being pregnant to care much for anything else." He closed his eyes. "There was this party before we pulled the prank . . . ."

"I know the one," Scott said slowly, trying to eliminate surprise from his face. It was the night he and the rest of the guys at Peninsula High had watched the most stunning cheerleader make her pick. Scott had still been mending from his broken relationship with Elli Grayson and hadn't paid much attention.

But now he wondered why the statement was such a revelation. He'd glimpsed Marianne sidling up to Ty that night, keyed in on their interlocked fingers, the proximity of their bodies, saw Marianne whisper something in Ty's ear and watched him follow her up the stairs without the slightest hesitation. They'd been inseparable ever since, but had become more distant with each other over the last month or so, now that Scott came to think of it.

"Yeah, I think everyone remembers," Ty said as if this was something he was no longer proud of. He tucked his thumbs into the tops of his jeans. "Thing is, she said she might be . . . pregnant a few days before all that Jesse situation . . . and it's kept me up so many nights. All I could think about was that . . . . I would have done so many things differently if I could go back."

Scott could see the water standing in Ty's eyes. While this hint of emotion was uncharacteristic of Ty, it wasn't enough for Scott to absolve his teammate or let him off the proverbial hook. "So what are you going to do?" Scott asked. "You can't keep ignoring her." He counted on his fingers. "She's at least five months along now. So how is avoiding her going to do anything other than hurt you both?"

Ty closed his locker tight and turned to give Scott his undivided attention. "You're right . . . I can't keep running . . . . It's not fair to her . . . . It's just that we had our whole lives in front of us, and we stand to lose so much . . . I might not ever play football again . . . ."

"At least talk with her," Scott said, refusing to commiserate with his teammate even if Ty's fears were understandable. "You've got to start somewhere and this . . . it isn't something that gets better on its own or by pretending it isn't happening."

"You're right. I'll talk with her," Ty said, seriousness etched into his features, erasing the rest of his boyishness. Then offhandedly—"Thanks for the pep talk."

"Look," Scott said, clasping a hand on Ty's shoulder. "It won't be easy, but it will be worth it. You're doing the right thing by her."

"How do you know that?" Ty asked, as if he wasn't quite so certain of himself. "You and I—we aren't exactly guys who know what it's like to do the right thing."

Scott felt the pang of those words but decided to let them fall to the ground.

"You know what it's like to do the wrong thing and what it's like to want to do everything in your power to fix it," Scott said. "Look, even though she's . . . going to have a baby . . . your life isn't over. It might be harder. No—scratch that—it will be harder, but it isn't over. It doesn't have to be."

"Well, so now you know," Ty said, giving one more glance to his locker and heading toward the exit doors. He had a cigarette in his mouth before they were even out of the building.

22

Different Lives

1976

*I*t was right before Christmas break and there was a rare moment when his dorm room at UCLA sat idle, though the chaos his roommate had left in his wake still surrounded him. Instead of attempting to tidy up after the guy—throw cast-off clothes into laundry bins, straighten notebooks and forgotten papers—Jesse drank in the stillness and the silence. His bag for the holidays sat waiting by the door and he found his thoughts tugging back to Elli again.

He fished around for his last letter from her. There it was, shoved between two sketchbooks. And here he was, allowing her words to leap off the page and fuel him again.

> *...I wish you could redesign the set for us, Jess. It's not my specialty, but anyone with a critical eye can see there's nothing original about it. You would know how to give it that spark that matches our performances. Want to transfer?! ...*

He had expected that the camaraderie he and Elli shared was enough to keep them close over their college years. But sometimes time and distance worked in its natural, unintended wedge and made the connection between two souls less certain—though they could never return to being mere strangers.

They'd intended to keep in close touch, even once their acceptance to universities took them in different directions. Elli entered the Department of Theater and Performance at Stanford, and Jesse enrolled in UCLA's Department of Architecture and Urban Planning. But the more than 300 driving miles was enough of a blockage, and their early letters and phone calls to each other phased out over time while trying to balance varied schedules and conflicting demands.

In their first semester, Elli was consumed with her role as Laura in *The Glass Menagerie*, and Jesse spent endless hours drawing and constructing models. As he worked with the barest amount of light at night—trying to be considerate to a roommate who loved his sleep—he'd think of her amused smile, the glint of her warm chocolate eyes. She hadn't written back to his last letter a few weeks ago. That was so unlike her. Elli was the most organized and precise person he knew other than himself.

He thought perhaps she'd gotten distracted and meant to reach him. He considered calling her, but it never seemed like the right time. If he got back from Perloff Hall or the library early some nights, his roommate Blake was usually waiting for him, wanting him to accompany him to the dining hall for a late-night snack. Blake was so puppy-dog eager for company that Jesse couldn't easily turn him down. He could have done without Blake's incessant talking at times, though much of what his roommate had to say amused him—pithy observations about professors' neuroses and their preferred styles, so out of alignment with the times. He also could have done without Blake's complete lack of organization.

Sweaters draped over the back of chairs, half opened bottles of Coca-Cola on his desk—on any free surface. His satchel occupied the center of the room, papers spilling out the sides. Occasionally, when flustered after tripping across the room at some ungodly hour, Jesse mentioned the need for more order. But usually, on catching Blake's hurt expression, he let it go.

Busyness drove Jesse forward. His professors had taken note of his natural gift right away, and his peers sometimes set aside their pride to ask him to examine their work. These circumstances cover the twinge of regret he felt when he thought of Elli.

Yet here he was, about to leave for Christmas break and feeling guilty again for letting her slide through his fingers like grains of sand. But hadn't she let him go first? She hadn't responded to his last letter. He'd attempted to give her a panoramic view of his world and in turn, had asked about hers. Could the last letter have possibly been lost in the mail? What a fool he'd be if he discovered that his letter had never arrived and he'd chosen his pride over the risk of vulnerability, or even rejection.

Blake walked in as he sat ruminating on the letter. A sheepish expression crossed his face. "When you go home, are you going to see that girl?"

Jesse blinked, trying to decide how much of his feelings to divulge.

"You mean Elli," he said tightly, knowing that Blake was aware of her name and that they weren't officially dating. He'd talked about her nonstop in the beginning, when the two of them were getting to know each other, and taking all their meals together in the student union building.

There was the picture Nicole had taken of the two of them right before they left for university framed on his desk. They sat closely together on a park bench and Elli's hand rested on his shoulder. He could still feel her fingertips whisper across the fabric of his flannel. Her touch had felt so certain then. How could it be so fleeting, to the point that he had to ask himself if she'd ever touched him at all? If they'd ever really kissed at all?

"Yeah, Elli," Blake said, his eyes flashing at the brisk correction Jesse had given him.

Blake was so earnest—it was as if he sensed his own outlier status, how he didn't quite fit in and tried to compensate with overwrought friendliness toward everyone on campus. "Do you think you'll see her?" his question seemed hesitant, but Jesse supposed he was grappling for something to say.

"I don't know," Jesse said slowly, staring down at the plush green carpet. "She didn't respond to my last letter, and that's so unlike her. I sent it mid-November and asked her enough questions to get a response. Elli's not the type to let a letter fall through the cracks."

Blake raked a hand through his disheveled hair and winced as if he'd been hit in the side. "Oh man, I'm sorry. I meant to tell you that she called a few weeks ago. I . . . I answered and spoke to her, but I was in the middle of putting that poster up," he motioned toward the image of Wonder Woman, and Jesse thought fast, training his tongue not to say something he'd regret. "It was only that once, but I'm sorry I forgot to mention it. That she called you and wanted you to call her back."

Frustration welled up in Jesse's chest. She'd called him at the beginning of the month, and Blake hadn't thought to mention it until *now*? How could he be so forgetful and careless, indulging in endless details about comic books, but not remembering to tell him something that bore actual weight?

Blake stammered; his cheeks turning cherry-red. "You're not angry with me, are you?"

Jesse tried to swallow a burst of laughter. This guy had no idea how aggravating he could be sometimes. "It's just that I thought she'd forgotten me this past month."

He made a mental note to return to school with a "while you

were out" notepad so Blake's attention wouldn't be so easily diverted next time she rang.

"Go see her when you get home and tell her your dumb roommate forgot to relay the message," Blake said, his expression glum yet hopeful.

"No use staying mad at you," Jesse gave his downcast roommate's shoulder a squeeze, though he was still irritated. Couldn't help it. "Have a merry Christmas, Blake. 1977, here we come! I'll see you in January."

·✦·

Jesse chastised himself as the Grayson's dark blue house came into view beyond a canopy of evergreens. Why hadn't he called ahead? A silver lighted Christmas tree glowed from behind the sheer white curtains. He'd borrowed his dad's new Chevy truck and its wheels crunched loudly over the gravel, announcing his unexpected arrival. It was two days before Christmas, and he wanted to surprise her with an impromptu visit.

Jesse wore a pair of dark-wash Levi's, a red and blue flannel shirt beneath a light jacket. He felt his recently shaved chin and smoothed the waves of hair back from his face. He was glad he'd finally traded out his thick glasses for contact lenses. He wondered what Elli would think of them, given that she'd worn glasses herself all through their high school years.

Why hadn't they ever made their relationship official? He hated that they'd denied themselves the significance and the formality, all the while laughing off the thought of going steady, and saying they were "too busy" to ruin a good thing by giving it a title. Jesse deplored this trivial thinking. It left them on such uncertain ground. He hoped he wasn't catching the Graysons in the middle of dinner, but still he edged his way up to the front door and rang the doorbell. The high-toned chime rang out and there was no going back. *Please let it be one of the girls*, he prayed. Courage could be fleeting and he didn't want to have one of those moments when his tongue tripped over itself trying to explain his presence to her intimidating father. Unlike times from the past, there was no tangible purpose for his being here—no deadline on a project they needed to complete.

Much to his satisfaction, it was Elli herself who answered the door. It wasn't always in her nature to greet visitors. Her cheeks were strawberry-tinted, her eyes sparkled with life, and she wore the most beautiful dark blue velvet dress Jesse had ever seen. It was only when her lips parted in question after greeting him that Jesse realized her warmth wasn't the result of his presence here.

"Elli—I . . . I want to apologize for not being in touch with you sooner. My roommate . . . he's not the most organized guy, you see . . . and he forgot to tell me that you called. I thought that after you'd received my last letter and that maybe you weren't too interested, or you were too busy to . . . ." He was talking too quickly and intentionally bit his tongue. *Stupid.* He'd never been like this with her before; what was causing him to falter now?

"I did wonder why you didn't respond," Elli said, crossing her arms over her chest. "But I didn't take it too personally, Jesse. I know we're both ambitious—you and I . . . we embrace the pressure and we get swept up in what needs to be done."

"Y-yes," Jesse stammered, while inwardly groaning *no*. "We're both hard-working, but that shouldn't stop us from connecting with each other. In any case, I'm sorry I didn't respond sooner." He smiled sheepishly, felt the small box—Elli's Christmas present—jab him in his coat pocket, right beneath his ribs.

She smiled at him too, but there was something akin to unease in her eyes and she didn't invite him in. His throat started to close in on him, but he fought to get the words out first. "If it's not a good time for me to be here . . . ." he said, rocking back on his heels and wishing he could accept what he'd spoken aloud. Why shouldn't it be a good time for her to invite him inside? It was practically Christmas, and it didn't appear that the Graysons were in the midst of a lavish party.

The door behind Elli opened, and a tall, golden haired young man stepped out on the porch. He gave Elli's shoulder a gentle squeeze and said, "I was just starting to wonder where you were, Elli-Belle. The show is starting soon." He stopped, as if realizing that he ought to introduce himself to the stranger on the porch. He tilted his head, curious, and stuck out his hand, which Jesse was reluctant to take.

The gears clicked into motion and Jesse was awash with the real reason Elli hadn't suffered from his silence. "Bryce Donahue," the guy said. "And you are?"

Elli, in a fit of nervous laughter so unlike herself, said, "This is one of my best friends, Jesse Sander."

Nice recovery, Jesse thought glumly. The phrase "best friends" did little to hearten him or make the situation easier to bear. He was relegated to the "friend" role, and maybe she'd never felt anything more. Maybe she'd only met his lips with her own because the intensity of that dark November had called for it. It had summoned everything that was dormant and brought it to fruition.

"One of your best friends? Oh, you mean the architect, your old lab partner?" Bryce said, looking proud that he'd remembered.

Elli's smile was small, perhaps because she knew it wasn't sufficient. "That's right," she said softly. "He's the one."

"You want to join us and watch *A Christmas Carol?*" Bryce asked, looking optimistic, as if he was doing the charitable thing. "Not sure if you're as into theater as we are, but it's a classic, you know. Hard to go wrong with Dickens."

He laughed, though no one else did.

Jesse was already shaking his head, a smile plastered on his face. "Thank you for the invitation, but I'm busy." He cleared his throat before Elli could extend her own offer.

The corner of the jewelry box prodded his ribs and he pondered what to do with it. Damn it all. Should he give her the present, even if it the trajectory of their friendship had altered? He certainly had no use for it. Swallowing his pride, he reached in his pocket, took out the black box and clutched it tightly. Voice shaking more than he wanted, he took one step closer to Elli and said, "I have something small for you. Just wanted to give you a Christmas gift, Elli, and wish you well with your next play."

Her eyes hinted at sadness, and she stammered before saying, "That's so kind of you. Thank you, Jesse."

Bryce pointed toward the front door and said, "I'll start the popcorn. It's ... it's nice meeting you, Jesse."

As soon as Bryce closed the front door, Elli spoke. "Bryce ... his parents work as medics overseas ... and he didn't have anywhere to go for the holidays. I didn't want him to stay at the dorms, alone, so I invited him here and ...."

"You don't have to explain," Jesse said, keeping his voice level and trying not to betray the pain he felt at being replaced so quickly—the first semester away from each other, in fact. "It was kind of you to invite him home for the holidays. I know what that's like, having a parent away."

He pressed the jewelry box into her palm, feeling the flow of undeniable relief. Who knew if she would wear it, but at least it was with its intended owner.

"You don't have to open it now," he nearly whispered, almost praying that she wouldn't.

"I'd like to ... if you don't mind," she said, her voice certain and strong. The question leaped in her eyes and he could scarcely tell her no.

He did mind. He minded entirely too much. Seeing her reaction would mean another last memory of her to replay when there were no longer moments for the two of them to spend together. But he didn't have the heart to tell her not to open it now.

"Alright," he said softly, waiting as she opened the box and fixated upon the delicate silver chain he'd found for her and the deep blue stone it held at its center. "It looked like you," he said, as if it required an explanation.

She smiled, her eyes taking on a sheen in the winter moonlight. He couldn't have dreamed of a better response to his gift, this evidence that it was stirring her heart and yet ... he couldn't enjoy it the same, knowing that what they had was fading, disintegrating into the wind.

"Could you ... could you help me put it on?" she asked.

As his fingers grazed the nape of her neck, he prayed his cold fingers wouldn't fumble with the chain. She felt as real to him as she'd ever been. She turned around and opened her arms to embrace him in a big-hearted hug. It defied logic to be losing her at all. Her eyes barely held the tears. "Will you still write me, Jesse?" she asked.

He swallowed so hard it hurt. He was immersed in his studies, and while he was good at what he did, his time was not his own anymore. And Elli—she was giving all her hours to the theater. Naturally she would become closer to her castmates there ... like tall, golden Bryce. Jesse couldn't compete, nor would he try. He must simply recognize their friendship as a temporal gift, something to feel gratitude for no matter how long it lasted.

She seemed to see the inner hesitation manifest on his face. So she amended her request. "At least let me know what happens with your designs. I want to know about all the things you create."

He nodded. "Of course. And you send me playbills from all the plays you're in."

She cracked a smile, one that wasn't contrived or tinged with sorrow. "I have lesser-known parts most of the time, especially as an underclassman."

He shrugged. "It doesn't matter," he said, "It will be my theater education. I need a break from my projects anyway, as much as they keep me on my toes."

She drew toward him for another embrace, and he was the one to take a step back, even though he didn't want to break from her warm apple scent, the evergreen clinging to her hair. The curtain swayed gently in the living room and he sensed that Bryce was more than ready for her to come back in.

"It was nice seeing you again, Elli," he said. He couldn't bring himself to say goodbye, even though their relationship wouldn't be the same going forward. "I'm glad you like your necklace."

She drew a hand to the small gem and her eyes leaped up at him. "I love it. Thank you. I wish I had something for you."

Jesse shook his head. "Don't worry about that. It's just good to see you. Have a good night, Elli. And merry Christmas."

"Merry Christmas, Jess," she said softly, delaying her return to the house and sounding as if she wanted to say more. How could she feel so close to him and yet be so far away? He was on the outside of the shop window looking in at what he couldn't have. He turned toward her and raised a hand, "Merry Christmas to you too, Elli." He'd already said that, hadn't he? She smiled sweetly at him before turning toward the house.

·⟷·

In the months that followed, the nostalgia faded for them both as they tackled more pressing tasks than staying in touch. Jesse made one attempt to visit her during the summer, but stopped short as he rounded the bend to her house and caught sight of

Bryce beside her on the front patio swing. Her head tilted back, and she laughed at something he whispered in her ear. It didn't take long for him to hear it confirmed in the Harbor—Elli had brought her tall, golden boy home for the entire summer, and it was apparent Mr. Grayson had taken an instant liking to him. He was often sighted with her father on the golf course, at the home repair shop, and in the pew with her family on Sundays.

Jesse forced himself to stop imagining Bryce and Elli studying together, running their lines. He tried his best to avoid common areas in town where he might meet her and Bryce. He was somewhat surprised when she called him late one summer night to say hello, a hint of longing in her voice. He was surprised when she remembered him the fall of her sophomore year, sending him playbills. *Our Town—A Midsummer Night's Dream—A Streetcar Named Desire*—and on and on through the rest of their college years.

He, in turn, sent her copies of his drawings, photos of models he'd made, clippings from the *Daily Bruin* on architecture lectures. He read each playbill she sent him and let his eyes stop at her bio, even though he knew it by heart. He didn't hear from her beyond these exchanges. But he never stopped sending her those clips, and she never stopped sending him those playbills, even as their words to each other became scarce.

23

Cold Winter's Night

Christmas 1999

*J*ared's eyes had stung with anger before he even stepped into the car with his dad. He hadn't possessed the self-control to keep from lashing when his dad started questioning him about what had gone wrong at practice that day. Whereas his dad was fast, agile, and able to catch, Jared was simply fast. He knew his performance on the court was a disappointment. Especially that afternoon—tripping over his feet, dropping the ball, unable to make a shot. Coach hadn't yelled at him, but some of his teammates had chided him and murmured beneath their breath.

Last practice someone had taken his clean clothes and towel from his locker and hidden them. He'd shrugged it off and told everyone he'd shower at home. Today there'd been a scrunched-up note left on top of his duffel bag. *Just quit. You're not your father*, the folded paper had read.

There was no knowing who'd written it, but Jared had his suspicions. He thought maybe it was Logan Waits, an up-and-coming forward on the team. The guy looked put out every time Jared made a mistake and made more of a show of rolling his eyes than anyone else on the court. Jared had folded the note away in his backpack, but the words were still hot off the press for him. Why did his father have it all without having to try half as hard? *You're not your father.*

The hot chocolate had only been a consolation, and he couldn't take it. He didn't want to fall apart in the front seat of the car. It wasn't only today's practice that was disheartening; it was the inevitable truth that he didn't have what it took to be a force on this sports team or any other. So as calmly as he could, he'd told his dad he needed to walk home and hopped out of the car.

His coach and several other players were still chatting it up in the parking lot, so he did his best to remain unapproachable as he began his trek home. He pulled up the hood of his sweatshirt, drew the drawstring tight, and tunnel-visioned it off of the school premises.

The wind was wreaking havoc and he felt it lash his face despite his efforts to shield it. He thrust his hands in his pockets and kept walking, knowing that he had about five long miles ahead. He'd made the right decision, though he hoped his dad wouldn't take his walking home too personally. There was nothing to talk about with him. When had his dad ever suffered the same limitations on a court or a field?

And was it worth staying on the team? The question nagged at him. Most afternoons he blocked a few shots, defended well, and scrambled down the court. He was a contributor even if he wasn't putting up most of the points on the reader board. Why had his performance gone so horribly flat today?

His dad's car passed him on the road and Jared set his resolve for his walk home. He'd needed space. And his dad hadn't known how to provide it. Instead, his dad had pigeonholed his frustration under the "angsty teenager" file and raked up other shortcomings—like not being attentive to his grandparents. Maybe he was mistaken, but it didn't seem like his father was spending as much time visiting them either.

Jared braced himself against the cold. He was already spent, but maybe once the other players and the coach cleared the area, he'd jog some of the distance to cut the time. Once he got home, he could take a hot shower, then hibernate in his room and maybe draw in his sketchbook.

But no sooner did the thought of running home cross his mind than he heard his name being called.

"Jared! Hey, Jared!"

He spun around and raised a hand to acknowledge whoever was trying to catch his attention. Pete Slade, the starting point guard for the varsity team paused beside him in a blue sportscar. A lot of the students around these parts were affluent, but Peter didn't strike him as a guy that put on too many airs. The upperclassman had stopped to talk to someone on JV, after all.

Until now, Jared didn't even realize Pete knew his name. He gulped, still not recovered enough to talk much. What did he want?

"Hey man, want a ride home?" Pete asked, momentary concern etching lines on his forehead.

Jared shook his head. "No thanks," he said as brightly as he could muster. "I told my dad to go on ahead. Thought I'd run part of the way home. Doesn't hurt to get a little more conditioning in."

Pete's eyes widened. "Coach didn't run you hard enough? Man, I'm dedicated to the team, but I can't think of any time I *added* to a practice."

While Jared appreciated the praise, he wished that Pete would speed on by so he could start moving toward his house. It would be dark before the hour was up.

"You sure?" Pete said.

Jared nodded. Pete zoomed on past and Jared did a quick search over his shoulder. At least three more players were exiting the school parking lot now in their cars. He couldn't know for certain which one had left that note for him in the locker room and he couldn't trust anyone.

He closed his eyes tight. Why hadn't he considered this all before he'd told his dad he'd rather walk home today? Who would really believe he was heading home on foot for the sake of extra conditioning?

The best way to take care of his dilemma was to hide, so he did what anyone seeking an ounce of privacy would do—he scurried off the shoulder of the road in favor of the woods below. He'd wait until they'd driven away to emerge back onto the street from behind the trees. This afternoon was hard enough. He didn't want any more varsity players pulling over and feeling sorry for him.

The pathway to the trees was a steeper decline than he'd expected. The Douglas firs and underbrush were stacked more tightly than he anticipated—scarce sunlight in between them—and he had to reach out a palm to break his chance of a fall as he stumbled down the slope. Particles of tree bark embedded in his skin, and he winced at the immediate sting it gave him. A flow of red met his eyes when he pulled his hand back. He stanched the stream with the sleeve of his sweatshirt, so focused on stopping the blood that he didn't notice his foot hadn't come down flat.

It was only after he'd picked out some of the small splinters of bark and grown accustomed to the jabbing pain in his palm that he tried to move, and when he did, his found that his foot was on its side. It was numb at first. When he tried to pull it free, he felt just how much he'd twisted his ankle.

Gritting his teeth, Jared steadied himself against the tree that had broken his fall, and looked up. He glimpsed a sage green house with smoke spiraling out of its chimney in the distance. It would be a hike to make it there—and it wasn't where he wanted to go. His heart banged loudly against his chest, and he tried not to let worry invade his thoughts. Had he known how steep it was off the road he never would have headed down here. Best try to climb back up to where he'd come from ... steep incline or not. The green house was too far in the distance.

His ankle throbbed and swelled by the moment, but perhaps he could reach the street with an uphill crawl. Dirt and debris and thorned shrubbery would make for a strenuous time of it, he was certain. But he had to make the most of it now. Give it half an hour, even, and the light would begin to bleed from the sky.

If he could make it back up to the road he could try to hitch a ride. He'd never make it five miles on his ankle. So much for maintaining his pride. It was the last thing he cared about now as he pushed himself forward, determining that he'd make his way up despite the injuries he'd accrued. Fear grabbed at him like a pesky fiend, but he kept his gaze ahead, his eyes fierce, resolute.

·⟨↔⟩·

Sadie had gone upstairs. Scott sank into his chair in the living room and tried to read the most recent copy of the *Gateway*. But the words swam before him, even doubled when he tried to decipher a headline. This onset dizziness had everything to do with his unrest with the way things had gone with his son. Should he give Jared space when he arrived home after his five-mile trek? Scott didn't think he could bear it. If nothing else, he'd learned that the failure to acknowledge and confront his problems did little to diminish them.

No, he would have words with his son as soon as Jared stepped in the door. Scott would apologize for his insensitive timing, and Jared, hopefully, would say he was sorry for overreacting to a bad practice in the parking lot—before an audience. If Jared wasn't prepared to apologize, so be it. Scott was the adult in the scenario and he would be more mindful of his son's triggers going forward.

Scott finally tossed the newspaper down on the coffee table. He didn't have the mental capacity to read it. Not when the grandfather clock was ticking the passing minutes. Not when he could hear Charlotte loudly rummaging through the kitchen cabinets. Not when he had no resolution to the argument with his son.

"Daddy," Sadie said, ushering herself back into the living room and taking a stand beside the Christmas tree, where she began fiddling with the ornaments. She'd asked for all white lights this year, but made sure the most colorful ornaments adorned the tree. "Do you think Jared might have gotten lost out there? So many of the roads look the same."

Scott shook his head. "Your brother has an impeccable sense of direction. Don't worry about him, Sade."

"I s'pose you're right, Daddy. Jared isn't known for getting lost."

Scott looked at his daughter, wanting to distract her from her singular focus. "Why don't you get a head start on your homework, Sade? That way we could watch *The Wonder Years* tonight. By then I'll bet Jared might even want to join us."

She nodded, enough for her ponytail to bob. "We're reading *The Phantom Tollbooth* right now, and I have some discussion questions. I actually don't mind answering them." Before he could respond—he remembered reading that one back in the day too— she was almost to her room.

Scott passed half an hour in aimless tasks without finishing a single one. He avoided the kitchen, aware that Charlotte was inwardly fuming at him for not taking their son from point A to point B, as she did daily.

What could he tell her—that he hadn't been looking for conflict with their son? Lord knew he had plenty of pressures at work. He didn't know how to navigate a relationship with someone with whom the slightest comment could be spun out of context. Why did trying to relate with Jared make him feel that he was reliving his senior year of high school all over again? Why did his son flinch at words that weren't even intended to harm him?

Scott was setting a crumpled blanket on the back of the couch when he sensed Charlotte's presence at the periphery of the room. Before he could even meet her gaze, she spoke.

"It's been over an hour and a half now, Scott. I know he's walking, but Jared is fast . . . and it shouldn't take him this long to get home."

Scott stepped toward her and said, "He'll be home soon enough. You have to remember, Char, that he expended a lot of energy at practice today and that the cold might be slowing him down."

Charlotte folded her arms over her chest and looked up at him. "Either you go out and find him right now, or I will. We both know that Jared's anger doesn't sustain itself for very long and that he's probably almost over whatever was bothering him. In any case, he doesn't have to walk every last step of the way." Her words came out clipped and tight.

Scott swallowed, hating her disappointment with him. He wasn't worried about their son, though he'd rather be on the other side of this fallout—Jared safely in his room working in his sketchbook, while the rest of them watched a show.

"Okay. I'll go out and find him, bring him home," Scott said, hoping that he and Charlotte were both right, and that Jared would care more about the warmth of the car than stewing over his dad's "insensitivity."

Charlotte tucked a blond strand behind her ear and said, "I'd like you to call if you don't find him soon. And I want to know if he's with you."

Scott placed a hand on her shoulder and was grateful when she didn't recoil from his touch. "I will, Char," he promised her before picking up his keys and placing his wallet into his back pocket. Maybe Jared had changed his mind and wanted something warm to drink after all. Doubtful, but cold weather was known to alter minds and hearts.

24

An Unexpected Guest

*I*t didn't take more than a few minutes for Jared to realize that his task—climbing back up to the street he'd come down—was not going to be a seamless effort. *Could you possibly be any more of a bumbling idiot?* He almost had to laugh at the tragicomedy of events.

First he'd had two left feet at practice, and now he might as well have no feet at all. Some contender. What had he gone and done? His attempt to escape his father's observation and his teammates' pity had instead banged him up enough to ensure the notice of everyone.

While his internal critic wanted to sound off some more about what a hopeless case he was, he shook his head and told himself that this brand of defeated thinking would be his ruin. So he hadn't had a shining practice out there today, and it got under his skin—so what? He was human, and he didn't need to agitate himself over what he was or wasn't on the court. He just needed to get home before dark. The right foot was swelling, prodding him with throbbing and undeniable pain. His ankle was strained enough that he was sure it was purpling. The attempts to grab at the brush didn't come without a cost. Debris shook from the bushes as he edged forward a few inches at a time in a slow climb. This wouldn't be an easy feat.

But he had to make it up to the road, foot be cursed. If he didn't make it up in a matter of minutes, his dad would start wondering at the time it was taking him and come out looking for him. As frustrating as his dad could be, he hated thinking of the level of stress he'd put him through with not being able to find him. He could imagine it now: his dad's blood pressure going through the roof, his mom's worried tears, his sister's detective mode. Still waters ran deep with that little sister of his, but he didn't want to cause her quiet distress either.

Mind over matter, Brighton, he told himself, borrowing one of his dad's long-used and sometimes irritating phrases. He needed it now. He needed to override his temporary pain and tap into the mental strength that would bring him to the road.

"You can do this. Mind over matter," he said aloud, crawling some more and then leaning against a sturdy tree trunk. He didn't allow himself to rest for long before he repeated the cycle—crawl a little, rest against a tree trunk, take a deep breath, avoid further injuries as much as possible, repeat. "Mind over matter." And finally, "Please help, God."

He looked up at the distance he still had to cross and bit back tears. This was no death sentence. Even if, at worst, he didn't escape from the wooded development before night crashed around him, he would eventually make it to the road. And it was a well-trafficked route. But it was the uncertain allotment of time from now until he reached there that warred with him. He could only muscle himself up so fast. He would forfeit his precision and his placement if he let his bursts of energy take the upper hand. And he didn't want all his efforts to come crashing down on him.

He was working on calm, deliberate placement of his limbs when he heard a rustling in the brush behind him. The kind of rustling that made his blood go cold and not want to look, though he wanted to see what he was up against. The impending footsteps behind him were swift and far too light for a bear's, though there were occasional sightings in the Harbor. He heard sharp intakes of breath and pictured—with dread—a coyote or a rabid guard dog.

Hair standing on end, he turned to face whatever was on to him. If there'd been time to pray, he'd have asked for a dose of courage. But he couldn't manage the entire thought before he instinctively turned and raised his elbow as a shield over his face.

He found himself looking into curious, large, dark blue eyes from about ten feet away. A girl about his age waited beside the tree that had broken his fall and rewarded him with small splinters for daring to touch its trunk. He noted her wide stance, a red coat large for her petite frame. She, having seen and pursued him for a while, looked like she was able to gather her thoughts a lot faster.

"Mind over matter it is," she said pragmatically. Her echo back of his words would have normally riled him, but there was nothing mocking in her tone. She moved closer, her fluidity as natural as water flowing. She was at his shoulder before he could utter a word about it being slick up the hill and deceptively harder than it looked.

"You're doing well, my friend, but you shouldn't have to go it alone," she said, her voice a few tones brassier than he would have expected for a girl of her small stature. Stronger too.

"H-how long have you been here, and where did you come from?" he asked, trying to size her up. He half wondered if he'd also struck his head when he so painfully clashed against the tree. He hadn't caught a glimpse of her when he'd run down from the main road, and it seemed unlikely that she, with her red coat, would have appeared out of nowhere.

Was he losing his mind, or had God sent an angel from heaven to intercede on his behalf? He'd met several people who insisted that their interaction with strangers must have been angels in disguise. Maybe she was no different.

"What the hell," she muttered, scanning the inner contents of her satchel for heaven knew what.

Possibly not an angel, Jared thought wryly, assuming that the heavenly host didn't slip up in their language with near the same frequency as mortals like himself.

She raised her chin and smiled. "I could have sworn I had a bandage in here somewhere. My dad ... he insists that I travel with a first-aid kit no matter how close I am to our house." She laughed and peered over her shoulder, motioning to the light green house in the background. "Ah, here it is," she said, drawing out the brown bandage and settling it gently in his hands. "Perhaps it's not such a bad idea to carry this stuff every day." She laughed to herself. "The calamine lotion helped after I walked straight into a beehive. And when I fell off my bike and landed in a bunch of poison oak. And now ... this wrapping is meant for you."

"Thanks," he said, grateful that she'd appeared out of seemingly nowhere to lend him a hand. He felt far less alone now that she was beside him, first-aid kit at the ready. "So you live in that green house over there."

She smiled, repeating his words back to him. "I live in that green house over there. I just so happened to be working on my fort to your right away back ... right where those huckleberry bushes are ... when I heard you take a tumble and came over to see who was on our property. I figured you hurt yourself from the sound of that clatter."

Jared felt himself redden. His lips twitched. He wanted to interrupt her narrative and insist that she'd heard it all wrong—he may have had to break his fall forcefully, but he hadn't collapsed near the tree. It wasn't like that at all. But he swallowed his pride. It didn't matter if she thought he'd taken a desperate tumble down a hill he had no business to be on in the first place. What he truly needed in this moment was her help out of this situation.

He brushed some wayward dirt from his sleeves and planted himself on the slanted ground.

"I s'pose I did hurt myself a little." He peeled his sock down and began to wrap his swollen ankle with the bandage she'd given him. "Thanks for coming to my rescue." He glanced up at her again and began to actually look at her, now that his heart had stopped hammering.

Her dark hair fell around her shoulders like a curtain. There was a dusting of freckles on her nose and cheeks. Her eyes held an adventurous spark. She was beautiful. How was it that he'd never seen her walking down the halls at school? He kept to himself often, nose buried in his studies, but he would have noticed her. The scarlet coat was one he'd never seen before. He was certain of that.

"So I'm going to help you get to the house," she said, looking over her shoulder at him. "But are you going to tell me what you're doing in our neck of the woods?"

Moving beyond humiliation and awash again with the urgency of making it back to the road, Jared pointed up the hill. "I need you to help me make it up there instead."

Sensing that she wouldn't be so inclined to offer further support without a hint of explanation he continued, "I got in a fight with my dad and decided to walk home from school. Didn't want to be pestered by my teammates and thought if I came down here for a minute, all the cars would leave the parking lot and guys would stop offering me a ride." He stammered. "It was a mistake, as you can see. But if you're going to help me, I need your assistance going up, not all the way over to your house."

She crossed her arms over her chest firmly and shook her head, a dash of stubbornness knit across her brow. "If your dad and your teammates have all driven off, what sense does it make to go back up there? It will take longer to walk back to the school than it ever would to walk over to my house. And don't tell me you have any plans to hitch a ride from a stranger. Because that's the stupidest way to end an already lousy day. Even in Gig Harbor."

He swallowed hard. What could he say to that? He felt she was a chess player, already anticipating his next three moves. "What's your dad gonna say to your outdoor adventures when you come back to the house with a strange boy?"

Now was her time to color. He noticed her cheeks tinge with a brush of berry and felt his heart quicken. Man, she was stunning. Why was he thinking this *now*?!

"He might not like it at first, but he'll listen and let you use the phone," she said, reaching for his cold-to-the-touch fingers and directing him toward the opposite direction from where he had headed. "Here. Take my shoulder," she said, swinging her satchel to the opposite side. "You want to move quickly, don't you? I know the fastest route back to the house. Trust me on this. It's far better than going back to the road."

Jared so wanted to believe her. She'd come through for him already simply by being at the right place at the right time and having the wrap that he needed for his busted ankle. If only it were so easy to cast out the image of his dad driving back down the road, eyes trained toward both sides of the street in search of his son.

What sense was there in reaching the green house and requesting the use of a phone when there might not be anyone home to answer it? He closed his eyes for only a second. One of his parents—most likely his mother—would surely stay home.

"I'm Greta," she said, interrupting his thoughts and offering him something he'd want to remember. "In case you're wondering, I'm a sophomore, but I only take some of my classes at the school. What's your name?"

"Jared Brighton," he said, glad his voice didn't crack like it did when he was twelve. "I'm a sophomore at Peninsula too, but I take all the ordinary classes." He winked and she laughed, a hint of embarrassment deepening the berry of her cheeks. "I used to play basketball, but it looks like I might only be able to paint for a while after this."

She paused and he gave her arm a momentary break, though she drew him back to her shoulder. "You're an artist . . . ." she said, interest coloring her tone. "Not so ordinary after all."

·⟨↔⟩·

The Christmas music played at a low thrum in the car as Scott searched for his son. He forgot that it was still on. Yet another background chorus that didn't fit the moment. There were limited roads between the school and their house, so it wouldn't take him long to track Jared down if he was still out here. Where else could his son have gone in such a short amount of time?

Jared had tossed his backpack and gym bag on the back seat, so it was unlikely he had much money on him. Before Scott left the house, Charlotte had phoned his parents and nonchalantly asked if Jared stopped by. Not wanting them to worry, she'd kept her voice upbeat and said he must have gone out with his friends for a root beer float.

By the time he made it to the near empty, darkened Peninsula High parking lot, Scott had to collect his breath. He'd taken the road slowly, and he hadn't seen a kid in a sweatshirt and sweats on the shoulder of the road anywhere. Jared might have been hotheaded when he'd jumped out of the car and told him he was walking home, but his temper wouldn't have held for over an hour and a half.

Since he had been a little boy, Jared both ignited and simmered down quickly. Scott had to continually remind himself that his son wasn't a missing four-year-old; he was almost sixteen. Whatever reason there was for his not being home yet would shortly be explained.

Scott rested his head on his steering wheel and thought about what his next course of action should entail. There was a dull ache in his head and he prayed against the splintering that sometimes followed when he felt overwhelmed. Before he could plot his next point, he heard a rapping on the passenger window. He tried not to startle too much as he raised his head.

He found himself looking into the eyes of his old teammate, Randy Clauson. They'd run into each other briefly at Spiro's Pizza a few weeks ago and talked business in those few moments. Randy had been nothing but gracious—as was his gentle way even back in high school, but Scott couldn't help but wonder if Randy still thought negatively of him for getting involved with the wrong crowd when they were seventeen.

Randy was good-natured even back then, but refused any invitation to cheat on a test. He'd done alright in chemistry. And he sure as heck made it clear he wasn't about to get caught in the mix of any retaliation scheme that Bobby orchestrated. His mother had kept him under lock and key after hours back when they were young. Plus, there wasn't a mean bone in his body. Scott could see the wisdom in the guy now that they were this many years removed from the fact.

Snapped back to the present moment, Scott saw Randy's son was standing shoulder to shoulder with his father outside the window. Randy's son wore a green football jersey and could have been Randy, but for the shorter hair in place of the afro his father wore back in the day. Scott would have said something about the uncanny likeness were his own son not out there in the dark somewhere.

Scott hadn't thought he'd enlist anyone's help in the effort to find Jared, but Randy stood in front of him, his expression quickly growing to one of question and concern.

"Hi Randy," Scott said before he'd even finished rolling the window down. "My son said he was going to walk home. It's about five miles to our house. I waited more than an hour and a half and he hasn't shown. That's not like Jared at all. He's pretty fast."

Randy took this in, nodding all the while and laying a hand on his son's shoulder. "We'll help you find him," he said, already locating the car key on the chain in his hands. He asked Scott where he lived and said, "We'll scan the area front and back and if we don't see him, we'll start knocking on a few doors."

Scott was about to protest, tell them Jared wasn't the sort of kid that would take a detour and introduce himself to the neighbors in the woods, but Randy was on to his next strategy before Scott could point that out. "I have the team roster in my glove compartment since I'm working with the Athletic part time department this year." Randy said, "What we'll do is scan the names of streets and see if there are any students Jared might know living in the area."

Scott ran a hand through his overgrown hair, thinking of the time that could take. Any remaining light was diminishing fast and even if Randy's idea was time consuming, what were the alternatives? If for some reason Jared had been convinced to stop in at a teammate's house, Scott had better start looking for him now.

As if reading his thoughts, Randy leaned down toward the window and said, "There aren't as many neighborhoods in a five-mile radius as you might think. Marcus and I will drive around the area and look for him. Why don't you stop in at your house and find out if anyone's heard anything? If not, let's meet back on school premises and start going through the team roster to find out if anyone lives nearby."

Scott was heartened that cool, practical Randy was here to help him out, but he braced himself for regret if he made it the five miles to their house to find there was still no sign of his son. He anticipated the deep pools of Charlotte's eyes as she reckoned with the fact that it was because of him Jared was out there in the Harbor somewhere—missing.

25

Green House in the Woods

*I*t took concerted effort for Jared Brighton to push back his apprehension in order to enter the front door of the green house. Greta had graciously lent him her shoulder, and yet she was so slight, he'd hesitated to put any pressure on her. He'd ended up putting far too much weight on his injured foot but was at least grateful it was wrapped. This was the type of injury that needed inspection, possibly even x-rays. He didn't need a doctor's eyes to know that. He was probably out for the rest of the season, but he couldn't let that disappointment trouble him now. First things first—he needed to get to a phone.

Greta opened the front door with urgency, and they stepped into a room with a beautifully vaulted ceiling. The scent of warm cinnamon and apple swept over him. He could see the family's Christmas tree from the entrance and was struck by the beauty of it, the strings of white lights and carefully placed glass ornaments in purples and blues he wouldn't necessarily associate with Christmastime. Somehow it worked and he knew his mom would love it. She was always looking for fresh and innovative concepts for her little boutique in the Harbor. Greta gestured toward a bench inside the entrance. He seated himself and tried not to wince too much at the persistent pain in his ankle as he removed his sneakers and set them to the side. The sound of younger children laughing upstairs interrupted Jared's attempts to mask his pain, and he glanced around the entrance where several cast-off backpacks and pairs of boots and sneakers signaled an active family life.

As if reading his thoughts, Greta leaned closer to him. "My parents thought I'd be an only child, but my twin brother and sister were born six years later. They keep life . . . vibrant. At least they're laughing right now. They're just as likely to be at each other's necks, which is why I don't let them build forts with me as often as they'd like." She rolled her eyes.

Jared smiled slightly, wishing he could he enjoy this unexpected introduction to Greta and her family more. "Should you tell your parents I'm here?" he asked nervously, thinking that it might take her father aback if he were to enter the room and see Greta so close to a boy she'd never mentioned before.

Greta reached out her hand, which Jared took in spite of his nervousness about her parents' first impressions. Unfazed, she kept talking as she guided Jared to a comfortable blue chair in the living room. "My mom's probably the only one home right now, but I'll let her know you're here. You don't have to look so worried, Jared." She smiled, and it made something stir within him. "They're not the sort of parents that easily startle at a guest . . . even a boy."

He bit down on his lip and scanned the beautifully outfitted living room for a phone. He couldn't help but be impressed by the built-in bookshelves filled with hardbound classics and the matching coffee and side tables boasting crystal lamps.

A painting of a young woman from the early nineteenth century occupied one wall. She stood before white foam waves. It fascinated him and he suddenly felt more interested in this family's artistic leanings than calling home. But he pulled his eyes away and located the phone on a side table far across the room. He swallowed mild irritation, not wanting to feel anything but gratitude toward this sweet girl who had stopped working on her fort to help him. Why wasn't she getting him to a telephone faster?

She drew a hand to her forehead. "I didn't sit you close to the phone. I'm sorry. I just saw the most comfortable chair in the living room and thought you should have it."

He shook his head, already in the midst of rising to his feet and steadying his uncertain footsteps. "That's all right," he said, any twinge of annoyance evaporated. "I got it."

He reached for the phone, started wending his fingers around the numbers and waited for someone in his household to answer his call.

His mother answered on the first ring. He easily detected the hum of anxiety in her hello. So much for her getting more Christmas orders knocked out today from the quiet of their home, as she'd intended.

"Mom," he said quickly, seeking to put her at ease. "It's me. I . . . I'm sorry I'm not home yet. I actually sprained my ankle in the woods, and I'm at a house close to the school . . . ."

"Oh, thank God," she said before he could even give an address. She sounded mildly concerned about his father being out there and having no way to deliver the message that he was found, but said she'd drive around, see if she could track down his dad now, and then come to his aid.

"Mom, I'll be fine. I'm . . . I'm safe . . . . I met this girl that helped me in the woods. She brought me to her house, and from the looks of it, her family is normal." He tossed Greta a playful smirk as if he'd known her much longer than the past hour. "In fact, you'd love their Christmas tree. You should talk to her mom." He stopped talking as soon as he saw an older, darker haired version of Greta enter the room. Her deep brown eyes were questioning, but also welcoming. She was dressed in dark-wash jeans, a peasant style blouse, and wore dangling earrings the shade of dark water. Her hair was tossed in a messy bun at the top of her head, but she looked bohemian beautiful. Effortlessly so.

"Mom," Greta said, walking across the room to stand at her mother's shoulder. "This is my new friend, Jared. I ... we met in the woods, and he was hobbling around on a hurt ankle. I brought him here so he could call his parents ...."

Jared's face flamed red. "I'm sorry for trespassing. I didn't realize this was your property, and I was trying to take an alternate route home." He cleared his throat and tried to shake off this new burst of humiliation. "It won't happen again."

Greta's mom smiled, no hint of wariness across her features. "I'm glad my daughter found you and brought you here, Jared. Is there anything I can get for you? Some chamomile tea or some hot chocolate, perhaps?"

He couldn't help but laugh to himself. What was it with the offer of hot chocolate this afternoon? Figuring maybe he was meant to have it, he concealed his amusement and said, "I'll take some hot chocolate, please. Thank you."

She turned promptly toward the kitchen, and Greta met his curious gaze. "She's gone a lot working in Seattle, but I love when she's home."

Before he took his first sip of hot cocoa, the front door opened again, and a warm tenor voice filled the house. "Family ... I'm ho—me!" the man sang out, eliciting a response from the upper echelons of the house.

Energized feet paced down the stairs. High-pitched laughter and delighted squeals touched the rafters and Greta rolled her eyes though she ended up smiling. "It's like this every day for the twins when Dad comes home from work."

Jared smiled, though he couldn't stop from thinking how her dad would react to seeing him sitting in his living room once he settled in. He was grateful when Greta's mother fled to meet her father, presumably to break the news that they had a visitor.

By the time Greta's father materialized beneath the door frame, he wore a warm smile that made his eyes crinkle in the corners. His arms were crossed over his oxford sweater, and he looked quite the professor with a high-quality pen still behind his ear. "Welcome," he said, offering his right hand. "I'm glad Greta here was prepared to help you out there. I'm sorry you got hurt. Did I hear that your name is Jared?"

·❦·

The half hour that Scott spent driving around the back roads of the Harbor seemed to last forever. He was heartened that Randy was so committed to helping track down his son, motioning him over to the side of the road every few minutes, to discuss possible students' homes where Jared might have ended up. Yet it was hard to keep his quiet desperation at bay. There was a chill in the air that hinted at impending snow.

What if Jared had been overwhelmed and lost his sense of direction? The roads out here were long, meandering, and darkened without the benefit of a lamplight's glow. What's more, they went on for miles without stores or gas stations in sight. His son was more likely to forge his own way home than knock on a stranger's door to admit he was lost. Unless they came across a teammate Jared regularly mentioned on the list, it wasn't likely he'd gone to any of these houses.

Headlights came toward him in the dark and Scott braced himself. There hadn't been many drivers out on the road. Coming a little closer, he could see the maroon Honda was Charlotte's. He paused on the road and began to roll down his window. While he thought it highly improbable that their fifteen-year-old son had been kidnapped or fallen off a ledge somewhere, he was bereft of answers, and he hated to admit as much to his wife.

She rolled down her window. "Scott ... Scott ... Jared called me, and I know where he is. He took a fall, but he's alright. Ankle's twisted is all."

Scott felt as if his heart would burst at the welcome news. Relief flooded him, and yet he knew he looked worse for wear. Dark circles under his eyes, scruffy hair, desperation moving across his features.

She paused long enough to assess him. "He's alright," she said. "Mostly just going through that angsty teenage stage that used to get the best of us sometimes." She rolled her eyes heavenward before looking back to him. "Since it appears you have help," she gestured over her shoulder where Randy and his son sat in their vehicle waiting for the next word, "I'll go on home and wait with Sadie." She waved in Randy's direction and handed Scott a torn sheet with the address and directions.

"Hey, you're still mad at me," Scott said, having taken note of her curt manner with him since she'd paused to give him this update.

"Yeah, I s'pose I still am," she said, tapping a hand to the steering wheel. "I don't think I will be for long, though." She summoned a half smile at him, and Scott tucked that assurance away, that they would make it through this night just fine.

She turned around and headed for home, and Scott hopped out of his car to tell Randy and his son that he had an address for Jared. Randy brightened immediately. "I'm glad he's safe. I wouldn't like not knowing where this guy was either," he said, turning to his son before offering Scott an empathetic smile.

Scott chuckled and thanked him once more and waved as Randy drove off into the night. He might not want to admit it, but he still envied Randy's resistance to Bobby's whim those many years ago. How it must have saved him on regret if he'd followed suit. At least some people got it right, he thought, wondering what life must be like for someone who'd said no to Bobby. As it was, he couldn't imagine life without that shadow hovering, muting treasured moments and making them gray.

Less than five minutes later, Scott found himself parked before a beauty of a green house. The driveway which led to it was long and meandering, and the canopy of trees over him immense as he pulled up to the number scrawled on the piece of notebook paper. So eager was he to reach Jared that Scott didn't pause to glance in the mirror to smooth out his hair or review his first words—*Hello. My name is Scott Brighton, and I'm here to pick up my son, Jared. Thank you for taking good care of him*—or something to that effect.

He had no pretense left to offer. No effort at a first impression to cast forward. He still felt the pang at not knowing where his disgruntled son had gone and the powerlessness of having to guess where to search first. So he peeled back the screen and rapped his knuckles against the front door. His knock had enough force to shake a few stray sprigs from the holly wreath hanging above him.

Before he could reach down to pick those sprigs up and nonchalantly tuck a strand or two back in the greenery, the door began to open. He'd already walked himself through what he would say, but no words made it past his mouth.

Elli Grayson stood in the doorway. More than twenty years may have passed with all their seasons—she might have a few lines at the corners of her dusky eyes, a strand of gray woven into her equally dark hair—but she was so much the same that he caught his breath and tried hard not to show it. Was she ever beautiful.

Her ready smile left her face and her eyes went a little dull, actress though she was. This wasn't the stage, and the honesty of the moment swept over her features.

"Elli," he said, his voice resigned. Out of all the homes in the world, *this* was where his son would end up.

Before she could utter a word, her daughter surfaced at the door, at the back of her shoulder. His surprise showed as he took her in: a near replica of her mother, but for the dusting of freckles over her nose and cheeks, a lighter shade of eyes, and an absence of glasses. "Oh, hi. I'll tell Jared his dad is here," she said, throwing Scott a curious expression before turning to leave the room.

Scott clasped his hands closely at his sides and felt his heart rise to his throat. He never should have returned to the Harbor. Should have known that he wouldn't be able to shed the past that haunted him. Should have known his very presence here would re-traumatize the people he'd hurt. He should have heeded his inner hesitation, but he'd fooled himself into the belief that it was ancient history and that the past wouldn't come back to bite him. But what could he do now? The adrenaline coursing through his veins told him to leave and yet, he couldn't. His son was waiting inside, and he was the entire reason he was standing here.

"Thank you for taking him in," Scott said softly, glad when his voice didn't come through as weak as he felt. "I got the call from my wife that Jared hurt his ankle and that a family helped him to safety. I didn't know it was . . . you. Thank you, Elli."

Her name sounded foreign on his tongue. He hadn't spoken it in so long.

"It was my daughter that helped him," Elli said, folding her arms across her chest. Her features settled into seriousness, and she maintained her stance at the door, not an inch closer to having him cross the threshold.

Small wisps of white were starting to fall from the sky, drifting into his hair, brushing across his cheeks as he stood awkwardly on her front porch. Perhaps realizing that she sounded harsh she explained. "My daughter has a fort in the woods, and she found him first since she was outside working in it for a few hours this afternoon."

Scott nodded. "I'm really grateful."

Elli looked at him, her expression still somber. "I don't know why I didn't see it before. He looks like you." Just when he thought there was a hint of tenderness there, she spoke again. "Wait a minute, and I'll get your son." She edged the door all the way closed. Scott's eyes smarted at the needles dropping from the Christmas wreath. It no longer served as a welcome.

26

A Strange Reunion

*T*wo minutes passed, and Scott still stood on the front porch, where Elli had left him. He supposed he could settle back in the car, let the heat warm him instead of feeling like an imposter here. But he continued to stand outside the Sander's house, indifferent to the first drops of snow falling on his head.

The door opened again before he could gather his thoughts. He expected to see his son hobbling out to meet him and was surprised to find Elli for a second time. Her eyes were still undecipherable, but her voice had lost some of its edge. "I'd rather you come in and wait for your son."

He paused, about to tell her that standing on her front porch was fine. But who was he to refuse her offer to come in from the cold? He couldn't stake a claim that high school history took away his right to be there. Just how many years had passed since he'd held her in his arms and lost himself in her kiss? It had come to such an abrupt end with her that it might not have happened at all. He remembered the catch in her throat after asking why he'd cheated on his chemistry test and how agonizing it had been to break away from her. She'd severed her tie to him when she'd found what he was made of and it had taken so long for the dull ache of it to go away.

The role he'd played in that whole debacle was no mystery to her. Still she'd held the door open to him and told him to come inside. If the circumstances were lighter, he might have laughed at this turn of events.

And yet, as he followed Elli in, there was a question that stuck on his tongue—*would Jesse want me here?* It didn't make it past his lips. They were all middle-aged now and if anyone was Jesse's gatekeeper, it was Elli. Why was he imagining he even had significance in their lives? He was there only as a father picking up his teenage son.

"It was kind of your daughter to help Jared out," Scott told Elli as soon as he crossed the threshold. Humbled with the new turn in this parenting gig, he was tempted to unpack it all—how he'd had a standoff with his son in the school parking lot, how he'd thought Jared was running most of the way home, how he'd started to really worry after about an hour and a half when his son was nowhere in sight. But he kept it back.

"He wanted to walk home today, and I don't know why he veered from the main road. We live about five miles from here."

Elli turned to look at him over her shoulder. "He's what, fifteen, sixteen? Kids like to wander at that age. Don't you remember?" She granted him a wry smile. "Why don't you take a seat for a moment?" She gestured toward the wooden bench at the entrance. Beside it there were discarded coats, mittens, several backpacks, shoes. He glanced his son's sneakers among the pile. "They're all out in the kitchen, making small talk. Or deep conversation, is more like it. Seems your son shares some common interests with Jesse."

Scott felt the hairs on the back of his neck stand on end. It wasn't his overactive imagination spinning story lines; had the two of them been peers, his son and Jesse would have made good lab partners. They might have even been friends. Their quiet spirits and their introspective minds were stunningly alike. He took his seat on the bench, clasped his hands together, and waited with an internal plea that this unexpected reunion with Jesse Sander wouldn't evoke too much discord within either of them.

He heard young kids laughing upstairs, dashing down the hallway from one room to the next. The tick of the oven timer. The kitchen radio playing the "Dance of the Sugar Plum Fairies." It never grew old, only more endearing with time. Then he heard the low voices in the living room interrupted by the whispered tones of Elli, and he braced himself for the exchanges that would follow next—perhaps a terse reception from his son, followed by a regrettable exchange with Jesse. He ground down on his teeth, hoping that wouldn't be the case.

Slowly his eyes traveled to the cream-colored walls behind him, across the beautiful family pictures that lined the walls. Jesse. Elli. Their three children through the years. They were proof that high school perspective had its limits; no one would have suspected that the two kids who'd hung out in the science lab could have created such a picturesque life together.

Jesse stepped into the room, alone. He still wore his work clothing—an Oxford sweater rolled up to his elbows, khaki pants, a large white gold watch on his right wrist. He looked as if he'd recently had a haircut. He wore frames that made him look far more GQ than nerdy.

Before Jesse could reach him, Scott instinctively stood to his feet and prepared to extend his hand. Jesse reached out his hand first and wore a faint, if uncertain, smile.

"Hi Scott," he said, maintaining his close-lipped smile as they greeted one another. "I enjoyed talking with your son," he said. "Smart kid. It's a bummer that he twisted his ankle."

Scott laughed nervously. "Well, he shouldn't have been on your property. Should have stuck to the main road." He didn't mean to berate his son, but he couldn't dance around truths, big or small, with Jesse of all people. He'd always felt the guy had the ability to see right through him.

Jesse smiled politely. Scott was distinctly aware that he was on Jesse's turf, not his own, and that the beautiful design of the home was due to the rare talent of the kid he'd once looked down on for being different, not enough, less than.

"So how does it feel being back in the Harbor?" Jesse asked, a gracious attempt at conversation.

Scott wondered why his son hadn't materialized near the door yet. He clenched and unclenched his hands at his sides. "It's a beautiful place to live, if not a little rainier than my family likes. But no, really, it's good to be back. My father is struggling health-wise, and my mom needed some help around the house—but beyond those reasons, it's a great community."

"It's hard seeing our parents get older, isn't it?" he said, crossing his arms over his chest. "I practically had to write my father a dissertation on why it's no longer necessary for him to blow fir needles off the roof. He's in his early 70's now and active as ever, but there's no good reason for him to be up there."

Scott marveled over how seamlessly Jesse was speaking with him. It was as if they could lock ancient history in an old school supply room and refuse to look over their shoulders. Here they were, two successful men with families roughly the same age and more in common than he could have imagined.

Not so fast, he told his overeager mind, encouraging himself to put on the brakes. Who knew what Jesse might truly be thinking behind the commonplace words?

While Scott was gathering his thoughts, about to ask Jesse what project he and his firm working on, he happened to glance toward the spacious kitchen and saw Jared limp into the room. His son was biting his lower lip and trying to conceal the extent of his injury. His complexion was ruddy and his hair tousled, but Scott could see that his earlier melancholy had lifted—that he seemed far lighter than when the two of them had parted company. It could be due to Jared's inability to maintain his anger, but Scott sensed it might have something to do with the presence of his newfound friend. She walked in just behind him with her mother, equally lovely.

Scott sought his son's eyes. "Hi Jer. Thanks for calling as soon as you could. Your mom and I were worried about you." He motioned toward his son's foot. "We'll have to get that looked at."

Jared said okay in agreement, but his expression was unreadable.

Scott reached out a hand toward Jesse again and said, "Thank you for taking care of him." He turned to Elli, appreciation brimming his eyes and said, "Merry Christmas to you . . . all."

His gaze drifted to the top of the winding staircase where Jesse and Elli's ten-year-old twins—a boy and a girl—watched him, curiosity painting their features.

"Merry Christ—" Elli started to say to him.

Greta broke in— "Oh, we'll be seeing each other before Christmas, you guys! Jared told me he'd come back after school since he can't play basketball anymore. He's going to help me build the fort."

No one in the room spoke—not even the twins on the stairs. Greta looked from one parent to the other. "That's alright, isn't it? You wanted me to find someone my age interested in building . . . ."

Scott was about to interject a gentle refusal—one his son would question to no end. Jesse went over to his daughter and rested a hand on her shoulder. "So far as no further injuries accrue, I don't see why not. You're more than welcome to come back, Jared."

Scott felt his body temperature rise, but what was he to do? Bluntly refuse this kind offer in front of his son who was searching for a hint of acceptance? No, he couldn't rightly interfere. Funny how Jesse had recognized this truth and surrendered any internal resistance for his daughter's happiness. He wasn't dwelling in the worst of high school days. Why was Scott gridlocked there?

So he smiled his assent. "Thank you again."

"Bye, Greta," Jared said, and the two of them, father and son, exited the green house.

Even before he opened the car door, his internal voice filled with regret. *Yet another run-in with Jesse and an apology isn't any closer to your lips.* He frowned, but tried to neutralize his expression in case someone was watching from the window. He had every reason to let gratitude evaporate the fog and weariness. Not only had his son been located, the man who might have had it in for him had treated him with a graciousness he didn't deserve.

·❦·

Jesse startled awake in the early hours of the morning to an eerie dance of winter's branches moving in shadow across the bedroom wall.

"Jess. Are you alright?" Elli asked, reaching for his forearm.

He winced at awakening her. His hair was damp, but thankfully he hadn't sweat through the sheets as he had on occasion, amidst dreams of entrapment.

"Yeah. Yeah. Just another one," he said, his voice flat.

"Let me get you some water," she said, tossing the comforter back and sliding from the bed before he could protest.

He sighed and rested against the headboard.

Most people never noticed his hesitation to examine small spaces or even his reluctance to step on an elevator alone. These triggers didn't derail his life. But his reluctance to lock doors until he was familiar with the mechanism and his apprehension about going somewhere without clearly marked exit signs was something that he'd never shaken. Not even after the strenuous hours spent in therapy where he was encouraged to wrap his arms around himself and repeat aloud, "I am not trapped anymore. I am safe."

He'd handled that exchange with Scott Brighton well enough to feel proud of himself and yet it had cost him something emotionally. He'd told Elli how he'd wanted to respond should they ever encounter any of the guys who'd harmed him years ago. He was proud of her for inviting Scott inside. And yet . . .

Forgiveness was a current. He'd released those three football players from his mental clutch years before. He knew that wishing them vengeance—giving them space in his mind even—would hold him back. But wishing them well and inviting them into his home were two different things. Yet he'd asked Elli to show unexpected kindness, should they ever be placed in such a predicament.

He hadn't liked the hesitation he'd shown Scott upon being recognized at the Christmas party. He wanted to do better. He wanted to acknowledge that twenty-five years had passed and show that he didn't wear the smoke from that fire.

Strange how he could be miles away from the awkward boy he'd once been and still feel his defenses so quickly leave in the presence of his bullies. He had to give himself a larger measure of grace for doing what was right, even when it was hard.

Elli came back with his glass of water and her dark, observant eyes swept over him. "You're kinder than I, Jess," she said, her voice cloaked with sleep. "I wanted to make him wait for his son on the front porch. I almost did."

Jesse smiled and adjusted his pillow. "It's not as if we invited him for a helping of apple pie, El," he said.

Elli propped herself up on one elbow and peered down at her husband. She took his hand up in her own and drew his fingers to her hair. He didn't take for granted that they'd knew they were meant to be after grad school. There was no one who understood, respected or loved him like Elli. He only wished it hadn't taken her so long to realize it. He wished she hadn't rushed into the arms of that actor, married him so quickly, and had his baby all before they'd graduated from college.

But God was kind, bringing them together in their mid-twenties after her failed first marriage. Her first husband had left her for another actress, and he was glad that little Greta took such a shine to him. It also made it easier that her biological father spent so much of his time overseas.

"No, Love. We didn't serve him a piece of pie, but we might as well prepare ourselves for the future probability of that . . . ." Elli said, her voice dry. "Don't tell me you didn't sense the immediate camaraderie between his son and Greta. You heard how Greta invited him back again . . . without hesitation. She doesn't usually warm up like that to her peers, but it doesn't have to go on." She hesitated. He hadn't taken his eyes off the ceiling.

"I'm not going to stop it," Jesse said finally, turning to look at her. "And you don't have to either. I don't like the idea of those two disappearing for hours to work on a fort alone, but if they want to be innovative out there with one or both twins there to assist, let's let them be."

"Are you sure?" Elli asked, the dark curtain of her hair falling close to his lips.

Jesse nodded. "I don't necessarily love that she's met Scott's son, but who am I to stop their friendship from growing?"

Elli nuzzled back into the covers and rested her head on Jesse's shoulder. "You're a stronger man than you realize, Jess. It would be so easy to tell Greta we aren't comfortable with her spending time with him—she'd never have to know the reason. But you're letting her make her own decisions, no matter what went down in the past."

Jesse tried to smile. "He's a nice kid. I could actually see some of myself in him when we were talking there in the living room—but he's not as much of a science nerd."

Elli smiled against his shoulder. "No, but he's not a jock like his father was either. Makes you wonder what life has been like for him."

Jesse placed a hand on her cheek and said, "Probably just fine, El. Scott's not some caricature athlete anymore. Though he still looks the part." He pulled a grin and glanced over at Elli to catch her response, but chided himself for doing so. Her expression barely wavered.

Still, he couldn't help but wonder what had led Jared Brighton to enter right into his woods after practice. There was so much to fathom in the things left unspoken.

27

Winter's Bloom

*H*ere it was: an opportunity to apologize to Jesse Sander staring at him as clear as his reflection in the glass. What more was he waiting for? Losing his son out in the woods and not knowing where or when he would find him should have knocked out all the pretense. But Jared hadn't gone missing for hours on end. He'd been relatively easy to find. And perhaps the lack of desperation had put his self-preservation front and center again.

Besides, what if an apology was the last thing Jesse wanted? The guy was an incredible success. People from all over the world sought out his talent, and he lived here, in the small town of Gig Harbor. What could Jesse want with an apology from a guy who had done nothing to mend his wrongs back when it mattered?

If Scott wasn't meant to offer up those words, however, why did he keep feeling the nudge to say something? Why was he provided with yet another opportunity to connect with Jesse if he wasn't meant to say how sorry he was that he'd been a bully back in high school? In the midst of conference calls at work, and even at the closing of presentations before the board, Scott found his mind tugged and considering his next meeting with Jesse.

"Char." Greta had phoned the house to ask if Jared wanted to help her create some shelving for her fort. Now his ongoing communication with Jesse in some form was inevitable. "Char, I need to talk to you about something."

She surfaced in the kitchen wearing her reading glasses and her blond hair done up in a knot on her head, looking very much the librarian, which he loved. The list in her hand preoccupied her, but she set the paper down on the counter, responding to his serious tone.

"I don't know how to tell you this, but back in high school—my senior year—I . . . I was involved in this stupid revenge plot." He stared at his shoes before raising his head up to meet her cool blue gaze.

He gulped before steadying a hand on the kitchen counter and divulging the rest, every now and then glancing up to see Charlotte absorbing the unsettling story the best she could. The disappointment wrote itself across her face. He'd seen it before, and he hated it so much, but he couldn't stop the disbelief from filling her eyes. Even though it had happened a few years before they met. Even though he recognized his wrongdoing and admitted his shame. Even though he told her it was one of his greatest regrets.

"And all this time, Scott, you never told me about any of it?" Charlotte said when he finished speaking. "As much as it pains me to hear you were such a bully at one time in your life, did you think that I couldn't get past it? That I wouldn't marry you or something because of it? Is that why you never spoke of it?"

"No, no, it's not that at all," he said before falling upon a simple phrase. "I'm sorry." The words made his throat sore. "I wanted to outrun that part of my life."

"Yeah, well, life doesn't work that way," his wife said, the blue in her eyes only deepening in their fury.

He wiped his nose with the back of his sleeve. "I know ... I know that now."

"Is this the misdemeanor you got slapped with in high school?" Charlotte asked, a frown now taking up residence on her face. "I thought it was because you went on that property. Trespassing charges. If I remember correctly, you didn't even steal anything from the place."

"I didn't steal anything," Scott said, his tone emphatic, "but it would have been better if that's what I'd come there to do. I helped kidnap a kid and *left* him there. I planned to return for him, but as I've told you, that never happened."

Charlotte frowned, her dissatisfaction with his past actions evident.

"I didn't give you the full story," Scott said, "and I'm sorry."

"It could have made a difference if you had," she said, bracing her arms across her chest. "I might have been able to encourage you to mend some fences earlier or to stay away entirely if we weren't wanted here. Did you think of that, Scott? Whether we should have come back here? Because I'm sure that what you're about to tell me next is that you've had some run-in with one of these guys you got in trouble with."

"Of course, I've thought of telling you," he said emphatically, before recalling he was at her mercy. He softened his tone. "I'm sorry, Char. Yes, I've thought of it. I guess I thought it was so long ago and that it wouldn't really matter if ...."

Charlotte shook her head and nearly laughed through her frustration. "You forget we've been married almost twenty years. You can't fool me. You've always told our kids that *everything* they do matters. That every action has a consequence." She chewed on the inside of her cheek. "How could they slap that poor boy who's in the wheelchair the rest of his life with a misdemeanor? Weren't his real-life consequences hard enough?"

Scott shoved back a curl that was falling in his face. "Jesse's dad demanded justice for his son, as he should have done. Deputy Morgan sat down with Ty Parsons and me and our parents. Not the most glorious moment. We had to come clean about the rest to our folks. I've never seen my father so disappointed in me . . . ." He looked at the kitchen floor. "Sometimes I don't know if he's recovered from that moment. So Ty and I . . . we took the fall for the rest of it. We begged and pleaded with that deputy to leave Bobby Minter alone, and he did. I could see he hated giving us a penalty when it had all spiraled so far out of control."

"Well, that misdemeanor's been wiped from your record for years now! What did they even have you do—community service around town?"

Scott nodded, his jaw muscles working. "Picking up garbage and meeting with a guidance counselor for the next few months. But that wasn't the painful part. Not after what we'd already been through."

"But there's a reason you're telling me this now," Charlotte said, taking a step closer to him.

His ruffled his hair. "Yes." He paused. "Jared ended up at the house of the guy we bullied. Jesse . . . his name is Jesse. And his wife, Elli. I . . . went to high school with her too."

"Jared is hanging out with their *daughter*? Oh, Scott, that's not good. You have to put a stop to this! It's too close. It's only asking for—"

Scott was already shaking his head, which he saw exasperated her. "I can't ask him to do that."

"No," she corrected him, "you *won't* ask."

"I won't . . . since he and Greta haven't done anything wrong."

"What if one of them develops feelings for the other and the other doesn't, and it turns into an emotional upheaval? We don't need that . . . ."

Scott leaned forward and pressed his elbows on the white-tiled island between them. "I've thought about the potential of all these scenarios . . . and I still don't feel l should get in the way," he said frankly. "Believe me. If I didn't have this strong conviction to leave it alone, I'd tell Jared to leave it . . . but I don't think it's right for me to interfere because of my mistakes."

Charlotte leaned across the island toward him. "Do you think you might tell him about your and Jesse's history? In case it gets brought up?"

Scott turned his head toward her and said, "I don't think so. No. Either one of them . . . Jared or Greta might ask if Jesse and knew each other back in the day. I'll tell them we were in a few classes together but didn't run in the same circles. I don't know what Jesse would say, but it would surprise me if he wanted to revisit the past. If he does, we'll cross that bridge when we come to it."

Charlotte lifted her chin. She didn't look convinced or satisfied, but she let it go. "Then we'll let the teenagers be, Scott." Then a moment later: "I still can't believe you didn't tell me the whole story. As if it wouldn't come out in the end."

She was scrubbing at a spot on the counter with a dish towel. She looked up at him suddenly. "What became of Bobby Minter?"

Scott straightened his shoulders and pondered his words before speaking. "I've heard a few things here and there, Char. We . . . we haven't spoken in so many years. I guess you could say our lives drifted apart."

He watched the light leave Charlotte's eyes, but didn't want to ask her why this mattered to her. Then he'd have to think of an explanation for why keeping up with Bobby hadn't mattered enough to him.

·✦·

"I'm dedicated, but not *this* dedicated," Greta laughed as the rain started pelting down like arrows on their skin. No amount of tree coverage could protect them from the winter shower.

Jared chuckled. He glanced around her meticulous fort, impressed that she spent time out here when the weather changed. "Me either," he said, motioning his still-injured foot. He'd recently replaced his crutches for a boot, and it made getting around less strenuous.

"Let's go inside," she said, arm reaching out to help him up.

They were on Christmas vacation and had abandoned their textbooks during their two weeks off. There were plenty of other ways to spend their time: trying their hand at ceramics (under the guise that the mugs were intended for the fort), cooking experiments (sampling dense blueberry muffins that might keep their stomachs full when they could once again go outside), and refurbishing used furniture (also for their outdoor hangout).

Jared thought ahead for these ventures, strategically planning what supplies they would need and asking one of his parents to drive him to the grocery store ahead of time.

"You really like that Sander girl, don't you?" his father remarked, when he asked to visit Greta for the third time in a week.

"You mean Greta," Jared said, delaying an answer to his father's pointed question. But when his dad simply nodded and glanced over at him, Jared said, "She's fun to be around. She doesn't care what people think of her like some of the other girls do."

Thus far, all their time together was spent at her house and not his, mainly because of their central focus on the fort. But also, Jared sensed, because her mom was protective and preferred for Greta to stay close to home. She was only a sophomore and more insulated from the world's edges than so many students their age.

She wouldn't know the first thing about lighting a cigarette or having an acquired taste for liquor. Her earthiness was evident in her knowledge of the outdoors, her ability to ignite a fire on her own, or create a meal with few ingredients.

Jared couldn't help but notice his father's intake of breath whenever they got closer to the Sander's green house. More than once, his dad turned down the radio, tightened his grip on the wheel, and came to an abrupt stop in conversation as they approached. Though Jared found this shift in his dad's demeanor curious, he filed it away, too excited to jump out the car and spend time with Greta. It was probably work pressure getting to him again, Jared assumed.

The ten-year-old twins, Owen and Nora, warmed up to Jared quickly. They wanted to take part in whatever he and Greta were working on, though Greta told them they needed to focus on their own art projects. Greta's mother approved of him—at least she offered him baked goods a whole lot. Even her dad didn't seem to mind when he stayed for dinner.

Still, Jared determined to get his license as soon as possible so he wasn't relying on his parents for transportation. It made him feel far too juvenile, asking them for drop-offs and pick-ups because of his crutches. If it weren't for his ankle, he'd make the trek to her place on his own.

"So when should I pick you up this time?" Jared's father asked him as soon as the tires stopped on the asphalt in the Sander's horseshoe driveway. Though late afternoon was still fading, the white lights already beckoned from the eaves of the home, a stunning contrast to the periwinkle blue and lavender sky of the early evening.

"I'd say eight-thirty or nine," Jared said, quickly escaping the passenger seat and looking at his father from the still-open door. "They've invited me to stay for dinner tonight, and sometimes it takes a while to serve dessert." When his father didn't say anything, Jared added, "It's the best part."

His father gradually relented. "Especially this time of year, no doubt." He patted his stomach, though there was no discernible layer of fat there. For all his chiding about the aches and pains of middle age, Scott Brighton wasn't one who had softened like a lot of the dads, reminiscing about their football and baseball stints some twenty-five years before.

Jared let out a laugh, "Seems I won't have to worry about putting on the pounds if I take after you. The twins are perfecting a death-by-chocolate cake," he said. "Last time it was delicious, but a little on the dry side, so they are attempting it again."

By the time Jared finished explaining, his father had lost both his interest and his smile. Jared didn't have much time to ponder his response, as the front door opened, and Greta's mom ushered him in. She made him think of a no-nonsense professor tonight, even in her simple dark-wash blue jeans and crisp, tailored white shirt. A wave toward his father was brief and direct.

She greeted Jared, on the other hand, with a wide smile and a motion to come forward. It was starkly different from that wave and he wondered if it was only because he was a kid. Somehow, he didn't think so. Mrs. Sander was unapologetically herself in all the occasions he'd interacted with her. Though quick-witted and intelligent, she wasn't given to stiff manners in front of her husband or her children. She was keen on licking the cookie dough straight from the bowl, dancing full-hearted whenever a song came on the radio that she took a liking to, and she'd kissed the family dog unabashedly on the nose.

A question occurred to him that he didn't ask out loud: *Dad, how well did you know Greta's mom in the day? How about Greta's dad?* His dad's energy bottled up when in their presence. Perhaps he'd ask him later tonight if he remembered.

The Sanders were the most welcoming people, and he couldn't wait to enter their home each time he arrived. They didn't treat him like the kid who'd stumbled—trespassed, really—on their property. How quickly he'd turned into a welcome guest without doing a thing. The beauty of it was that he was simply himself.

·❦·

After dropping his son off at the Sander's that early evening just before Christmas, Scott determined that he would reach out to Jesse and ask if the architect had any interest in meeting with him. He wouldn't lead with a heavy apology, but he'd mention his regrets about the past, in spite of how awkward it might be. He *was* sorry, and the unspoken words were eating him up. Presumably Jesse felt this too. Now that their kids were spending so much time together, it was far better to wade through the discomfort rather than act like he wasn't treading murky waters.

If his apology fell flat and Jesse let it bounce off of him like nothing had ever happened, he could at least live with that outcome. He could rest, knowing he'd tried to do what was right. But there was no moving past what wasn't acknowledged.

When he got home, Sadie rushed out of the kitchen and handed him a napkin with a warm peanut butter cookie, a Hershey's Kiss pressed in the middle. She dusted her hands off on an apron that read "Pike Place Market" and beamed at him, waiting for his response to his favorite treat.

"Mom and I just made two more batches," she said, smiling. "And we're gonna make two more, but don't worry—he said one batch is going to your office and another is going to the shop."

He took the napkin from her hand, not wanting to crush the still-warm cookie and said, "These look delicious. In fact, I know they are. My girls are incapable of making anything less than the best." His response seemed to satisfy her, because she turned with a flourish back toward the kitchen where the beaters were humming, the air teased with sugar and Bing Crosby singing "White Christmas."

Meanwhile, Scott shuffled into the home office he and Charlotte shared. Not as much attention had gone to this room as the others, but there were framed seascapes of the Oregon coast on the walls. He cleared off a small pile of bills resting across the keyboard, set down the napkin, and opened his email. He started a new message to Jesse titled "Meeting Up," and without further hesitation, got to typing.

> *... I should have reached out before, but now that our kids are spending time together, I wanted to ask if we could meet up for a conversation. Despite the passing of time, I have deep regrets for how I behaved in high school and wish I could change it all. I'd appreciate the opportunity to talk with you about putting the past to rest and moving forward for the sake of our kids ....*

In his message, he gave Jesse an out, but suggested that the meeting could transpire at the Sander's house, at a local coffee shop like Austin Chase, or anywhere that Jesse preferred. Before he could talk himself out of it, he hit send and sat back in the leather swivel chair. Some might suggest that there was no ounce of courage in sending an email twenty-five years after the fact, when his back was almost against a wall. But for whatever reason, Scott felt led to compose it. He didn't want to catch Jesse unawares or put him on the defense over a phone call, forced to answer in real time and not in the manner Jesse wanted. And he welcomed the dose of relief that came after it was done. No matter how late or how clumsily, he would bend his heart toward what was right. Let the pieces fall how they may. Any control he'd ever thought he had in this was only an illusion.

·❦·

Hours later, Scott stood hesitating at the Sander's door. He shut his eyes tight and tried to collect himself. He didn't know why he hadn't waited until *after* he'd picked Jared up to send that email. Jesse might not check his messages after work hours, but he'd set himself up for uncertainty when they met again.

What was he to say if Jesse was the one who answered the front door? Would he be able to see it in Jesse's eyes if he'd received his message and how he felt about it? Should Scott act as if he'd never said anything at all? Since the unknowns were enough to make his head spin, he decided he'd say nothing of the message unless Jesse brought it up.

Scott drew his fist up to the door, half wishing he'd told Jared to watch for his headlights through the window. An unfamiliar green Ford Bronco in the driveway was reflected there. He found it curious, but perhaps it belonged to Jesse or Elli and spent most of its time in the garage. The Christmas wreath on the front door beckoned to him as he waited, no longer a taunt.

Jesse came to the door, a polite smile on his face. His light blue work shirt was untucked from his khaki pants. "Hi Scott. Jared's wondering if you're in a hurry."

He obviously hasn't seen my message, Scott told himself, squeezing his hands into fists at his sides. He didn't know if that was good or bad in this situation. Scott glanced at his wristwatch. It was close to nine o'clock. He'd dropped his son off three hours before, giving him more than enough time for dinner and dessert. "No, we're not in any hurry, but I thought with you having work the next day . . . ." his voice drifted.

Jesse smiled at that. "Same for you. No rest for the weary sometimes." He cleared his throat. "No, I was actually wondering if you wanted to come in and say hello to our dinner guest. He said he hasn't seen you since high school days if you can believe it."

Scott felt the air go out of him. Someone who hadn't seen him since high school days. He had no idea who might be waiting inside, but he found himself saying, "Sure. I have a few minutes. Jared and I . . . it's still early for us. We're both night owls."

Just then Jared came swinging out of the living room, a look of hostility filling his eyes as he met his father's gaze. When he closed in on his father, he looked away and reached down for his Vans. He slipped a shoe on his good foot and said over his shoulder, "Thank you, Mr. Sander. Dinner was delicious. Dad, come on. I'm ready. Let's go."

Scott was thrust into the realm of confusion. He reached for his son's forearm. "Jared, there's no hurry. Jess—Mr. Sander said there's a classmate of ours I haven't seen in years."

Jesse hung back, quietly, his hands hovering at the front pockets of his pants.

Jared locked eyes with Scott, and this time he could detect a certain woundedness that hadn't been there before. "Why didn't you tell me about some of this stuff *before*?" Jared whispered.

Scott felt a sinking sensation wash over him, but he couldn't stop the questions from moving past his lips, not even for the sake of propriety. He reached for Jared's sleeve. "Tell you what, Son?" he asked, though he had a serious suspicion he knew what this was about.

"Who you were when you were my age and what you did at that abandoned boat." He tugged free from his father's loose grip but didn't race out the door. Scott could see the temptation there to flee, but Jared resisted it. Perhaps he had learned from his last experience that fleeing in no way resolved the issue.

Jesse spoke, his face losing all color. "I . . . I don't know what to say, Scott. It came up in the conversation at dinner—my friend didn't know your son had never heard about what happened . . . . I thought we'd all moved on."

Scott looked down at the oak floors beneath his feet, and when he turned back to Jesse, he was awash with shame. "Jared wouldn't move on from hearing something like that about me. Truth is, he isn't meant to. None of us are since it's not something we can forget."

He looked at his son, whose eyes were sending sparks of fury across the room. Jared was still within arm's reach but seemed so far away. Was he starting to lose him? Had he already lost him?

"I wanted to protect you . . . ." He stopped. "No—I wanted to protect myself from something I was ashamed of in the past, and I'm sorry." Steeling himself—he had no right to show emotion when it was he who had wronged—he continued, "I can see that I've only made things worse."

No one in the room responded. Not Jared, who folded his arms across his chest. Not Jesse, whose pallor remained. Scott sought words he didn't have. How had he thought that coming back here and not saying a thing about his wrongdoing would ever suffice? How had he thought that he'd be received as a good-hearted guy and that his reputation would subsist on his father's good name and all his parents had done for the community? It had already crumpled for good at age seventeen.

Greta surfaced in the room and grew immediately attune to the tension filling it. Scott could see her assessing, taking everything in. Her beautiful face marred with worry, she sought out Jared. "Please, Jared, go on a walk with me. We should talk."

Her father stared at her, bewilderment crossing his brow. "Right now? It's starting to snow, and it's dark outside."

"I don't care, Dad," she said, jutting her chin out, her voice resolute. "When has a little snow ever stopped me?"

Jesse shook his head, and a wry smile etched its way on his face. "Here, take a flashlight and don't be long. We don't need anyone coming down with pneumonia out there."

She turned to Jared, her eyes beseeching. "Will you please walk with me?" There was a hint of vulnerability in her words, behind the persistence. Before Jared could form the words, Greta moved toward him and took his hand up in her own. "Will you please go with me? There's something I'd really like to show you."

He took her hand, and the two of them—his son and Jesse Sander's stepdaughter went out in the dark, snowy landscape.

Scott and Jesse stood alone at the entrance. An occasion to exchange words for the first time without an audience hung before them. No sound between them but the tick of the grandfather clock and the beat of Scott's uptight heart.

28

When the Past Catches Up

So much could change in an hour's time. Just an hour before Jared had sat down to enjoy a hearty meal with the Sanders, his mind had been as far away from his father as could be. He wasn't mad or irritated with his dad—his thoughts were simply centered on Greta Sander and what he might get her for Christmas. Something sweet, but not too overwhelming. He'd known her only two weeks. He didn't want to scare her off with a gift that felt too personal or too heartfelt and so he settled on several strands of durable white lights for her fort.

In the short time he'd known Greta, life had gone from a muted gray to a promising blue, despite the dreary Northwest rain. Jared was drawn to her intuitiveness, her quick wit, her effortlessly beautiful smile. Though his heart tugged toward her already, he didn't want to move past friends just yet. He'd never been in a relationship before, but he'd watched too many of his peers in friendships that curdled as soon as they became romantic.

But try as he might to be cautious, to maintain focus on their daily activities—whether baking, crafting shelves, tracking down outdoor supplies, and what have you—Jared couldn't help but imagine how it would feel to lose his fingers in her dark curtain of hair, to press his lips against her own, to feel her heartbeat rise against his cotton t-shirt. He didn't want to stop imagining these things and yet he had to watch himself. He didn't want to make it weird between them.

His mind's wandering was curtailed (perhaps for the better) as he caught the scent of chicken fettuccine Alfredo and home-baked sourdough bread. His stomach growled. They were in the midst of their second round of Yahtzee and the notion that he was about to sit down for a meal with her entire family pulled him up short.

A decisive knock at the front door startled him. He paused with his cards in his hand and looked at Greta, but she shook her head. "Oh, it's only one of my dad's old friends from high school days. He's home from Alaska, where he works on fishing boats. He's funny and smart, and I think you'll really like him."

Jared didn't think much more of the Sander's guest until they sat down for their meal and he found himself sitting next to a weather-worn man around his own father's age. He wore a Mariners baseball cap backward, had shaggy blond hair that brushed past his collar and blue eyes that crinkled when he smiled. He reached for the pitcher of ice water on the table and Jared saw that the man's hands were deeply calloused. A stark contrast to the artist hands belonging to Jesse, or his even own.

He couldn't keep from wondering how the two men had formed a friendship. One worked on fishing boats in Alaska for most of the year; the other was most comfortable behind a cherry-wood desk in an office.

The man reached out his hand as soon as Jared sat down. "Bradley Parsons," he said, "It's a pleasure to meet a friend of Greta's." He beamed at her from across the table. "She's a selective one, as she should be. Any friend of hers is worth knowing, if you ask me."

"Nice to meet you. I'm Jared." He could picture this man with stark clarity, out on a boat, reeling in one of those heavy nets over and over to deposit sizable halibut and salmon on the deck. He hoped he could find enough to say to this man for the next hour or more. Somehow, he didn't think that talking art class sculptures would appeal to him.

"Jared. That's a great name," he said. "You ever seen that show *Big Valley*?" He grinned at the reference to the main character. Without waiting for an answer, the man proceeded. "Your family been in the Harbor long?" He picked up his cup of ice water and took a long sip. Jared watched as a bead of water tangled itself in the man's dirty-blond beard.

"I guess you could say I'm third generation . . . kind of," Jared said. "My grandparents live here, but my family only recently came back. We've been back since September since my dad took over the family business."

Bradley tilted his head to the side, curiosity sweeping over his features.

"He's a Brighton," Jesse said, reaching for the plate with the warm sourdough bread and helping himself to a slice before passing the plate to Elli. Jared didn't miss her questioning expression as she glanced at her husband.

Bradley set his ice water down hard, unable to conceal his surprise. "No way. You mean to tell me you and Scotty Brighton are friends after that stunt he pulled on you back in high school?" His eyes were incredulous, and he gestured wildly with his hands. "When I saw you that day, you told me that you'd never . . . ."

The color immediately drained from Jesse's face and he pressed his lips together in a thin line. Bradley adjusted his baseball cap and mouthed a quick apology to Jesse over the table. Jesse merely glanced down at his lap, as if willing this conversation to end.

"W-what is he talking about, Dad?" Greta asked, her voice pointed.

The dining room suddenly filled with silence. Even the twins stopped their chattering and were quiet enough that one could hear napkins dropping into laps. Not a single fork had been lifted yet, as the creamy chicken Alfredo waited to be served. Elli, who'd been standing over the pot, paused with a ladle in hand. Her typically sparkling eyes turned somber.

Jesse let out a long, exasperated sigh and looked down at his hands before raising his eyes to meet his stepdaughter's questioning gaze. Jared's mind was a flurry of possibilities. He felt his heart throb in his throat.

"Back in high school, there was a revenge incident that some other boys and I . . . were involved in."

Disbelief filled Bradley Parsons' eyes and he shook his head, nostrils flaring. "Jesse, it's not fair to pretend that you were involved when you were the one *targeted* the entire damn time."

"Not fair to whom?" Jesse asked, his tone stripped down. "It was so long ago. We were all kids back then . . . I don't see the need to rehash the past."

Jared fumbled with his napkin and watched it swirl to the floor before he could catch it. His face burned. He'd been right to think there was unspoken tension between Mr. Sander and his dad. Not wanting to believe there was anything more to it than two men who'd led entirely different lives, he'd ignored his gut and kept on seeing Greta, as if the friction between their fathers was inconsequential.

"You're right," Bradley said, scratching his forehead. "It was so long ago, and I was wrong to assume that you would never move past it. My little brother never really could, though he's a good pretender. A good stoic, that one." He finished adjusting the strap on his Mariners cap.

"Don't mind me, you guys. I still live too much in the past. Vietnam might have a lot to do with that. In fact, I know it does. In any case," he waved his hand, "your families are a good testament to the beauty that's possible if you draw a line in the sand."

"What line in the sand?" Greta asked, rising to her feet and searching her parents' bewildered faces. "What is there to your relationship with the Brightons that you haven't told me? Because it sure sounds like Jared and I deserve to know if there's a history there. Please. Don't keep secrets from us."

Jared let his napkin rest under his feet at the table. He'd lost his appetite, rumbling stomach or not. How could he think about lifting a fork to his mouth after learning that his father was most likely not the person he'd thought he was?

He watched Greta's mom lock eyes with her husband. Without asking him a word aloud, questions leaped from her gaze and he nodded in answer. She set the ladle on the table and sank into the empty seat beside him, uncommonly quiet.

"I can only tell you from my perspective," Jesse said before looking from Jared to his stepdaughter. "Every guy that was there that day was affected. No one thought it was worth it . . . after the fact. The price they paid was too steep, and I'm not even the one that was impacted the most, though I'm the one they were after." He took a deep breath and proceeded. "There's this abandoned boat in the woods near this old yellow farmhouse . . . that's where they took me."

29

What Remains

Jared's mind was shaken with learning his father was once a bully, but Greta's determination to take him somewhere forced him not to linger too long on that revelation. Neither of them had stopped to find gloves, and her hands were cold as his own. He clutched her fingers, hoping to generate more warmth.

She led him to the left of the house, where she'd never taken him before. He'd only recently surrendered his crutches, but she was considerate enough to pause every few minutes to make sure he was tracking alright. Fortunately, the ground was level this time, and he could get around alright with his boot.

"Greta," he said finally, "What's going on? Where are we going?"

"It's just a little bit farther," she said, her voice breathless and her cheeks the red of holly berries.

In less than five minutes, they were standing before a small blue work shed that Jared had never noticed before. It wasn't visible from the onset of the property, tucked behind expansive trees.

Before telling him why they were here, she pressed on the door, and the hinges gave way. She pulled a cord on the ceiling, and light poured over them fast, before he could ask any more questions or process why she'd taken him here. He'd been inside her father's larger, more visible shed to the right of the property more times than he could count already, and the reason he'd built another eluded him. Baffled him even.

"This one is mine," Greta said, extending her hand and showcasing the interior of hers, much more disheveled than her father's, whose tools were organized in bins and labeled meticulously. "My dad and I built it a few summers ago."

A worktable stood in the room, littered with an assortment of goods. Anything from pocketknives to a compass to a lantern.

"It might not mean a lot after what you just heard, but my dad taught me to fend for myself from an early age because of experiences he'd been through. So I know how to ward off an attacker, I know how to change a tire ridiculously fast, I know how to escape most confined areas. My father didn't tell me about what your dad did," Greta said, refusing to look away, "but I don't think it would change anything, had I known. You're not your dad. And he's not that seventeen-year-old kid anymore. Look, no matter what went on in his past, he's raised a good son. A kind one."

Jared sucked on the inside of his cheek, trying to make his emotions indecipherable. "Well, my dad should have let me know." He squeezed his eyes before glancing at her again. "Look, Greta, I really like you . . . to the point that I thought this was almost too good to be true. But I don't know what to do right now . . . or what this means for us. All this time I thought my father was someone to look up to and that I'd never fill his shoes. To find out all this time that . . . I mean I wouldn't do that to someone, leave them locked up in a hold of a boat. You wouldn't either."

He glanced away. Felt her cold fingers wrap around his own as she drew closer to him. She stood so close that her breath grazed his face.

"Jared . . . Jared, I know it's a lot. But what if you started seeing your father as who he is today . . . as who he is right now?"

He looked at her because her question called for it. Her dark hair fell around her face and he wished he could weave his hands through it, kiss it, kiss her. She extended grace when he wasn't even asking or begging her to, and that was beautiful.

"Greta, thank you . . . I . . . ."

She pressed a finger to his lips and smiled as if telling him he didn't have to try so hard. There shouldn't be any strain. Not so much trying to shape and bend what was out of his hands to control. He should just be still. It was possible, and she intended to show him.

·⟨⟩·

Scott looked at Jesse, feeling ever the trespasser in the Sander's house now that his son was no longer there. Jesse hadn't turned away. "I'm sorry to intrude on your night like this. And sorry I've brought this . . . unrest into your home . . . and for being a culprit in that cruel stunt." He wanted to shut his eyes at the shame which rose to a river current within him. He hated how he put the onus on Jesse to respond to his too little, too late apology. If he could make a beeline toward the door right now, my God, he would do it.

Jesse's blue-gray eyes were earnest, but his expression remained impassive. He wasn't easy to read like he was back then, when he was a sophomore, full of more zeal and devotion to a chemistry book than anyone he'd ever met before. Perhaps he was offending Jesse, acting like this isolated incident still mattered. The architect had apparently moved beyond it.

For Scott, it still acted as the thorn in his side. So many complimented him on being a kind person, a man of integrity, an underdog's champion. Oh, but you don't know, he'd wanted to correct them, but never could. Bobby hadn't held a gun to him, making sure he'd followed through. How fragile he'd been, how much a farce beneath the shoulder pads and black paint beneath his eyes.

The dining room door swung open, and in stepped Ty Parsons' big brother Bradley. The veteran's bright eyes swiftly darkened as he took in the visitor. Bradley moved forward, his work boots pounding on the floorboards without apology. "Brad, it's alright . . . go back . . . ."

"It's not alright," Bradley said, his agitation working its way into his jawline. Making him seize up. "You finally decided to show your face. What took you so long, you son of a bitch? What took you so goddamn long to do the right thing?" His nostrils flared. "Did you know that you're the *last* one—the only one who hasn't said *anything* to Jesse about that night?"

Scott stiffened. His friendships with Bobby and Ty had disintegrated into nothingness after that disaster. They still had classes to get through, another football season to finish, but that was it. He hadn't expected either of those guys to go out of their way to apologize to Jesse—especially since they'd been physically worse off than the kid. Now, all these years later, he was being told otherwise.

Bradley edged right up to Scott's face as he screamed these words. Scott glanced down and saw the brawny man's hands close in tight fists, and he felt a shiver of fear rush up his spine. Adrenaline coursed through him, but he searched for his breath, prayed against acting out impulsively. Told himself to take whatever he had coming to him, within reason. It would be ugly otherwise.

Instinctively Scott drew back from him and bumped into the bench at the entrance. Hard. He winced. Bradley's eyes were saucer-wide, his mouth was curled above his lip.

Scott tempered his voice. "You're right. It did take me too long to apologize. But you wanna know what else? That's something I carry. It's something that doesn't ever go . . . away."

Bradley remained speechless, but he was breathing through his nose—his chest still inflated, ready to take on the predator in his midst. Out of the corner of his eye, Scott saw Elli materialize near the door, lines of worry etched into her brow.

"Bradley, don't . . . ." she said, her voice a command.

He looked at her and crossed his arms over his chest. Then he looked back at Scott, whose jaw was worked into a hard compression, whose eyes shone with tears, trepidation too.

"Well, you should know you are the last one. The last culprit in this revenge prank to apologize. Did you know that Bobby made amends years ago? That even my little brother wrote him a letter with all he had going on, with Marianne knocked up and all? Did you know that Ty tried hardest to get Jesse out? That he asked me to help Jesse even though it cost him?" Bradley's blue eyes were intense, but his righteous indignation was starting to simmer down to a mist.

Scott let his arms drop to his sides. "I didn't know," he said, regret cloying his voice. "I don't see either of them anymore. After the accident, we went our separate ways. It was too . . . painful trying to pick it back up where we left it. How could we? We were no longer kids after that day."

Bradley feigned a laugh. It came out dry and brittle as fallen leaves. "Tell me about it, Scotty. I know a thing or two about having your childhood taken too early. There was this thing called the draft."

Scott closed his eyes, taking on a new layer of shame. He hadn't thought his words through, had he? What he and his pals had been caught up in that time was minuscule—winning football games, hoping to do well enough on tests, gain notice of the right scout, drive an enviable car, catch the eye of a pretty girl.

"Look," he said, his eyes falling upon Bradley and then slipping over to Jesse. "All I can do is apologize. Words sound trite, but what else can I offer? I am deeply sorry. More than you could know."

For the first time, Scott heard the music playing in the background, took note of the melody and the lyrics. Christmas carols, of course. He'd always tempered the restlessness of this season with them. This time it was Nat King Cole and his silk-smooth "Cradle in Bethlehem." Only now the melody didn't calm him. He waited with suspended words for someone to react, for Jesse to kick him out of his house. For something to shift the unwinding narrative playing out *before* him.

"I accept it," Jesse said finally, glancing down at the kitchen floor before lifting his head and looking directly at Scott. "I accept your apology, Scott. I don't want you to carry this anymore." There was earnestness in his eyes. "Look, it was awful what happened. All of it. I think we can all agree that day shouldn't have happened. But all we can do now is move forward, teach our kids . . . ."

Scott swallowed down the last of his remorse, felt compelled to step forward and at least shake Jesse's hand. He'd half expected the architect to shrug him off, armor himself against such dated apologies and tell him it was time to leave. He had company to tend to. But Jesse Sander had done none of those things. Scott watched as Elli pressed a palm to Bradley's shoulder and led him back to the dining room, where she announced in a steady voice to her twins that a second helping of chocolate cake and mint ice cream awaited. "Here, Brad, I made you some coffee too," he could hear her say.

Meanwhile, Jesse proceeded to reach out his hand, shaking with Scott after all these years. He gripped Scott's hand firmly, and Scott saw the water swimming in Jesse's eyes. He never, not for an instant, thought this would result from the wrong he'd done. Not that he and Jesse would emerge from this as friends. No, sometimes the damage didn't allow for that level of repair, and the heart needed its own fortification.

But the forgiveness—an unwarranted grace washing over him now like bubbling wonder—that was real. The truth of it made him want to pinch himself, to make sure he wasn't dreaming.

He'd thought that he'd exist in a state of purgatory for the rest of his days, but if he did so, it would be his own doing. Jesse had refused to keep him down. Had proven there was no good reason for him to settle for a gridlocked past. Scott couldn't help shaking his head. He marveled at Jesse's reaction to Jared's identity—he could have put an immediate stop to a friendship with Greta had he wanted. Perhaps it wasn't Jesse's first choice, but he'd let it be, and that alone was a mercy.

The sound of Jared and Greta approaching the house interrupted his thoughts, Greta's optimistic energy intact, though she seemed to swallow some laughter as they reached the entrance. Jared had left spitting-nails mad at him, but Scott felt a sense of peace wash over his being.

He owed Jared an apology too failing to be forthright, for allowing him to believe for too many years that his light shone brighter that it really did. And he thought that Jared might forgive him soon. There was a compassion in the kid that made him so incredibly proud. He turned to his son.

"Are you ready to ride home?"

"Yes," Jared offered quietly.

Greta reached for Jared's arm and clutched it, "Promise me you'll drop by on Christmas Eve. I thought maybe we could work on a sign for our fort. We don't need any trespassers." Her eyes cut to kitchen, where Nora and Owen were in danger of tripping over each other as they grabbed their dessert plates.

Elli, silently redirecting them, overheard her older daughter and turned her head, "Yes, stop by on Christmas Eve, Jared, even if it's only for a little while." Her smile was direct and undeniable. "We'd love to have you here."

Jesse smiled shyly and studied his watch before glancing back up. He surprised Scott when he chose to echo his family's sentiments and said, "We like having this guy around."

A few minutes later as Scott and his son walked to the car, jingle bells still ringing from the wreath on the Sander's front door, Scott felt a tear trace its way down his cheek.

"He's a good man," Scott whispered, his son three steps behind and within earshot. One that he'd want to know better in different circumstances.

"Yep," Jared said, his tone distant. "Anyone can see that."

Scott's delayed atonement had cost him, and it would take time for Jared to come around. He wouldn't regain his son's trust and respect in one night. He reached for the car door.

Jared, his voice still shaking spoke. "Dad . . . I'm not ready to forgive you for not telling me yet, but you know you're one of the good ones, right?" He raked a hand through his disheveled hair and said, "You're so hard on yourself, and you don't need to be, all right? You've held yourself hostage for long enough, but you're meant to be free. To let others know they can be free."

Scott felt like the air had gone out of him. He counted Jared's kindness toward him a miracle. In truth, Jared looked just as stunned to have said these words as Scott was in receiving them. His mouth still hadn't closed all the way.

"I still wish you'd have told me. Like before I got interested in Jesse's daughter," Jared added, as he reached for the car door handle. "But what's the use of wishing for things to be different?" He glanced toward his still-healing foot and shrugged.

"I'm sorry I never told you, Jer," Scott said, refusing to look away, no matter that shame that wanted to stake its claim all over again. "I have so many regrets, still. But you can ask me anything you'd like, and I'll tell you. Greta's dad . . . just forgave me."

His eyes welled again, and he couldn't speak. He looked to the silver slice of moon, not wanting to lose his composure entirely. He couldn't turn his eyes away, not yet.

·❦·

Caught in the throes between waking and dreaming, Jesse Sander's Christmas Eve morning didn't have a quiet, peaceful start. His heart hammered like it was outside his chest. The sheets entangled him, held him down, and let him believe he couldn't get away. He was wading through currents in the Sound and there were heavy patches of ice overhead, a sinister blockade, a coffin's lid. He searched for a drifting branch, something to grasp onto, but it was as if he kept tunneling down into the eerie blue, his legs leaden, his breath fading in and out to nothingness. Adrenaline surged through his being, and his hands grasped for that indifferent branch once more. He faltered. Lost his grip.

He tried to cry out for someone, anyone to help, but his pleas were swallowed up by gushes of water, which turned his voice to nothing more than an anemic whimper. "Please, please help," he thought, though no one could read his mind, no one had the premonition that he needed strong arms to reach in and extract him from solitary depths.

He was murmuring his protest when suddenly, firm hands lighted on his chest, and he heard an urgent voice saying, "Jesse, Jesse, you need to wake up. It's only a dream."

Jesse tossed the comforter to the floor. He felt the sweat at the back of his neck before opening his eyes and meeting hers, the same two dark orbs that had brought him back to life before.

Breathe, he told himself, letting out gust after gust of air trapped inside. He felt his racing heart start to settle, but the edge of unease wanted to cling to him, keep him down. Just like it always had. Since he was a boy of fifteen.

"It's only a dream," she said, hand still on his sweat-drenched t-shirt, refusing to move away from this—one more nightmare in a series of many. There was no ridicule, no frustration, only concern etched into the lines of her forehead.

He squeezed her hand in response, still unwinding from the dread that wanted to overtake and drown him, steal his breath and blot it out. He sat up and leaned over with his face clasped in his hands. How gratifying it felt to go spurts of time without this restlessness, the returning guest of terror and helplessness. Where his power was stripped away and he was left to the mercy of those who decided he was better held down, beaten, boxed in, trapped, discarded. Sometimes when the night panic returned, he chided himself for not moving past, for still wearing the ashes of what he'd endured. But he didn't want to lean into the remnants of the returning nightmare now, so he scanned the surroundings of their room. Dust motes rose from the dresser where a photograph of Palo Alto sat framed in the corner. His watch rested on the bedside table. He stopped scanning the room as his gaze settled on *her*.

He rushed to his feet and said, "Get up, Elli." He ripped the blue sheets off the bed, not wanting to make either of them suffer through their dampness. One would have thought he'd run a marathon from the amount of perspiration on his body.

Before he could say a word, Elli was reaching for a fresh change of sheets in the bathroom closet and returning to him, compassion in her eyes. "I'm sorry, Jess," she said as he tossed his drenched t-shirt in the laundry basket and sought another from his drawers.

Once sheets were back on the bed, she sought his hand, placed her own inside his and lay her head on his shoulder.

"You know how to shake it off. You've always done it. It's Christmas Eve, love. I don't want you to miss the wonder of it. Jesse, you know how to overcome this. You don't let anything defeat you."

"I know," he said, staring at the ceiling before turning to look at her. The girl he was grateful for then, the woman who held his heart even now. "Neither do you." He ran his fingers through strands of her hair and said, "I'm not there anymore. Even if my dreams want to play tricks on me. I might hate it when it happens and I really do, but when I wake up, I'm right here with you."

She smiled against his shoulder. He drew her closer and her warmth made his heart full to bursting. It was only then that he felt a cold stone against his arm. She was wearing something she hadn't worn in an incredibly long time—the dark blue necklace he'd given her when they were freshmen in college. The moment he was almost certain he'd lost her forever. He didn't know she still had it.

"That's the way the story always ends, Jesse Sander," she said. "Me here with you."

His gray-blue eyes met her dark brown eyes.

"Thanks for helping me remember," he said, taking her hand up in his own and never wanting to let it go.

30

Harbor Spring

A sheen of sweat clung to his t-shirt from an afternoon of weed whacking and mowing his parents' front lawn. Scott found his heart surging anyway. It was fulfilling to be back where he grew up and to lend a hand where he could.

He felt more a visitor than a resident returning to the familiar blue house, but it didn't prevent the waves of nostalgia from taking over. His parents had kept traces of him and his siblings everywhere—framed photos of school pictures, trophies, textbooks, that black Mustang he'd worked on with his dad, stored here for years. It had become bittersweet to him after everything with Jesse, but he and his dad had still worked on it together his senior year. That project of theirs had kept him going, though sometimes he felt that it was merely going through the motions.

His dad wasn't one to sit idle, even with his current medical setbacks, and he'd been out front planting rhododendron bushes with Scott's mom while Scott took care of the more pressing tasks. The close proximity to his parents was more than worth the hiccups he'd experienced since moving back here. The gray poking through his dark hair reminded him how finite life was, that he didn't know the number of years he had left with them. When he thought of his edgy banter with them, his distancing techniques through his high school and college years, he cringed. But he still had the present moment, and he wasn't going to take it for granted.

On his way out, Scott's mom caught him by the elbow. "Next time bring that grandson of ours over here too," she said. We'll pay him to trim some of these huckleberry bushes. But truth is, it would just be great to see him."

Scott wiped his forehead with the back of his hand and cracked a smile. "I'll bring him by more often, but hope you don't take it personally, Mom. Char and I are seeing him less these days too. He spends whatever free time he has out at the Sander's house with their daughter, Greta. He kinda likes her, you know."

His mom sent him an amused look over the top of her glasses. "Funny how life turns out sometimes, isn't it?" She squeezed his shoulder, "It's good of you to let his relationship with Jesse's daughter develop as it's meant to, though it can't be easy having that constant reminder . . . ."

"I actually dropped him off the other day and didn't think about it," Scott said. "Jesse was out picking up the mail, and when I waved at him, I didn't feel sick to my stomach. I rolled down the window, and we had a short conversation about the Maritime Festival, if you can believe it."

His mom looked at him earnestly. "That's how you've felt after all these years, Son? Sick to your stomach?"

"Yes. You have no idea, Mom," Scott said, feeling new beads of sweat materialize on his forehead now that he was cooling down. "It's why I almost didn't come back . . . home . . . But I'm glad I did and that we're not as bound to the past as we might think."

"You asked for his forgiveness," his mom said, a statement instead of a question. Her dark eyes exuded understanding. "So you know that the only way to the other side is through. The only way we learn this is through experience. Live as long as me, and you'll know there are no shortcuts for any of us."

·✦·

Now that it was warming up and slated rainfalls weren't the norm, there was something Scott had to do. He hadn't returned to the yellow farmhouse since the day they'd kidnapped Jesse, but he'd felt compelled to go there ever since Sadie had brought it up. Back when he was seventeen, he'd known nothing about the family who lived there. Only that his friend's hangout was taken over by new owners.

Hours after he'd woken from his state of unconsciousness, he'd learned the name of the other driver in the crash—Jake Halvorson, the new owner of the abandoned property. What he hadn't known until recently was that the property had never fallen from the family's possession. A quick Internet search had told him the Halvorsons were early Norwegian immigrants to the Harbor. He'd felt goosebumps rise on the back of his neck at this revelation, though he didn't know why.

The house had sat vacant for decades—boards rotting, paint peeling back, the overgrowth of brush wrapping around the front porch, and he'd thought it was utterly forgotten. Written off. What had prompted anyone to come back after all that time? And even more, it intrigued him that the Halvorsons remained in the yellow farmhouse after the accident, when it might have been easier for them to pack up and leave soon after. And why had they kept the boat despite its disrepair and the shameful history that became synonymous with it? Their granddaughter, Linny, had found it fitting to mention the boat, and he really wanted to know why.

Scott tried to convince himself to let sleeping dogs lie and to stop tampering with the past. Hadn't that property owner endured enough without him bringing that long-ago accident to the forefront of his mind?

If I'm not meant to be here, let no one be home, Scott repeated to himself as an entreaty, even as he inched his car forward, heading past the newer homes on the outskirts of this development. He eventually parked his car before the Halvorson's gate and cut the ignition. *What's the use in being here? What more can be resolved?* He sat in the silence of the car for a few minutes, and then, taking a deep breath, he opened the door and stepped out.

Please let no one be home, he thought before looking toward the bright yellow farm house. A wrought iron gate marked the border of the property and an older man stood nearby working away at it. A quick glance told him that the hinges were giving way and that this man, who wore dark green flannel and faded Levi's, was on a mission to set it straight.

He gulped. After all these years, the owner was still trying to maintain the boundary between his place and the outside world. Or so it seemed. Scott wondered if high school kids were still prone to head up this way, but he strongly doubted it.

Since he'd been a kid in the Harbor, there were so many more places to explore, and a discarded boat up on a hill didn't hold the same appeal. Not when it wasn't outfitted as a fort. His heart dropped when he thought of Bobby and all he'd lost since they'd been idealistic kids and the sun had shone on their shoulders.

"Anything I can help you with?" the older man asked, pausing his handiwork before Scott could utter a hello. Mr. Halvorson squinted at him, but Scott hoped it was merely the sunlight hitting his eyes. He almost murmured something about taking a wrong turn, but he hadn't come all this way to take shortcuts with the truth.

So he summoned a small smile and walked over to Mr. Halvorson, silently praying that his bid for closure wouldn't undo the other man's attempts to heal. If he at any turn received less-than-willing answers, he'd call it a day. But the only way to know what he came here to find out was to launch right in.

"Yes. I hope I'm not intruding," he gestured toward the gate and immediately felt himself color around the collar. "I'm hoping to find out a little more history about this place. You see, I used to come here as I kid, and it was only a few months ago that my daughter, Sadie, came home from school telling me that your granddaughter . . . ."

"Linny."

"Yes, Linny," Scott said, glad he'd asked for it. "She told Sadie that the property has been in your family for years, and not only that—there's a reason you kept the boat."

"Aah," Mr. Halvorson said, as if contemplating his next words. His expression was so impassive, it was hard for Scott to know if he was at ease, or questioning, or irritated by his presence here.

Scott began fidgeting with the loose change in his pockets.

Mr. Halvorson squinted again, tilting his head to the side as if analyzing a rare species of birds. "Took you a long time to come back," he said, not unkindly.

Scott's breath halted at these words. He felt like punching his own eye. He had never seen Jake Halvorson the afternoon of the accident, but this man, the driver of the blue Mercury, had clearly seen him unconscious in the back of the red Chevelle. Still, it was impressive that the man recognized him this many years later. They'd never had a proper conversation, never made eye contact, never crossed paths since that unfortunate time.

Scott took a step closer to Mr. Halvorson. "You're right," he said. "I shouldn't have been here that awful day. I probably should have apologized to you in person. I'm sorry for skipping that part." He bowed his head, sheepishly.

Mr. Halvorson set his drill down on the ground and walked

forward until only six inches stood between them. Scott felt rooted to the spot, a thrill of fear anticipating whatever words might come next. Mr. Halvorson looked at him and then reached for Scott's right hand. "I appreciate that, but it's not needed," he said as his own hand closed around Scott's. He let go, but his voice remained empathic. "You were a kid. What kid doesn't trespass at some moment in his life?"

"Well," Scott said, not wanting to let himself off the hook quite so easily. "It would have made your life so much easier if a bunch of hoodlums hadn't come here, up to no good that day."

"Yes. Yes *and* I've adjusted to how life is now," Mr. Halvorson said, his eyes a wiry blue. "Walk with me?"

He pushed open the gate, and Scott found himself falling into lockstep with the man before he could give it a second thought. He felt as if these following steps were predetermined for him and that he'd merely agreed to show up. He knew where they were headed from the start, but if that's the way Mr. Halvorson wanted to answer his question, he'd agree to it. The old cabin cruiser, the *Linnea*, was merely a structure. He didn't believe it carried negative energy; it was the key players, himself included, who had done that.

Despite his wariness in where they were headed, Scott first admired the fresh, sun-splashed coat of paint on the farmhouse and swinging flower baskets in red and purple bloom. Seven or so chickens frolicked around the green grass in front of the house. But Mr. Halvorson continued to effortlessly climb the hill, so Scott turned his attention to the long ascent before them.

Still unready, they reached the top and he could see the weathered cover that shielded the boat after all this time.

"So the *Linnea* . . . ." Scott started in, hoping the man would just tell him what he knew before he instructed him to climb that rickety ladder for a visit to the interior. It's not that he couldn't do it, but what was the need? He remembered the dimensions of the hold, the pink graffiti on the back wall that screamed at Bobby for what he'd done, the boarded-up windows.

"Linnea was my mother," Mr. Halvorson said, his voice managing to be wistful and proud at once.

Scott stopped walking toward the boat and looked at Mr. Halvorson, aware his expression was one of surprise.

"This boat was my father's pride and joy. Our family—Mom, Dad, my younger brothers and I— had the best memories out on the Sound growing up. Dad called this boat his investment, though I think its greatest return was his kids' happiness. We went out on this cabin cruiser come rain or shine. And it rains a lot out here, as you know." Mr. Halvorson chuckled. "So guess where I spent most of my time."

He smiled knowingly.

"We had this little farmhouse, built at the turn of the century, and lots of chores growing up. But we also had the *Linnea*, and somehow that was enough to make us feel like the luckiest kids alive."

"Wow," Scott said, unable to contain his astonishment at the unimagined connection. He'd expected to be told that the boat was too expensive to fix. That it was a young man's pipe dream. That it had been traded out for a newer model. He didn't expect to hear from Mr. Halvorson that it was a central artifact to their family, an actual treasure. "And your father brought it here . . . ."

"He brought it here when my mother died in her forties from cancer," Mr. Halvorson said soberly. "My brothers and I would have taken it out again, but he said it had served its purpose and that it was a shell of what it once was. He invested a lot into keeping it here, though I don't know why. We moved to eastern Washington, away from all the water. We let that boat become subject to the elements. And then a boy found it, made it into a fort . . . ."

"Bobby," Scott said quietly.

"And truth is, I didn't mind so much when we moved back . . . I knew we'd have to crack down on any partying, which is why I put the chain over the door. I thought I'd run into the kid sometime and have a conversation with him about how badly he wanted to come up here. But it never happened ... I thought maybe he grew up and left childish things behind."

He lowered his head to the forested ground just as Scott lifted his chin to examine the *Linnea*. The enduring covering was the same, but unless his eyes were playing tricks on him, so much was different. He refocused his gaze and cut his eyes to Mr. Halvorson. "Mind if I ...."

Mr. Halvorson shook his head. "Not at all. You asked me why my granddaughter, Linny, mentioned this boat, so I wanted to show you."

Speechless, Scott closed the distance to the steel cruiser. Sure enough, his eyes weren't deceiving him. The hull was painted a deep ocean blue. Bright white lettering spelled out "*Linnea*." The rickety ladder had been exchanged for one of solid wood that wouldn't upend him or anyone who wanted to take a look inside. Once on deck, Scott saw the floorboards had a sheen to them.

Mr. Halvorson hadn't joined him. He turned over his shoulder and called down to him, "Aren't you coming up?"

Mr. Halvorson didn't waste any time. "Nah ...." he said. "I 'bout broke my back renovating the place. Go take a look in the hold."

Scott edged forward and placed his right hand on the door handle, but found it harder to go any further. A memory of stagnant air, images of Jesse being held against his will, the whole absurdity of the failed rescue plan rose in his mind. He didn't want to step any further into the memories. But Mr. Halvorson had asked him to enter. Mr. Halvorson had been put through so much more than he ever deserved, so he opened the door.

By some grace those ugly words on the back wall had been blotted out. A new coat of dark blue paint coated the walls. Laminated newspaper clippings hung at intervals. As Scott came closer, he grasped their content, highlights of good taking place about town: a Peninsula Seahawk who collected coats for a clothing drive, a Tide who created a compliment jar for fellow students, another Seahawk who rallied a recent year's football team to do yard-work for the elderly in the community. Scott wanted to sink down onto the floorboards, if only so he could find his way back to words.

In one corner stood a cooler with the instruction: *Take one. Leave one. Clean up after yourself.* Popping the lid, he saw cans of Coca-Cola waiting for the next thirsty soul. A galley table was spread with gently used card games, Checker boards, Stratego—all the games he liked to play before he and the guys began to think they were too cool for them. He smiled. And beside it was a partially filled journal with the simple prompt: SAY SOMETHING KIND AND TRUE. The pages were filled with short messages from kids who had visited there:

> *Keep going. You've got this. / You're stronger than you think. / The person reading this has really great shoes. Your hair's pretty awesome too. / No, really. You've got this. God loves you, too.*

The hands were all different, the lettering at this slant or that, but the encouraging thread was unbroken. There were still empty pages, but the last one was taken. The last one was a punch to the gut. He read the signature before he swallowed the words.

Dear Gig Harbor kids, Purdy kids, Bremerton kids, Tacoma kids:

When I was seventeen, I was on top of the world. Confident. Athletic. The life of the party. The big fish in a small pond, you might say. Unfortunately, I got some friends to help me in a stunt that I still regret to this day. We got turned in for cheating in school and had to sit out some football games senior year.

We—but mostly me—shut a kid up here in the hold of this boat to punish him for turning us in. We planned to let him out at a certain time, but we didn't make it back. It was a violently rainy day, and I collided with another car. I came away from the accident paralyzed from the waist down. Fortunately, the boy escaped. That took a lot of strength if you ask me.

I tell you this in hopes that you won't be like me, and that you'll think before you act. That you will pause before retaliating against someone who rubs you wrong, and that you'll weigh your choices. Seventeen sounds invincible, but it's not. Varsity football player one minute and on my back in a hospital bed the next.

Why do I write this sad story in a fort re-purposed for encouragement, you might ask? Because I pray to God this isn't you and that your story will be different than mine.

Today I have more blessings in my life than I deserve, and I'm not the same jerk I was back then. At least I hope not! You are capable of being kind to the kid you don't like and of making his day better. I promise. Please—stick to being kind. You won't regret it.

Bobby Minter

I don't believe this, Scott thought, wondering what strategies Mr. Halvorson had employed to get Bobby to write this letter. Bobby had been sorry, but Bobby was still . . . Bobby. He had humbled himself even more than Scott had expected, coming out with this public confession.

When Scott emerged from the Linnea and eventually climbed down the ladder, he was lightheaded, mind swimming. He didn't know what he'd been expecting when he followed that internal nudge to come here today, but it wasn't this. Not by a long shot.

Mr. Halvorson waited for him, a quiet smile hovering on his lips. He held out a bottle of water to Scott. "I keep a stash up here since that hill's a beast. Or so I've been told."

"I . . . I can't believe it," Scott said, still short on words. But did he ever want to bring Jared here. Sadie too. He wanted them to absorb Bobby's words. Stand-ins for his own.

"Minter and I have kept in touch since the accident," Mr. Halvorson said quietly, "in case you wondered about that. I told him my granddaughter wanted a fort here, and he came up with a lot of the vision for what it is today. It was his idea to fill in the last entry."

"It speaks well of him."

"Yes. Yes, it does."

"So other than the goodness of your heart, what prompted you to restore this place?" Scott asked, no longer afraid to ask to-the-bone questions.

Without delay, he said, "I wanted my boat back. Or you might say . . . *our* boat back. I wanted all the positive memories to start filling this place and start drowning out the sorrow that took place here."

Scott ran a hand through his tousled hair and knew there was no sense in regretting that he was only getting to know this man now.

"I love it," he said finally, his gaze still on the *Linnea*. A sparkling showoff in the sun. "I love how you returned her to her former beauty. I bet kids love coming here."

"Ah," Mr. Halvorson said, "She's her true self now. I could have taken her out on the water again, but I think her purpose is more fitting here. Dad made me promise to buy a new boat when we first moved here, so I did. She's called the *Linnea II*, and we take her out on the water often. I think a lot about my mom when we're out on the Sound."

"That's wonderful," Scott said, finally uncapping the water and raising the bottle to his lips. "Thank you for sharing this with me.

You don't know what this means. It gives me more hope, you know. It reminds me that we can return to the people God intended us to be if we listen. Even when it's hard." He smiled. "Especially when it's hard."

Mr. Halvorson placed a strong hand on the back of his shoulder and began to walk down the hill with him, a guide through that former night of the soul. This was a place Scott had never wanted to return to until now, with the sun melting like golden honey above the tree line. It was suddenly so much less daunting. He felt his shoulders come down. His jaw unclenched. He knew the *Linnea* would await his return, and that he too would add his voice of newfound reason and encouragement to a page somewhere in the middle of the record. He paused momentarily and raised his line of vision past the top of the trees, nodding heavenward. Thank God there was still time.

Acknowledgements

*T*hank you to those who helped me see this third novel to completion! My first and sometimes repeat readers I'm grateful to include:

Joni Bennett, Hank Buchmann, Connie Hampton Connally, Ashley Corbaley, Steve Durgin, D. L. Fowler, Marissa Harrison, Patty Mausolf, Judy Prisoc, John Schrupp, Amanda Snyder, and Greg Spadoni.

Thank you to the Gig Harbor Historical Society for allowing me to peruse the archives. To Bill Braun for getting me started, and to Greg Spadoni for giving me keen insights that only a lifetime local would know.

Thanks to Elli Seifert for being my continued editor, typesetter & typographer, and for saying yes to the idea of having a character with your name. I love your creative range.

Thanks to Nancy Archer for your graphic design talents with our third cover together. It's a blessing to work with you!

Thanks to Sage West Photography for graciously taking my author headshot as a last-minute request at our family photoshoot.

Thank you to E. Hank Buchmann and D. L. Fowler for continual guidance, and Connie Hampton Connally for reading every line and helping this novel spark. My gratitude also goes out to the newly assembled Greater Gig Harbor Literary Society.

Thank you to my family: Steve and Kim Triller (Mom & Dad) and my younger siblings Kaeley Harms, Meagan Shaw, Christie Palmquist, and Heath Triller for believing in me.

As always, my gratitude to my husband, Justin, for promoting my work and loving me. To our kids, Trenton and Josie, thank you for encouraging me with questions such as, "So when are you going to publish your third book, Mom?"

Last, but most importantly, thank you to my Lord and Savior for being steadfast and faithful.

About the Author

*A*lisa Weis is also the author of *Swiftwater* and *The Emblem*. When she isn't thinking up new plot lines, most of her time is spent teaching English to secondary students at a private school in Bremerton. Alisa enjoys HIIT and running, visiting coffeehouses, and meeting local authors in her free time. She lives on a small farm in Olalla, WA with her husband, son, daughter, and a host of animals.

Learn more about Alisa at her website: *www.alisaweis.com*